LOVE AT FIRST LIGHT

JENNIFER BERNARD

PROLOGUE

The first time Ethan James nearly died was at the age of six. He'd stumbled into a hornet's nest and gotten stung twenty-three times before his sister Olivia had dragged him away. The next time, he was ten. He went into a brief coma after reacting badly to anesthesia during surgery on his leg. No one thought he'd pull through, but lo and behold, he did. Close shave number three came when he was twelve and he'd decided that climbing a tree with his leg in a cast would be a good idea.

The brushes with death didn't stop after he'd—despite the setbacks—survived childhood. Over the course of his career as a private investigator, a few more near-death experiences followed.

By the time he was about to turn thirty, he'd almost gotten used to the idea of flirting with the Grim Reaper.

But this one felt different.

For one, he'd never nearly drowned before. That was new. The man chasing him with a car—the cheating husband he'd been hired to follow—had forced him onto a bridge with a flood-swollen river below. It was either jump off the side or get run over by a Lexus. If he had to decide between death by Lexus or death by drowning, that wasn't a hard choice.

He probably should have picked a less torrentially rainy day to track his target to his motel tryst outside of Fresno. Flash flood season in California could be so damn dangerous. Every year people died when they got trapped by floodwaters. He hoped everyone driving this route would be extra careful—though it might be too late for him. When his car had refused to start, he'd been forced into fleeing on foot.

Without any further thought, he leaped off the bridge, the speeding Lexus nipping at his heels like the dogs of the Underworld.

The churning water rushed toward him. He knew he had to do his best rag-doll act when he hit the water. *Don't resist. Surrender. Now. Do it.* He filled his lungs with air, went limp and closed his eyes as his body collided with the river. *Cold. So cold.* And fast and wild. The current batted him around like a cat playing with a mouse. He tried to right himself, to work with the flow, to find the surface. He was running out of air, his lungs aching, the urge to suck in water irresistible.

And then his head hit something brutally hard and the black pain erased everything around him. No more river, no more rapids, no more Lexus, no more fear.

He was somewhere else. A meadow. Tall golden grass waved in a gentle breeze. Butterflies flitted past him on important but obscure missions. The air felt sweet on his face; his sense of smell seemed to be amplified. How was that possible if he was dead?

And there was a woman next to him in a gauzy white dress. He couldn't see any specifics about her because the sun was shining right in his eyes. Was she an angel? The angel of death? He was dead, right? Finally? Sorrow made his heart heavy.

Then he realized that their hands were linked together. In her other hand, she held a bouquet of bright wildflowers.

A bride? Was it Olivia? Was she getting married? Was he her best man? Where was Jake?

No, none of that was right. In a flash, he understood. The groom was him. *He* was getting married. In a fucking meadow. He never spent time in meadows. West Covina didn't have any, as far as he knew. "What the...?"

He sat bolt upright, finishing that sentence with a very loud "fuck?"

The meadow was gone, replaced by a gaggle of medical types wearing masks and scrubs. A strong fluorescent light shone in his eyes.

"I'm not dead?" he asked.

A doctor pushed him back down onto the gurney. "Not anymore. Stay still, please. We're trying to keep you alive here, but you have to help us out."

He settled back down, heart racing. His body throbbed like one gigantic all-encompassing bruise. *Not anymore?* That implied he'd been dead, but survived. Once again he'd slipped from death's grasp. Incredible. Another near-death experience. And this one came with a vision.

Or, more likely, a delusion. Because one thing he knew for sure—he had no intention of getting married in a meadow. Or anywhere else, for that matter. With his medical history, he didn't seem like a good bet for anyone he cared about.

But the feeling of that vision—that delusion—clung to his senses as he drifted back to sleep. The scent of antiseptic had joined the flowers and grasses of the meadow, all just as strong as before. He knew from experience that almost dying could change a person. Could it enhance his sense of smell? Would it do other things to him?

When he woke up next, the medical crew was gone. His girl-friend Charley sat near his bed, tapping something into her phone. She must have come straight from an appointment with a client, because she always wore white during her life coaching sessions. She said it gave her patients a sense of calm.

A tailored white linen dress, in this case. Nothing like the one in his vision. But why quibble over details?

It seemed pretty clear what he had to do next.

CHAPTER ONE

Two months later

THIS WASN'T the first time Ethan James had found himself in trouble with the local authorities. As a private investigator, sometimes he worked with them, sometimes he got on their nerves. But they didn't usually arrest him and toss him in jail.

Welcome to Lost Harbor, Alaska, where before last night he'd mostly been worried about bear encounters.

"We have a new police chief," the arresting officer informed him as he fingerprinted him. "She runs a very tight ship. Sorry, man. Blame her, not me."

"Chief Maya Badger. Yes, I know. She's the one—"

"Nope." The sergeant threw up a hand to stop his explanation. He was friendly enough, with a sunny smile and a fringe of white beard, like a Santa in uniform. "I'm just doing my job. Letter of the law. Following orders. Not my fault. Filling out reports. Dotting I's and crossing T's. Just the way she likes."

Obviously this guy was hellbent on putting him in that cell.

Ethan gave in and handed over his personal items, which didn't amount to much—wallet, rental car keys and phone. He hadn't even checked into the Eagle's Nest yet. That was where he'd stayed on his previous trips to Lost Harbor; but those had been financed by clients. This trip was different.

Very different. He chuckled to himself as the sergeant steered him into the small holding cell tucked into a corner of the bullpen area of the police station. Its door had a small window, with bars in place of the glass. At the back of the cell there was another window that looked out on the inviting grove of birch trees behind the station. At least there was a view. If he had to spend a night in jail, he could do worse.

He spread his arms wide, realizing he could nearly touch both walls. "It's a good thing Lost Harbor has such a low crime rate so I have the place to myself."

"We're a little cramped for space here," the sergeant explained. "They're building us a new station, but for now, it is what it is."

"I'll have to come back in a year and get arrested again," Ethan said dryly as the cell door closed behind him. "I promise to rewrite my Yelp review."

"Funny. Okay then, Ethan S. James. Enjoy your night."

"It's off to a great start, can't lie."

The officer snorted and shuffled off. Ethan realized he hadn't been granted the traditional one phone call, but since it was three-thirty in the morning, he'd just suck it up until Maya Badger showed up.

She'd asked him to come here, after all. True, she hadn't asked him to hack into the police station's database and pull all the records related to one "Spruce Grouse," aka S.G. But old skills never went away, and with an antiquated system like Lost Harbor's, he could hardly be expected to ignore such a tempting opportunity to get a head start on this case.

He settled onto the bench that lined the back of the cell and stretched out his legs. His right leg was aching vaguely, with a kind of desultory whine, like a kid asking "are we there yet?" He rubbed it automatically, out of habit, even though what he really needed was a hot bath and a bed.

"You'll have to wait, buddy," he murmured to his leg. "Behave or I'll switch you out for a pirate peg leg." He'd gotten into the habit of talking to his troublesome limb when he was a kid, and had never quite shaken it.

"Eh?" shouted Sergeant Santa.

"Nothing," he called back. "Can you keep it down? Gonna try to get some Z's. Any chance you got some of those eye masks, like on a plane? It's so damn light in here."

"Teach you not to commit crimes in Alaska in the summer."

Ethan grumbled to himself and settled his back against the wall. Was "crime" really the right word? Maya Badger, the police chief, had hired him for this case, after all. On the phone, she hadn't set down any "rules" about "computer access." At worst, he was just an overeager new colleague.

The light from the little window above his head cast a shadowy blue glow into the cell. From where he sat, the other window, with its aluminum bars, gave him a view of the police station's acoustic tile ceiling. A sepia stain shaped like Florida spread across two of the tiles.

If only he could drag the bench to the front of the cell, so he could enjoy the view of the woods behind the station. Then his first night back in Lost Harbor would at least include some sight-seeing. He loved this little town clinging to the edge of the Alaskan wilderness. With its magnificent setting on Misty Bay, right across from the snowcapped mountains and deeply forested slopes of Lost Souls Wilderness, it had a special mystique that had stayed with him even back in the James Agency office in humdrum West Covina, Los Angeles.

This was his third trip to Lost Harbor. He'd met Maya on his first trip, when he'd worked with her to protect Padric Jeffers, the rock star, from death threats. He respected her, but they certainly weren't close friends.

This last time, the Alaska phone number had flashed on his phone in the middle of an argument with Charley.

His new fiancée.

Who wanted him to quit being a private investigator.

"You don't have a real schedule." She'd been ticking off her complaints on her fingers. "Your life is so unpredictable it's impossible to make plans. And what about all the people who apparently want to kill you?"

"But they keep missing the mark," he pointed out.

"You're not taking this seriously. Are you forgetting that I'm a life coach? This is exactly the kind of thing I advise people about."

"I'm not your client. And I enjoy my work."

"Oh, so you enjoy nearly drowning?"

"No, that was a low point. Gotta admit."

"Okay, what do you enjoy about it? How does it serve you?"

Ohh, that life-coach talk really got under his skin. How could he explain that it made him feel more alive than the computer work he used to do? He liked throwing his body into things. It was *his* body. Not the surgeon's or the oncologist's. *His*, to risk as he wanted.

She tried another approach. "You don't want me to worry, do you? Some things have to change when you get married. You have to accept that."

Just then, Maya's call had come in. He'd listened to her outline the situation. Spruce Grouse, known as S.G., was a mysterious runaway girl who'd been raised in Lost Souls Wilderness by a trapper who had found her as a baby. She'd recently become eager to find out her true origins, and had asked Maya to help her. With Maya's recent promotion to police chief, she didn't have enough spare time to investigate the mystery of a teenage runaway's origins.

He said 'yes' before they so much as discussed terms.

Before Charley could scold him, he took her hand. Cool to the touch, neutral nail polish. His future bride. Was this how her hand had felt in his vision? He couldn't remember.

"One last job," he told her softly. "It's in Lost Harbor, Alaska, and it won't involve any vengeful husbands or crazed Lexus drivers. It's a cold case, really. We'll be trying to figure out the true identity of a fifteen-year-old kid. I've been to Lost Harbor before, and it's a tiny little fishing town with a low crime rate. I'll be facing no danger. Should be back in a week."

"Just one week?"

"One week."

"Do you promise that it'll be your last job?"

He nodded, though it took everything in him to do so. If he was going to marry her, he should try to make her happy. "Last one. You can even come with me. It's a magical place."

"My schedule is beyond booked, you know that. Besides, Alaska..." She shivered. "No thanks."

One last job.

He'd never imagined that it would land him in jail on his very first night back in Lost Harbor. But whatever. It was just a few hours. As soon as Maya Badger came into the station, she'd spring him out of here.

Another thing he'd learned long ago was how to sleep in uncomfortable places and positions. He managed to doze off despite the sporadic sounds of phones ringing and voices and metal chairs screeching against the floor.

WHAT WOKE him up was a smell.

Not just any smell. A divine fragrance wafting through the bars of his cell door like Tinkerbell riding an air current—if Tinkerbell was bringing him spiced coffee cake. Ever since his near-drowning, he'd been acutely sensitive to smells. It was weird, and it hadn't faded in the months since the incident.

Light footfalls sounded on the floor outside the holding cell.

"Hello?" a female voice called. "Is anyone here? Maya?"

Ethan stiffly pushed himself off the bench to stand up. He wobbled there for a moment, gaining his balance. *Come on, buddy. Don't let me down.* "Hello? I'm here. Hungry as a horse."

The footfalls paused. "Who said that?"

"Over here. In the corner. Behind the bars. Don't worry, I'm not dangerous, though a little breakfast might help with that. 'Hangry' is a real thing, you know."

"Oh, I know, believe me. I see it firsthand every morning, as soon as the bakery doors open." Her voice came closer, and a few seconds later she was peering through the bars at him. Rich auburn hair backlit by the office fluorescents. Curious amber eyes, a merry smile. "Who the heck are you? I don't believe I know you."

"Ethan S. James. Nice to meet you." He gave her a little salute, like a military officer. "And you are?"

"Not about to introduce myself to a prisoner."

"Good policy in general. But I'm not supposed to be in jail. It's a mistake, and as soon as Maya realizes it she's going to be furious and full of apologies."

Her forehead crinkled. "That doesn't sound like Maya. She ruined my suede jacket in a snowstorm once and she still hasn't apologized."

Was this girl for real? He was in jail and she was ranting about a suede jacket? Talk about frivolous. She was pretty; maybe *too* pretty, the kind of girl who got by on her looks. The opposite of his sister and his fiancée. He liked brains in a woman.

But clearly she knew Maya, and maybe that meant she could help him out.

"Sounds like you're pretty close to her."

"Besties since third grade. Except for sixth grade, half of sophomore year, and part of our early twenties. Long story. Several long stories, come to think of it. I can tell you if you're interested, since you seem to have plenty of time. You're literally a captive audience. Our sixth grade fight was the worst, it started when she was sitting in front of me and I pulled her braid to get her attention. I only intended to offer her some Juicy Fruit but she thought I wanted to mess with her about the half-assed job her mom had done on her hair and—"

Oh my God. Was this story going anywhere? Was it worth listening just to pry some information out of her?

Good thing Charley was nothing like this. They might disagree about things like the dangers of PI work, but she was a practical, sensible person just like he was. That was why people trusted her life coaching skills.

"Are you sure Maya wants you spilling all her secrets like this?" he interrupted at the first possible moment.

"Oh, none of it's a secret. We had an epic fistfight right there in class. Hair pulling, eye gouging, the whole thing."

"Eye gouging?"

"Attempted eye gouging," she corrected with a shrug. "It was the class right before lunch and like you said, 'hangry' is a real thing. So is it appropriate for me to ask why you're in jail?"

He was pretty sure "appropriate" wasn't something that concerned her too much.

"Happy to tell you if you hand over one of those muffins."

"Do you mean these freshly baked, Rainier cherry buckwheat scones with lemon-cardamom icing?"

She lifted a cardboard bakery container to the bars to give him a look. The aroma made his head spin. Spice and citrus and sugar.

"Please God, yes," he said fervently. "Those."

"Perhaps you'd like some coffee with them too?" A metal thermos appeared on the other side of her face. Her sunny smile, combined with the promise of breakfast, made his mood lighten for the first time since the sergeant had knocked on his rental car window.

"You have no idea." His mouth was watering so much he could barely get the words out. "I have some money in my wallet. It's somewhere out there, wherever they put personal items. You know what would be even better? If you could find the key and let me out. That way I can get some cash for you. And Maya won't be quite so angry when she discovers that I'm in jail."

She pursed her lips and looked up at the ceiling, as if thinking over his proposal. "So let me get this straight. You want me to feed you breakfast, let you out of jail, and piss off my best friend by giving away her coffee?"

He snorted. Maybe she wasn't quite as flaky as he'd imagined. "Is that a no?"

"I'll think about it." She winked at him. "What's in it for me?"

"I'll tell you all about the dire acts that put me behind bars."

"Or...just spitballing...I could wait for Maya to show up and she could tell me."

"Yes, but you know how police blotters are, they're very dry and boring. I can tell you the inside story. All the juicy gory details."

"Gory? Is there blood involved? I'm not good with blood. That's why I picked baking instead of—"

"Medicine?"

"Fishing." She frowned at him. "Okay, how about this? Maya

never eats more than half a scone anyway because she gets so busy. I'll give you a nice big chunk of this scone if you tell me what a well-dressed, probably good-looking-when-not-so-tired stranger is doing in our humble little jail."

Probably good-looking. Not the most flattering description, but at least she was still talking.

"Throw in a sip of coffee and you have a deal."

"I can do better than that." She disappeared, taking her scones and coffee with her. He wanted to cry like a baby, watching them go.

In a minute, she came back with a paper cup of extremely dark coffee. She passed it through the bars to him. He took a whiff and made a face. "This is what's in that thermos?"

"Oh no, this is the station coffee, they must have made it last night."

"Good God." He sloshed it in the cup, where it left a poisonous-looking residue on the sides.

"Yeah. That's why I bring Maya *my* coffee when I want to butter her up." She flaunted the thermos at him, and he choked back a tormented growl. "But jailbirds can't be choosers. Here." She broke off a piece of scone and passed it through the bars. "This'll help it go down."

He set the coffee aside and devoured the scone in two bites. It was the best thing he'd ever tasted, hands down.

"Well?" She waited expectantly. "Juicy details please. As agreed."

"All right. I hacked into the police department computer system to find out more about the case Maya hired me for. Sergeant Santa got pinged that someone was on the network and decided I should contemplate my evil deeds during a quiet night in lockup."

She frowned. "That's it? Hacking? Not even the axe kind of hacking?"

"Not juicy enough for you? Sorry." The incredible cherry buckwheat concoction had hit his bloodstream, making him feel much more like a regular human. "I completely agree. They should only arrest people for more exciting crimes. So maybe you could find the keys to this place and—"

"What was the case?"

"Excuse me?"

"The case Maya hired you for?"

"I probably shouldn't talk about that. Maybe it's supposed to be confidential."

"Is it about S.G.? Spruce Grouse?"

He looked at her with surprise. Either it was already common knowledge or she wasn't a bad detective herself.

"I can see by your eyebrows that it is."

He forced his eyebrows back down to their normal position. "No comment."

She tapped her fingers on the thermos, barely paying attention to him anymore. "If she hired you to help with that case, something must be wrong, because she's been knee deep in that one for a while. What kind of help does she need? Who are you, anyway?"

"Okay, you can stop with the interrogation shit, Jess." The bakery girl's face disappeared, replaced by Maya Badger's. She frowned at him, the light sliding off her rich dark skin. "Ethan James? What the hell are you doing in there?"

"That's exactly what I've been wondering all night. Just so you know, I charge overtime for jail time."

A frown dented her forehead. "Did I say this was a paid job? You hung up before we got a chance to discuss it."

He sighed. Perfect end to a perfect night.

At least he'd gotten half of a perfect scone out of it.

CHAPTER TWO

Jessica Dixon stepped back as Maya unlocked the door of the jail cell. The man inside it—Ethan James—came limping out. Had he sustained an injury while being arrested in the parking lot? Maybe hacking was just as violent a crime as it sounded.

Ethan had wide shoulders, quiet hazel eyes, long legs encased in blue jeans. Wherever he came from, some stylist had done excellent work on his hair. Even after a night in jail, he looked good; he even smelled good, with some kind of clean citrus after-shave. Definitely different from the rough-edged guys she'd grown up with in Alaska.

And yet, she got the sense that he was pretty tough under that nicely groomed exterior. Something about his features intrigued her, as if he was a lot more than he appeared at first. Above all things, she trusted her intuition; it was probably the only thing that hadn't let her down at some point. Her intuition told her that Ethan James wasn't someone to mess with, and that there was a lot going on under his easy-on-the-eyes facade.

The way Maya treated him—with an unusual degree of respect—reinforced that impression.

"Let me guess," she told the man behind the bars. "You arrived here early and my sergeant got a little overeager last night."

"Don't blame him. I was crossing a line, I admit. I wanted to get a jump on the research."

"Shit." Maya set her hands on her hips. "I'm going to look like a hypocrite if I go easy on you."

Jessica waved the thermos of coffee and the box of scones at her. "Maya, I need to talk to you."

"Can we do it later, Jess? I have a problem on my hands."

She had a problem too; why else would she be here this early with coffee and bribery scones? "Okay sure, we can talk about my thing later. One crisis at a time, or so they say. Seems to me they always come in clusters."

Ethan shot her a vaguely amused glance. She got the impression that he didn't take her very seriously, as if she was a pesky little sister.

She didn't like that thought at all. She wasn't anyone's little sister, and just because she was a little offbeat didn't mean that she wasn't worthy of respect.

Or did it?

Lately she'd been wondering about that very question.

She realized that both Maya and Ethan were looking at her. "What? Did I miss something?"

"You said you were leaving. That we're going to talk about your thing later." In her police chief uniform, Maya always looked so stern, even though Jess knew better. Maya was the kind of friend you could always count on—well, except if she was busy with an unexpected perp.

"If this is about S.G., I don't mind sticking around. I could probably be helpful."

Ethan's half-smile felt wholly condescending. "Those scones

are sure helpful, I'll say that. Any chance you can rustle up a few more of those?"

A flash of anger swept through her. Just because she made sweets for a living and liked to smile didn't mean she was a dimwit he could order around.

"Sure thing, jailbird. I *live* to feed breakfast to inmates. They're so sexy, it's the lure of the forbidden and all that. Maybe I'll write you letters while you're serving your time, and then we can get married and have conjugal visits and—"

"Jessica." Maya could barely keep herself from laughing. "Take it easy on him. Ethan came up here from Los Angeles at my request. I have to deal with this situation before it gets even more awkward. But I'm grateful for the breakfast and we'll definitely address your problem as soon as I'm done here. I'll call you, okay? Are we good?"

As police chief, Maya knew how to manage a situation. Jessica wasn't used to being "a situation," but she could read the anxiety in her friend's posture. Right now, Maya needed her to leave, and so she'd do just that—but for her own reasons. Not because Mr. Bigshot from LA wanted another scone.

"We're good," she assured Maya, while casting a scathing glance at Ethan James. "No sharing my Guatemalan Organic Roast with the inmates, though."

Petty words to leave with, but she didn't take them back. She didn't appreciate being patronized, even by an attractive stranger.

Especially by an attractive stranger.

EVEN AFTER SHE'D ridden her bike back to the Sweet Harbor Bakery and B&B and gone back to work in the kitchen, Jessica's irritation didn't fade. She rolled out the lunchtime biscuits with twice the force she usually used, nearly bending her favorite cookie cutter in the process. It wasn't just Ethan she was mad at; they didn't know each other, after all. He could be forgiven for dismissing her with a smile and a light word about scones.

Could be forgiven, but might not be, depending on what he did next.

No, this wasn't about Ethan-the-handsome-jailbird. This was about *her*. Just because she'd been running Sweet Harbor since her mother had dumped it on her didn't mean she couldn't do other things. Just because she'd skipped college to take over the bakery didn't mean she didn't have a brain. Just because she'd never even left Alaska didn't mean she was trapped in her comfort zone of muffins and room rentals.

Or did it?

Lately, she'd been wondering if all of those things were true. Ethan James, whoever he was, had hit a sore spot.

She busied herself with making biscuits until she noticed that Sergeant Hollister was at the display case. Ethan had referred to a "Sergeant Santa," and he was the only one who fit that description.

With a glance at Nia, the blue-haired, nose-ringed server, she took over at the cash register.

"Good morning, Sergeant. Why are you trying to pay, you silly goose? You know all the Lost Harbor police caffeinate for free here."

He covered up a yawn with the crook of his arm. "Seems like that's only when you're around."

"Oh, well, the others forget sometimes." She waved off his money. "Hey, heard you had a busy night last night."

"Sure did. Following the new chief's orders. Doin' my duty."

Poor Maya. Taking over a department of ornery old dudes

was no picnic. Jessica admired her for shaking things up. If only she could do the same.

"We all appreciate everything you're doing to keep the town safe." She batted her eyelashes at him, knowing he was no match for her smile when she unleashed it. "Is it true you arrested a violent felon in the parking lot?"

"Nah, I wouldn't go that far. He came easily enough. Didn't have to fire my weapon, but I was ready."

"I just bet you were." Maya had told her that the Lost Harbor police rarely even drew their weapons. It just didn't come up very often. "He would have been no match for you, I'm sure."

He puffed up his chest. "Of course not. We're a small town, but we can hold our own. No hotshot PI's gonna get the best of me."

Oh ho. Ethan James was a *private investigator*. Very intriguing. She smiled again at the sergeant and patted his arm. "You should go get some sleep. Those overnight shifts must be killer."

"Thanks, dear. You're gonna forget I just told you that about our perp, aren't you?"

"Sure thing, Sergeant. You know me. Silent as a cheesecake." She winked at him. "I know it's supposed to be 'silent as a grave,' but that's just too morbid for me. Cheesecakes are equally silent, at least I've never known one to say a word."

He chuckled as he picked up his coffee. "Always nice to see you, Kiddo. Brightens the day. Say hello to your mom."

"Will do." Her smile dimmed as he left the bakery.

What was the point in passing along his greeting? Her mom wouldn't even remember him. It was ten years since they'd dated, and she had a new husband now. He was the worst of the lot.

She went back to her biscuits and saw that they had risen enough to be slid into the big commercial oven. When her mother had started Sweet Harbor Bakery over twenty years ago, she'd done all the baking in a tiny propane unit in an RV. As soon as she'd started turning a profit, she'd invested in a real commercial oven. But old framed photos of the original Sweet Harbor kitchen still adorned the wall. The infamous yellow RV with its cheerful curtains and abundant production of muffins and sweet rolls for the local fishermen was iconic.

The photo with Jessica as a little girl poking her head out of the window to take someone's order had even made it into a national magazine article about quirky offbeat eateries.

Yup, that was Sweet Harbor Bakery. Quirky and offbeat. Just like Jessica herself—at least according to everyone in town.

What would it take to shake that label? What would it take to inspire someone like Ethan James to look at her with something other than mild amusement?

She sighed, stirring a puff of flour into the air. Why should she care what Ethan James thought of her? He could "rustle up some scones" and shove them where the sun don't shine, as far as she was concerned.

She had much, much bigger things to worry about. Like the certified letter from her mother sitting unopened on her office desk. Her mother's new husband, *Gary*—she always mentally drew out the name in a sarcastic tone—had big plans for Sweet Harbor Bakery and B&B. He was pulling out all the stops to get her to sell.

That was why she'd rushed over to the police station with panic scones. She needed to talk this over with someone. It was such a big decision and she *hated* making important decisions. Little everyday decisions were no problem, but the big life-changing ones were her Achilles heel. Her fatal flaw. And Maya was *so good* at them.

The water pipes clanged, meaning someone had just turned on the shower upstairs. That reminded her that she had to fix the hot water heater today. Her B&B guests could handle some minor Alaska-style inconveniences, but not a lack of hot showers.

She left the biscuits for Nia to finish and hurried off to gather up her plumbing tools. Lost Harbor had very few plumbers, so she'd learned to handle such things herself. Besides, she'd much rather play plumber than make a decision. No contest.

CHAPTER THREE

Ethan only had time for a quick meeting with Maya before things got busy at the Lost Harbor police station. They squeezed in apologies on both sides and set an appointment for later that day.

"I have some homework for you before then," Maya told him as she turned on her computer. "Just give me a second to print my notes."

"Sounds good. It might have to wait until after a shower and a nap, though."

"Do I have to apologize again?" she asked wryly.

"No need," he assured her. She'd dropped the charges, and that was more than enough for him.

"The thing about this case," Maya explained as she tapped on her files, "it's not in my jurisdiction. Lost Souls Wilderness is a mix of state and federal land, and since we don't know exactly where S.G. was found, I can't say which. I know for sure it isn't Lost Harbor PD territory. So for me to work on it, I have to do it on my own time, after hours."

"Which probably doesn't leave you much time at all."

She crossed over to the printer on the other side of the room.

"Exactly. That's why I thought of you. Padric Jeffers vouches for you, and so does Darius Boone. I was pretty excited when you agreed to come up."

"My pleasure. It's always a good change of pace from California. It came at a good moment."

Part of him wanted to ask about her friend, Jessica with the divine scones. Before his near-death experience—and before Charley—he might have tried to see her again, because she was appealing and might be fun to pass some time with while he was in Lost Harbor.

But now, he was engaged. No more flirting for him.

"Any big news in your life?" she asked as they watched the printer spit out pages.

"Well, I did get engaged since the last time I was here."

"Congratulations."

He grunted. He still wasn't used to the idea of being engaged. For long stretches of time, he forgot about it.

She eyed him sideways. "Where's that disgustingly besotted look I usually see when couples get engaged?"

He rolled his shoulders, still getting the kinks out from his night in jail. "It's not that kind of engagement."

"You're not engaged to be married? You got some other kind of engagement down there in the Lower Forty-eight? We're always behind the times up here."

"No no, we're getting married. It's just not, you know, the sappy kind of engagement. Romantic. All that shit. It's the practical kind."

The printer stopped whirring and Maya collected a sheaf of pages. She handed them over to him. "I didn't get a chance to organize these, so just look at it as raw data. It's everything I've managed to learn so far about S.G. and Edgar Murchison, the fugitive who raised her in Lost Souls. He's in prison in Texas now on preexisting warrants."

"Have you interviewed him?"

"He's not talking. I have no leverage because the Texas authorities aren't too worried about a girl who survived. They have a bunch of murders they're pinning on him. He's a very bad dude and S.G. is a lucky kid."

Ethan wasn't sure he'd call being raised in isolation by a murderer "lucky"—but at least she'd survived.

"Will I be able to interview her?"

"We'll see. S.G.'s a funny girl. She either trusts you or she might pull her hunting knife on you. But we can talk about all that later. You go get yourself a hot shower and some rest. I'll see you tonight. Where are you staying?"

He opened his mouth to remind her that she should be covering his expenses, but then realized, once again, that they'd never discussed terms. Awkward.

"Never mind. Here, take this voucher for the Sweet Harbor B&B. I bid for it at the last auction and haven't got a chance to use it. Best breakfast in town. Well, you already know. You liked that scone, didn't you?"

"Yes," he said cautiously. He wouldn't mind more of those scones.

"Then you're all set. See ya later. I want to know more about these 'practical engagements' you got going on. I like the sound of that. If I was ever going to tie the knot, it'd have to be something like that."

Her phone was ringing and the next shift was arriving and she was practically shoving him out the door now. He felt as if he'd been caught in a whirlwind and before he knew it, he was outside the station facing his rental car, a red Jeep that had caught every pothole between here and Anchorage.

It was still not quite nine in the morning, but the blazing sunshine made it seem like high noon. He squinted and shaded his eyes, dazzled by the brilliant light bouncing off the cars in the parking lot. Everything—the blue spruce trees beyond the lot, the wild profusion of sunny buttercups at their feet--felt freshly washed and crystal clean.

He tried to catch up to what had just happened.

So wait ... he was going to stay at the place that made the scones Jessica had brought? Did that mean she was going to be there too? How did he feel about that? He felt some kind of way, but he couldn't pin it down.

His phone rang, making him start. A little knot of dread formed in his stomach. It was probably Charley, checking to see if he'd made it safely to Lost Harbor.

But it was his sister Olivia instead. He chose not to examine the sense of relief that came over him, and answered the call.

"Hey Liv, I can't talk now, I just got out of jail and I have to check into my bed-and-breakfast."

"Wait...*what*? Are you okay?"

"I'm grrrrreat."

"You sound drunk."

"Not drunk. Just excited to be a free man again."

"Are you talking about your imprisonment or did you break up with Charley?"

He also chose not to examine the hopeful tone in her voice. "Of course not. I don't break my commitments. Shame on you."

He clicked his key fob and got into the Jeep. He did a quick check to make sure his stuff was still there—laptop, overnight bag. Nothing had been disturbed by Sergeant Santa. At least something had gone right.

"Ethan, be serious. Seems like ever since the...you know...the incident..."

"The near-drowning."

"Yes." He could practically hear the wince in her voice. Olivia was used to the medical crises that involved his leg, but nearly getting drowned was a very different story. She'd been phone-hovering ever since. "You've been acting strange since then. Not yourself."

"That's because I'm a new man." He put the phone on speaker and started the car. He didn't bother to route it through the sound system. "I told you what happened. I had a vision."

"I know you said that, but is it really a reason to change every single thing about your life?"

"You're so dramatic. Jesus. Look, Liv, dying made me rethink my life."

"Stop saying that!" his sister exclaimed. "You weren't really dead."

"They told me I was dead for a whole minute. What do I know? I didn't think I was dead either. I thought I was getting married. Then I woke up and saw Charley."

He'd proposed to her with saline dripping into his veins and oxygen cannulas in his nose. He'd been a little shocked when she'd accepted.

"You weren't yourself. That was the worst possible time to make such a drastic decision."

"It's done. There's no going back. Besides, we're very compatible."

"Aside from her hating your job."

"My old job."

"Stop saying—maybe we should talk about all this another time." Olivia obviously didn't want to fight. He didn't either. He and his sister were very close; or at least they had been until she'd left the James Agency to go fall in love with Jake Rockwell. He and Olivia had always stuck up for each other. But Olivia's dislike of Charley might be a problem.

"I don't need to talk about it. I'm getting married to Charley and you're going to be my best man and there's nothing else to say. I'm getting off the phone now. I don't want to get arrested again. Once a day is enough for me."

"You know I'm going to need the whole story soon, right? Are you starving? Did they at least feed you in jail?"

"Someone showed up with the most incredible cherry scones you've ever tasted. Like an angel from bakery heaven."

"Someone?"

He recognized that hopeful tone of voice. "Someone who bakes," he said severely. "Don't go getting any ridiculous ideas. I don't know what your problem is with Charley, and I don't want to know."

"Are you sure? Because—"

"I'm sure. This is happening, Liv. As soon as I get back to LA, we're doing it. She's planning the whole thing right now."

"Of course she is," muttered Olivia. "Okay, I'll shut up now. I suppose I'm just annoyed because she made you give up the James Agency."

"Don't want to hear it!"

"The agency I started—"

"Olivia James Rockwell. Stop it."

"The agency you love, the job you love—"

He ended the call with his thumb and tossed the phone in the backseat. Sure, it had hurt to announce that the James Agency was closing. He didn't really look forward to shifting into tech work. But he was good at it, and it was a safer kind of profession. And it would make Charley happy.

He drove out of the police station lot, after a quick glance at the voucher Maya had given him. Sweet Harbor Bakery and B&B, located on Beach Drive, which he knew ran along gorgeous Seafarer's Beach. It probably had a spectacular view, since every place in Lost Harbor did. But right now, he didn't care if it looked out on the town dump. As long as it had a bed and a shower, he'd be a happy former jailbird.

A SARCASTIC ASIAN girl with blue-streaked hair checked him in at the counter of the Sweet Harbor Bakery. She rattled off instructions in between setting out fresh croissants and serving quad shots to a group of tourists. All the guest rooms were on the second floor. His room was the one facing the ocean. He could enjoy breakfast any time after seven in the morning, and oh, by the way, the water heater was broken. She handed over a key with a fob shaped like a cupcake.

"Wait. What was that last part? About the heater?"

"Water heater. It's broken."

"No hot showers?"

"You must be a detective or something. Correct."

God damn it. Why was everything going wrong on this trip?

"Is someone working on it? Is the problem going to be fixed any time soon?"

"The owner is working on it right now. But if it's urgent—"

In his opinion, showering after a night in jail was an urgent need, but he didn't want to make a scene. Especially because Sweet Harbor Bakery was like a gingerbread house come to life and it smelled like a sugar factory.

"It's all right. I'll wait."

"You sure?" She leaned forward and took a whiff of the air near him. "Just saying. You smell like you had a fun night."

"Oh yeah, it was quite the party. One for the history books. Or at least the police blotter."

She laughed, with no idea that he wasn't joking. "I hope I can still party when I'm your age."

"My—" Shaking his head, he let it drop. He was only twenty-nine, but people often thought he was older than that. He liked to think it was because he was a hard-boiled detective, but possibly it had something to do with his medical history too. He'd had to grow up early. He didn't mind the mistake, but then again, he didn't need a nineteen-year-old consigning him to an early grave either. "Hopefully I can find my room without my cane."

The girl laughed. "If I hear a crash I'll come running. Make sure to grab some firewood on your way up the stairs. The heater isn't working and a cold front's moving in."

"I suppose the owner's working on the heater too?"

"No, it's summer, we're not too worried about it. It's in the shop and the repair dude promised he'll get it to us by fall."

"Thoughts and prayers."

With another smirk, she pointed him toward a set of worn wooden stairs just past a display of fresh-baked bread. At the base of the stairs, opposite a side door, cut birch branches were stacked against the wall. He bent down to snag a bundle as he passed.

He found his room easily enough, since there were only four of them. Inside, he heaved a sigh of relief that it was clean and inviting, with a double casement window looking out toward the beach, and a four-poster bed with a quilt patterned with sandhill cranes. A vase of fresh sunflowers sat on the nightstand next to the bed. A small woodstove took up one corner of the room.

Dropping the firewood next to the stove, he abandoned his bags and flopped backwards onto the bed. *Bliss.* Apparently nothing felt quite as good as a comfy bed after a night behind bars. He should have gotten arrested years ago.

Laughing at that thought, he closed his eyes briefly.

At least he thought it was briefly, but when he opened them again, jerking awake at the sound of a shout, the light in the room had changed. It lay across the floor in strips of gold, making him wish he could skate across it into the glorious day outside.

A shout caught his attention, similar to the one that had woken him up. A woman yelled, "Need a hand up here! Anyone?"

Ethan waited for an answer, but no one came running up the staircase. He rolled out of bed and stretched his arms over his head, working out the kinks. He stuck his head out into the hall-way. "Still need help?"

"Yes!" a woman hollered back. "Unless you want the whole place to float away into the ocean."

Her voice sounded familiar, but he couldn't place it as he blinked the sleep out of his eyes. He locked his door and stepped down the hallway toward the room at the end, which had an old-fashioned WC sign on the door.

The owner must be working on the water heater. With any luck, maybe he'd get a hot shower after all.

He put his hand on the knob and pulled the door open, just as another shout rang out from inside the bathroom. "Watch out!"

Too late. A jet of water hit him right in the chest.

Cold water. Very, extremely, icy-ass-cold water that probably got pumped in from a Lost Souls glacier.

He swiped the water out of his eyes, scowling at the incompetent plumber who'd gotten him drenched from head to toe.

It was Jessica with the scones. She too was soaking wet, but at least she'd dressed for the possibility in a white tank top and paint-smudged cutoffs. Through the chaos of water he noted that her arms were strong and defined, and her auburn hair was pulled back from her face in a tousled ponytail. She had a wrench in one hand and was wrestling with some pipes behind a vintage water heater. Her legs were tanned and shapely, and she wore work boots with bright pink socks.

And despite the circumstances, he found all of that pretty freaking sexy.

Damn, this trip ...

CHAPTER FOUR

Jessica scrambled to her feet, not sure if she should help Ethan or fix the valve first. The poor man was staggering backwards into the hallway. The water had hit him dead on, like a bullseye to the chest, but it had so much force that it had drenched the rest of him too.

"Step back and close the door!" she shouted over the noise of water jetting from the pipe.

"Didn't you shut the water off?"

"Just get back!" She reached out with her foot and slammed the door in his face. Of course he would assume that they were on city water, because what else would there be in a place like Los Angeles? But the Sweet Harbor had a well, and she couldn't very well shut all the water off while she worked on the water heater. The bakery was still open.

So she'd closed the valve that allowed water to flow to the upstairs...except something had gone wrong. Someone must have reopened the valve without checking. It had happened before. The whole system was absurdly complicated, probably because the plumber who had installed it had gone on a bender halfway through the job. That was life in Alaska for you.

She scrabbled in her pocket for her phone, which fortunately had stayed safe from the gushing water. As she clicked on the downstairs number, she did her best to reattach the old galvanized pipe into its connection. This whole system needed to be replaced. She wouldn't be surprised if it all collapsed in a heap of scrap metal one of these days.

"Nia! Did you switch over the valves?"

"I don't know...maybe?"

"Ugh. Just flip that switch you're never supposed to touch."

"But I'm not supposed to touch it."

"Now! Before I drown in the bathroom or the entire floor disintegrates."

"Okay. What's that noise? Sounds like rapids."

"Nia!"

A second later, the water stopped abruptly. Jessica shoved her phone back in her pocket and grabbed the wrench. She reset the pipe into its socket and fit the head of the wrench around the joint. This was the part where she could have used a hand before, someone to keep the pipe from shifting. Hopefully she could get it this time, before she caught a cold from being sopping wet.

But she didn't have to do it alone; a strong hand appeared on the pipe wrench that she'd tried to clamp above the joint. Ethan, soaked to the skin, gazed down at her. "Go ahead, wrench away."

"Thanks," she muttered, though she didn't feel especially grateful. First he'd been snide to her at the station, now he'd made that little comment about shutting off the water. Clearly he thought she was some kind of dimwitted country bumpkin.

Quickly, she tested the plumber's tape she'd already wrapped around the pipe with the male end. Still good. Then she set it into the female end of the other pipe. She wrenched the fitting on until it was tight, then tested it with a tug. Solid. The entire time she worked, she was aware of Ethan's attention on her.

Probably looking for mistakes.

She was also highly aware of his physical presence. Her intuition, that part of her that sent out feelers to people and gathered information like a busy bee, told her he had a lot of inner strength and determination, that he liked to laugh but that he wasn't in a very good mood at the moment. He had a lot on his mind, she sensed. He'd been through something serious. And now he was here, laughing at her.

Not that she could blame him.

As soon as she was done, she took a step back from the overwhelming closeness.

"I appreciate your assistance," she told him, using a formal tone to create a distance. "Although I could have done it without you, and have many times in the past, it was certainly easier with an extra hand."

"No thanks needed if it means I get a hot shower. The surprise cold shower was better than nothing, but I'm still holding out for a hot one." He grinned at her, showing her a whole different version of the man she'd first seen in the holding cell. That smile could make a girl's knees melt right out from under her.

Some other girl, not her. She believed in destiny, and she knew for certain that she wasn't destined to meet her soulmate in a jail cell.

"You're at the head of the line," she promised. "It's not quite ready yet, but I'll knock on your door as soon as it is. I might have a tiny bit of cleanup to do first."

Since the floor was covered in a good inch of water, that was an understatement.

"Need a hand with that?"

She stared at him, trying to make out if he was serious or not.

Mopping a floor wasn't something most people were eager to volunteer for. "You're a paying guest. Absolutely not."

"Technically, I'm not. Maya Badger gave me a voucher."

"Did she? You must be a VIP. She's been saving that forever. I keep hoping she'll use it for a hot date. I don't suppose...?" She eyed him speculatively, remembering how Maya had treated him with such respect. With Maya, respect would have to come first—on both sides.

"I'm engaged," he said quickly. "Sorry to disappoint."

"Really?" Strange—she hadn't picked up any hint of a romantic attachment in her intuitive survey. Well, she'd never claimed one hundred percent accuracy.

"That's odd."

"Really, is it so odd?" he asked dryly. "Even jailbirds can find love."

"Of course. It's not that..." She shook her head impatiently and waded through the water to the wastepaper basket, which fortunately got emptied every day. She took out the liner to use the basket as a scoop. "It's nothing."

"What then?"

"Nothing. Really. It's nothing that you'd be interested in."

"See, that's the thing about me. I'm interested in a lot of things. Comes with the job."

"The private investigator job?"

Now it was his turn to look surprised. "Maya filled you in?"

"No, I have my own sources." When he narrowed his eyes at her, she just widened hers. Sergeant Hollister had sworn her to secrecy and she never betrayed a confidence. She filled the plastic basket with water and dumped it into the claw-foot bathtub.

Ethan disappeared, then returned carrying the trash basket from his room. He was barefoot and had rolled up his pant legs, revealing muscular calves and a long scar running up his right leg.

"The quicker we get this done, the quicker I get my shower, right?"

"Correct."

As if they were bailing out a boat, they both set to work scooping water from the floor into the tub.

"Still curious why you think it's so odd that I'm engaged," he said after they'd lowered the level of the water by about a quarter inch. "You don't even know me."

"You're right. It's completely not my business. Forget that I said anything, please." His feet were distracting her. They were very well-shaped. Not that she judged people by their feet. She was more into forearms. Forearms were definitely her jam. She stole a quick glance at Ethan's forearms, visible because he'd stripped down to a t-shirt when he'd come back into the bathroom.

Oh yes, he also had excellent forearms, well-muscled but not excessively so, with just the lightest scattering of hair.

"I'm here bailing out your bathroom after you water-hosed me. Don't you owe me?"

She couldn't deny that. "Fine. But you already think I'm a flake, and now you're going to think even worse of me."

"I haven't yet come to any kind of conclusion about you except that you bake a damned good scone and you have a way with a wrench."

She didn't believe that for a second. "I'm very good at reading people. I'm quite intuitive and I can pick up a lot about someone without them telling me. It's like an extra sense. You can laugh if you want, but even Maya agrees that I can sense certain things. For instance, I know perfectly well that you've formed a judgment about me. You don't take me seriously."

He looked up at her as he filled his container with water. "That was before I knew that my hot shower depended on you."

"Bow down to the plumbing queen," she quipped.

He went along with her joke, and ducked his head. Her irritation with him began to fade, since he was being such a good sport.

"I said it was odd because I didn't pick up any hint of you being engaged. Normally it's the kind of thing I can sense. There you go. You can laugh now."

He dumped his bucket of water into the tub with a shrug. "Well, it's pretty new. Maybe my aura hasn't caught up yet."

She gritted her teeth and sloshed her way over to the sink, where the big sponges were stored. "I see your mockery and raise you an 'I knew you'd react this way.' You know the funny thing? Everyone has the ability to be intuitive, but most people just ignore it. Haven't you ever done anything just because some sixth sense was telling you that you should?"

He straightened up as a smile slid across his face. "Yup. I got engaged."

Every time he referred to his engagement she got a strange sensation, like trying to swallow a moldy bit of cheese. It just felt wrong to her. But she could hardly tell a total stranger that she didn't have high hopes for his impending marriage.

"Congratulations." She sopped up water with the biggest sponge she'd been able to find and squeezed it into the bathtub. "And good luck to you."

He must have picked up on the doubt in her voice. "Won't need it. I don't believe in luck. I like to use my common sense, not count on good fortune."

What kind of person didn't believe in luck? Her opinion of Ethan James was once again dropping fast. Too bad he had such nice feet and forearms. And voice. She really liked his voice, which had an undercurrent of laughter to it that gave her the shivers. "So you got engaged by using common sense?"

"Exactly. Marriage is much too serious for anything else. You're talking about the rest of your life."

"Which is exactly my point. You can't rely on something as

limited as common sense for such a big decision. When I meet my soul mate, I'll know because I'll be using *all* my senses to identify him."

She'd imagined it so many times—the way her intuition would light up like a sky full of fireworks.

"Oh, here we go. The whole 'soul mate' argument. I think we can skip right to the part where we agree to disagree."

"But I don't agree to disagree." She shot him a sunny smile. "I'd prefer to talk you out of your mundane view of life. I'd prefer to make you acknowledge that not everything can be explained away with so-called common sense. That's where intuition comes in."

A funny expression crossed his face; maybe she'd touched a nerve. If so, it wasn't something he wanted to talk about, because he tucked the wastepaper basket under his arm and checked his wrist watch. "Sorry, I'm going to stick with mundane. That's what works for me. I have some homework to do before my meeting with Maya. Unless you can telepathically tell me what's in her notes, I'd better get to it."

"Mockery will get you nowhere." She squeezed out the sponge with an extra-vicious twist of her hands. "Good luck with your homework. I'll knock on your door when the shower's ready."

"I don't need lu—"

She waved him out of the bathroom and closed the door before he could finish. If he wanted to believe he had all the answers, so be it. All she had to do was wait patiently for her chance to say "I told you so."

Oh, how she'd enjoy that moment when it came.

CHAPTER FIVE

Ethan changed out of his wet clothes and draped them near the open window to dry. Maybe later he'd ask Jessica if there was a clothes dryer in the building. But he wasn't ready for any more conversation with her. Even though she was right about his assessment of her, she'd left out one thing. He also found her appealing. Too appealing.

Best to put the entire bathroom episode behind him as he concentrated on Maya's notes about S.G. It wasn't easy. Jessica had made some good points, damn it all. And she'd done it while competently fixing a pipe and wading through a flood.

Disturbingly sexy.

Focus. *Focus.*

He spread the notes out on the antique desk under the window. A sweet summer breeze filtered through the screen. The scent of salt air and wild roses filled the room, along with a touch of cinnamon and melted butter from the bakery below.

Were they making more of those incredible scones?

Charley rarely ate pastries. She was very disciplined when it came to her diet so she could provide a good example to her clients. He admired that about her, along with so many other things. What would she say about Jessica's butter-laden cherry scone? She'd be kind about it, but firm. *It's okay to cheat sometimes*, she'd say, *just make sure you get back on your plan as soon as possible.*

Instead of lectures, Charley relied on a kind of subtle disapproval, like a disappointed mother. It set his teeth on edge, to be honest.

Focus, damn it.

He forced his gaze away from the hazy blue horizon and the dazzling diamond-spangled surface of the bay to the pages Maya had printed out.

Facts: Spruce Grouse chose her own name because the trapper who had raised her called her only "Girl." Nate Prudhoe, the firefighter who had first found her hiding out in the firehouse, had shortened it to S.G. That was the name everyone called her now.

More facts: S.G. was an expert with a hunting knife, but had never learned to read or write. She had no memory of other people, just the trapper, who she called King because that's what he told her to call him. She didn't know how old she was, but Dr. Bethany Morrison estimated her to be about fifteen. There were huge gaps in her vocabulary and knowledge because of how she'd grown up. She was resourceful, ingenious, and independent, but also traumatized. She had no interest in leaving Lost Harbor for any reason. It was the only place she felt safe.

She was currently being fostered by a woman named Denaina Hopkins, a Native Alaskan woman. She'd made friends there, including Dylan, the newly discovered sixteen-year-old son of Darius Boone, the fire chief.

Another oddity: She believed that she could communicate with animals.

Which brought his thoughts back to Jessica. That seemed like something she would believe too, along with intuition and people-reading and soul mates.

He flipped over to the pages about the trapper. His name was Edgar Murchison, and he'd been a fugitive for twenty years. He'd fled Texas, where he was wanted on armed robbery and murder charges, and made his way to Alaska and then into Lost Souls Wilderness. He'd lived alone in a cabin there, trapping and dog mushing and trading furs for supplies, until the day he'd found a baby in the forest.

Was that really possible? Was there more to that story?

For fifteen years, S.G. had lived as a virtual servant until one day Murchison hadn't come back from his usual trapping run, but the dogs had. She'd taken the dog sled team and set off across the wilderness without any idea of what she would find. Somehow she'd ended up in Lost Harbor and hidden out in the firehouse, spying on the firefighters and eating out of the refrigerator.

Truly fascinating story. It felt like something out of another time. In a world ruled by the Internet and connectivity, it was hard to imagine living completely cut off from civilization.

He couldn't wait to interview S.G. for himself.

Maya had gathered all her theories about the case into one document. He was just starting to scan it when his phone rang.

Charley, checking up on him. It would be rude to ignore her.

"Hi sweetheart."

"Ethan, I've told you that we don't have to say that kind of thing." Her no-nonsense tone felt like a splash of cold water on his face. Bracing.

"Right. Slip of the tongue. How's LA?"

"I got a new client. A *celebrity* client."

"Anyone I would know?"

"Probably not. She's a YouTuber. I didn't know her either

until I looked her up. She's an influencer, which means that if I do a good job for her, I could reach a whole new client base."

"Wonderful. Congratulations."

"You sound distracted. Did I catch you at a bad time?"

"Relatively speaking, no. At least I'm not in jail or being attacked by a broken water valve."

"*What?*"

"Just another day in the life of a P.I."

"See, this is exactly why I wanted you to quit. You were in jail? I hope none of my clients find out about that."

Why should they care about something that had nothing to do with them?

Best not to argue that point. He didn't want to argue with Charley because whenever he did, doubts snuck into his mind. They hadn't yet mastered the art of arguing successfully.

"It was really more of a misunderstanding. Now I'm at a lovely bed and breakfast with a view of wild roses and glaciers and mountains. I may even score a hot shower. Things are looking up."

"Well, don't get too comfortable because I have an amazing surprise for you."

"Oh yeah?"

He scanned the "Theories" section as she talked.

Theory One: S.G. was on a small plane that had crashed on its way back from Aurora Lodge, in Lost Souls Wilderness, killing all aboard except her.

Pros: The timing fits, and the geography fits.

Cons: The only passengers were Anthony and Carole Berenson. No babies listed.

"Dr. McGee has offered to marry us. He's a licensed minister along with all his other skills."

Dr. McGee was Charley's own life coach, the one who'd

gotten her into the field. She often referred to him as her "mentor," in a tone of awe.

Did he want to be married by Dr. McGee? He didn't really trust the guy, but did it really matter who performed the ceremony? Not to him.

"That's good news," he murmured as he scribbled a note in the margins of Theory One.

Expand the timeframe for plane crash searches. Younger or older?

"There's a catch, though," Charley continued. "A big catch."

"Whatever it is, we'll work with it."

"He can only do it this weekend."

That got his attention. "Why? I'm working up here, Charley. I don't know how long it's going to take."

"You said no more than a week."

"I just got here."

"Can't you fly back just for the wedding? You know how busy he is. He's in demand all around the world. He's doing us a huge favor by squeezing us in."

"Am I supposed to be honored by that? He's *squeezing us in* for the most important day of our lives?"

"Yes, exactly. But he can't actually be there in person. It will have to be online."

Ethan ground his teeth together, determined to hold back the argument that was just dying to burst out. If this was what Charley wanted, why not just do it? How much did it really matter if Dr. McGee was just a bunch of pixels at the wedding? Maybe it would be better that way. The man got on his nerves.

"I'll think about it," he managed.

"What's there to think about? This is a life-changing opportunity."

He clenched his jaw so tight the muscle twanged. "Fine."

"You don't sound thrilled."

"I'm working on it."

"You're working on being thrilled?"

"That's as good as it's going to get, sorry."

"Honestly, Ethan, you can be so passive-aggressive some-times." Her cool critique made him want to bang his phone against the window. "I'll tell him you're working on being thrilled. Just let me know if you achieve it."

Before he could get in another word, she ended the call.

He stared at the phone, wondering where he'd gone wrong. What exactly was passive-aggressive, anyway? He'd been aiming for honest-without-offending-her. Apparently he'd missed.

A knock sounded at the door.

He tossed the phone aside, aiming for the bed. "What?"

Jessica stood in the hallway, as fresh as a just-rinsed summer peach. Her white tank top clung to the firm curves of her waist and chest. He forced his gaze away from her breasts. "Just letting you know that the hot shower is now fully operational and that I recommend you skip on in there if you want to beat Old Crow."

"Old Crow?"

"He's one of our local fisherman. He rents a room here one day a month so he can get his personal grooming done."

Amusement lifted his mood, like the first light of dawn on the horizon. "Once a month, huh?"

"Yes." She used her shoulder to flick away a long strand of coppery hair that had fallen from her ponytail. "As you can imag-ine, it takes a while. I just wanted to give you a heads up about that. Sorry to disturb you."

"No, no. It's fine. I just...got some news I'm still trying to wrap my head around."

Her expression softened from wary to sympathetic. "Sorry. If there's anything you need, either me or my staff will be happy to help. I always find there's nothing like a beach walk to help process bad news. It's only one block away, and you can walk for miles in either direction, depending on just how bad the news is."

"It's not *bad*, per se. It's more a...decision I have to make. About the wedding."

Her face shifted, as if a window curtain had drawn halfway closed. "I see. Well, whenever I have to make a tough decision..." She drew her lower lip between her teeth. "Never mind. I'm sure you'll make the right choice. Enjoy that shower."

She hurried down the hallway, as if fleeing from having to explain her method for making tough decisions.

Probably a good thing, because he was one hundred percent sure he would find her method ridiculous.

He allowed himself one quick glance at the sight of her disappearing around the corner to the stairs—those work boots really set off her long legs, and her cutoffs hugged her rear to perfection.

By now he was too distracted to absorb the rest of Maya's theories about S.G., so he grabbed his travel bag and the folded towel left on the bed and hurried into the bathroom.

The faint scent of cinnamon still hovered in the air, left by Jessica, no doubt. The floor was sparkling clean. The ancient hot water heater in the corner had been put back together with no sign that it had ever been dismantled.

He had to hand it to her; she had some skills along with her weird beliefs.

The hot shower was pure perfection. It felt so good to get the grime of jail and travel off his body. His leg appreciated it too; nothing worked quite like hot water to make the tightness of his scar tissue ease. He soaped himself vigorously, whistling a cheerful tune, shoving all stressful thoughts of weddings and mentors and runaways behind him.

A happy, carefree mood stole over him, for the first time since...maybe since his near-drowning. This trip might be mostly a disaster so far, but at least the pastries were good and the showers were hot and—

The bathroom door flung open. For a wild moment he thought maybe Jessica was back. Maybe she was going to strip off that wet tank top and step into the claw-foot tub with him.

But it wasn't Jessica's merry voice he heard out there—it was a deep male growl. It was accompanied by a rank stench that blocked out the scent of cinnamon. He identified notes of dead fish and several weeks' worth of sweat.

"Who's in my shower?" the intruder roared. "Get out or I'll toss you to the fishies and they'll use your bones for a playground!"

And thus, the disaster that was his trip to Lost Harbor continued.

CHAPTER SIX

Jessica believed that she was *mostly* a good person. But that didn't mean she didn't have a petty side. That side wished that she'd left her phone on record in the bathroom to capture the moment Old Crow scared the attitude out of Ethan James.

She'd just have to picture it in her imagination, savoring every delicious moment.

Unfortunately, that involved the image of a naked Ethan, which was regrettable. His forearms were temptation enough without throwing in a bare chest and muscular ass.

Also, regrettable in an entirely different way—a naked Old Crow. He always dumped his clothes outside in the hallway, in a garbage bag that he would then haul either to the dump or to the laundromat, depending on how disgustingly fishy they were.

No doubt, Ethan was currently experiencing a genuinely authentic Lost Harbor experience.

He'd mentioned sightseeing, after all. Well, he was definitely getting an eyeful.

Giggling to herself, she holed up in the tiny back office to run the day's accounting. A good day, overall. The summer was their busiest time, and this promised to be one of their best summers ever.

Her mood dimmed when she caught sight of that damn certified letter that had arrived from her mother. She couldn't put off reading it forever.

Big news, Japonica! Prince Cruise Lines is ready to make an offer for the bakery. Can you believe it??? Location, location, location. Of course they want to tear it down and start from scratch, but the place is falling apart anyway. This is it, sweetie!!! We could both walk away with a huge check. Huge!!! We're sending this certified because you keep ignoring our calls and emails.

Gary had also scrawled a note. *Need a decision ASAP. Exciting opportunity. We could use the funds. So can you. Listen to your mother on this one. Don't be foolish.*

"Of course I need the funds, *Gary*," she told the letter—out loud, because why not. "And I'll be foolish if I want to."

Why had Mom even hooked up with Gary Phelps? They were complete opposites. Gary was a taciturn businessman who liked to hunt in his spare time. Her mother was a flower-child free spirit who'd only settled in Lost Harbor because she'd gotten pregnant with Jessica.

Stability had never been Destiny Dixon's strong point. Instead of taking her from place to place, her mother's restlessness sent her from boyfriend to boyfriend. She'd finally married one of them—Jessica's least favorite, unfortunately. Gary had had his eye on Sweet Harbor Bakery from the very beginning.

But Jessica had been running the place ever since she was eighteen and Destiny had left for a retreat in Big Sur. Following the advice of Maya's father, Harris, who was virtually her second father, she'd gotten her mother to sign over part ownership of Sweet Harbor. Any sale would have to be agreed to by both of them.

At least, that was her interpretation of the "contract," which was written on a sheet of expensive watercolor paper. Jessica had added flowers and butterflies to it to match the menu chalkboard. She assumed it was legally binding, or else *Gary* wouldn't be pushing for her signature.

But she hadn't yet consulted with a lawyer. She'd been hoping the whole thing would go away. Selling Sweet Harbor felt like such an impossible decision. She'd been here literally her entire life. It was her home, her work, her nest, her cocoon, her comfort zone, her haven.

What would Harris Badger do? He always gave good advice. He'd probably say talk to a lawyer.

She picked up her phone and dialed her friend Kate Robinson's number. Kate was a lawyer who had recently moved back to Lost Harbor and fallen in love with Darius Boone, the so-called "hottie fire chief." Right now she was wrapped up in the peony harvest at her grandmother's farm, so Jessica hated to bother her.

She got Kate's voicemail, of course. She was probably out snipping stems in the peony fields. "Hi Kate, it's Jess, can you call me when you get a chance? It's a legal-ish thing, so if I have to make an official appointment just let me know. And if you want to wait until the harvest is over—"

Her phone beeped as another call came in—this one from Maya.

"Gotta go, the police chief's calling. I just love saying that. Hey, we should all hang out soon. Call me!"

She switched over to the other line. "Hey Maya. I was just leaving a message for—"

"Dad's in the hospital."

She froze. *Not Harris.* Town icon, retired Coast Guard, beloved father figure.

Finally she found her voice. "What happened?"

"I don't know exactly. I just got the call." Maya barely sounded like herself. All her usual calm was gone, replaced by freaked-out panic. "I'm headed there now. Can you do me a favor?"

"Anything."

"I can't reach Ethan James and I have a meeting with him. Can't even leave a message on his phone. Can you let him know I can't make it?"

"That's it? What else? There's got to be something else—"

"Yeah ... I don't know, I can't think right now." The sound of a horn honking interrupted her.

Jessica imagined her swerving across Lost Harbor's only two-lane street and running one of the two stoplights in town.

"You go, Maya. Get off the phone and take care of your dad."

'Thanks Jess. *Get out of the way!*" She was yelling as Jessica ended the call.

Jessica sent a quick blessing to both Maya and Harris. She held the image of the gentle man in her heart as she did so. Harris was so many things—a wonderful fiddle player, a knitter, a kind father, a man who'd raised his daughter alone after his wife left them. He'd always made room for Jessica at their home. With her mother's constant chaos, with boyfriends and projects coming and going, the Badger household had always been a safe haven. And now he was in the hospital and Maya sounded terrified.

She ran out of the office and dashed up the stairs to Ethan's room, where she knocked for a full minute before he answered.

He did so bare-chested, with a towel knotted around his hips and a bemused expression on his face.

She peered at him. "Is that a bruise on your cheekbone?"

"Yes, because apparently you can't have a hot shower in this town without wrestling an angry fisherman for it."

"Oh." Her hand flew to her mouth. The news about Harris Badger had made her completely forget about the prank she'd pulled on Ethan. "Are you okay?"

"Oh sure. We made up. Even got invited to the Olde Salt for happy hour."

Whew. At least she hadn't caused a catastrophe with her silly prank. "You should totally go. You'll hear some crazy stories with that crew."

"I have a few stories to tell myself. Like the time someone gave Old Crow's shower away to some out-of-town stranger."

She folded her lips together, wondering if he saw any humor in the situation at all. "He must have been in quite a mood. He's not always like that. Is, uh, is *he* okay?"

"If you don't count the fishhook scar in his gut. Or the old knife wound on his neck, or the broken rib that never healed right. I got to see those for myself. But he has no new wounds. I can't vouch for the state of his liver. Probably not good. Won't keep him from the Olde Salt, of course."

She let out a breath of relief. Her intention had been to engineer a lighthearted mistaken crossing of the paths in the bathroom, not a High Noon showdown. "I'm glad you two worked it out. He's a good person, once you get past his crusty exterior."

"You mean the 'crusty' part literally, I assume. Because I can confirm."

She shuddered lightly. "I sincerely apologize." She wondered if there was anything she could do to disable his access to Yelp or TripAdvisor. "How about a free breakfast, on the house?"

"Isn't that included with the voucher?"

Right. Darn, she'd really screwed up with her petty desire for revenge. "Yes. It is. Well, I'm sure we can find a way to make it up to you. Perhaps a guided beach tour or a fresh salmon. Anyway, I'm actually here with a message from Maya. She's been trying to reach you. She has to cancel your meeting tonight."

His smile dropped. "What happened?"

"That's for her to say. I'm just the messenger here."

He groaned and rubbed at the back of his neck. "Why is nothing going right with this trip?"

"I don't know, but this does free you up for happy hour at the Olde Salt. Tell Toni that your drinks are on me." Toni, the bartender, was another of her good friends. They traded drinks for muffins on a regular basis.

"That's nice, but I don't drink."

A private investigator who didn't drink? That sounded unlikely, unless...

"Ahh," she said. "I understand. We do have meetings here in Lost Harbor. I can direct you to—"

"I'm not an alcoholic." With an irritated look, he adjusted the towel around his hips. "Don't your extra-intuitive super senses tell you that?"

It was getting harder to keep her gaze on his face instead of his bare chest. She needed to get out of here—to get to the hospital and lend whatever support she could to Maya. Why was she lingering here with this grouchy bear of a customer?

"You know, they do actually, but I'm a little distracted." She realized that she'd just confessed to staring at his chest. "Not by your...you...that..." She waved at his bare torso. "It's not that, it's Maya. So uh, have a fun night and I'll eat you for breakfast...*see* you for breakfast tomorrow." Sweet goddess, this was spiraling out of control. "Bye."

She whirled around and fled for the staircase before she could embarrass herself any further.

CHAPTER SEVEN

The Sweet Harbor Bakery didn't serve food after the lunch rush, so Ethan chose one of the town's burger joints for dinner. The Burger Queen was mostly a drive-through, but it had a few picnic tables set up on a grassy knoll outside. If you could ignore the faint stench rising from the nearby mudflats at low tide, it was even scenic.

But Ethan wasn't there for sightseeing. The Burger Queen was S.G.'s favorite place to eat. Maya had noted that she loved cheeseburgers, perhaps because she'd never tasted such a thing before coming to Lost Harbor. He saw no reason to bring his investigation to a stop just because Maya had had to cancel their meeting. He'd flown all the way up here, might as well start poking around.

He'd already finished reading Maya's notes, and now he really wanted to meet Spruce Grouse for himself. Maybe even interview her.

To give himself the best chance of success, he'd stopped at the Lost Harbor firehouse on his way and invited Darius Boone and

Nate Prudhoe to join him. He knew both of the firefighters from his previous trips to Lost Harbor, and they both knew S.G. well.

Perfect chance to glean more information over some greasy hamburgers with a view of mud.

With a bag full of extra cheeseburgers and fries, he settled onto one of the picnic table benches outside the Burger Queen. A black bird landed on the grass about ten yards from the table. Raven? Crow? He didn't know much about birds, or wildlife in general, other than the mountain lions and coyotes who sometimes showed up in the hills of Los Angeles.

The bird cocked a beady eye his way and gave a croak. "That sounds ominous," he told it. "If that's some kind of dire warning, don't bother. I already nearly died before I came here."

He picked off a bit of his bun and tossed it to the bird. "But if you're just hangry, I got you."

"You must be new here." Darius Boone slid his big body onto the bench on the other side of the picnic table. He wore his regular clothes and a black cowboy hat, so he must be off the clock at the fire department. "The ravens will always outsmart you."

"Should I be insulted?"

"Nothing personal. They're just damn intelligent birds, that's all. I saw a raven figure out how to get a solar streetlight to go on so he could warm himself up. He covered the light sensor with his wing."

Ethan waved at Nate Prudhoe, who was striding across the grass holding a takeout bag. With his easy smile and playful manner, Nate was the first person Ethan had gotten to know in Lost Harbor on his first visit. Nate was close friends with Padric Jeffers, the rock star who was the cause of Ethan's original trip to Lost Harbor. On his second trip, he'd been sent to find Kate Robinson, who was now Darius' girlfriend.

That was small towns for you. Everyone was connected.

He stood up to grasp forearms with the firefighter. "Good to see you, man. Thanks for coming."

Nate grinned at him. "I knew you'd be back. What's this, your third trip? One more and we'll have to make you a resident."

"Don't worry, this is it for me. This is the famous 'one last job.' After I crack this case, I'll be a boring old married man whose biggest risk is ordering sushi from a food cart."

Darius put down his burger, eyebrows lifted. "You're quitting? Big news."

Ethan shrugged. "My fiancée doesn't want me getting into so much trouble. I have some ideas for apps I'm working on. I originally got into the PI game doing computer-based research for my sister, so I have the background."

"Congrats, dude. On all of it." Nate dipped a French fry in ketchup. "So what do you need from us? Maya gave us the heads up that you might want to ask us some questions."

"Actually I think I got what I need from her notes. The real missing piece is the girl herself. It'd be helpful if I could talk to S.G, but according to Maya that might be a problem."

Darius squinted at him from under the brim of his cowboy hat. "How so?"

"Maya said it can take her a while to warm up to new people. But she trusts both of you. I'm hoping that if you can vouch for me, she'll talk to me."

Nate nodded thoughtfully as he chewed his french fry. "You picked the right spot. That's how I earned her trust at first. I kept bringing her cheeseburgers until she stopped threatening to stab me again."

Ethan patted the bag next to him on the table. "I stocked up just in case. I heard she comes here just about every day."

Darius laughed. "Sounds like you have it all figured out. What do you need us for?"

"Nothing has gone right with this job." Ethan grinned at the two of them. "Consider yourselves my insurance policy for the next disaster."

The two firefighters exchanged an amused glance. "Have you heard the saying 'strange things happen around Lost Souls Wilderness?' You might be getting a taste of that," Darius told him. "I didn't believe it when I first moved here, but I sure as hell do now."

"I never doubted it," said Nate. "The best part is, 'strange' doesn't mean bad. Just...odd. Unexplainable."

Ethan ate a few French fries while he let that word "unexplainable" sink in.

It made him think of Jessica, of course, and her belief in intuition. But it also reminded him that he himself had experienced something unexplainable. The image of the meadow and the golden grasses flickered through his mind. He had no explanation for that...vision. Delusion. Whatever you wanted to call it.

But maybe someone with more knowledge would. Everything was explainable if you knew all the facts.

"I'm a stick-to-the-facts kind of guy," he said lightly. "That's what's worked for me so far."

"Fair enough. Hey, where are you staying?" Nate asked him. "We have extra space up on the hilltop. Bethany's taking some time off to get our wedding squared away. It'd be great to have company."

Ethan's stomach dropped at the mention of preparing for a wedding. The argument with Charley still bothered him. They always seemed to be talking past each other and he had no idea how to fix it.

"Maya gave me a voucher for Sweet Harbor. I'm staying in one of those rooms above the bakery."

"Then you scored yourself a sweet situation," Nate told him. "Jessica Dixon will take good care of you."

Ethan snorted with such force that he nearly inhaled a scrap of his bun. "I guess that's one way to put it. Just promise me that most of her guests survive. That's all I ask."

Darius lifted his eyebrows, while Nate frowned at him in confusion.

"What are you talking about?" Nate asked. "Sweet Harbor has a five-star rating everywhere. Jessica's famous for her hospitality, not to mention her cinnamon rolls. Most of her guests fall madly in love with the place and never want to leave. Some of them fall madly in love with *her*, but she'll never leave Lost Harbor."

Ethan had no idea how to respond to that, except to mumble something about "getting off on the wrong foot."

But it didn't matter anyway, because just then a teenage girl skipped across the grass from the drive-through line to the table. "Hi Darius, hi Nate. Do you have any extra cheeseburgers?" she asked. "I forgot my money."

It had to be S.G. She fit the description perfectly—blond hair in a braid, pale gray eyes, extremely blunt and direct approach to things like food. She wore a pair of overalls over a yellow t-shirt, along with muddy Converse sneakers.

Darius tipped his hat back, smiled at her, and gestured at Ethan. "I think my friend there does. S.G., this is Ethan. Ethan, meet S.G."

The girl barely glanced at him before homing in on the greasy paper bag at his elbow. "You have extra?"

"I do. Help yourself."

She opened the bag and peered inside. She sniffed a few times, big inhales of air through her nostrils. Then she fixed him with a revolted frown. "These aren't cheeseburgers. That's *fish*."

"Really?" He took the bag back from her and smelled for himself. Damnit, she was right, and the only reason he hadn't noticed before was that the French fry smell had drowned out the scent of fish. "Sorry about that. They must have given me the wrong order. Any chance you like fish?"

"I hate fish. Too slimy." She turned her focus to Nate. "Did you get an extra burger?"

"Not today, kid. I can share my fries though."

She barely waited for him to offer the fries before she took a handful. Ethan recognized the behavior; he figured it was the result of "food insecurity"—the uncertainty about where your next meal was coming from. Even though S.G. had plenty of food now, she probably still remembered what it felt like not to.

He cleared his throat to get her attention. "How about I buy you a burger, to make up for the slimy fish?"

She shook her head, keeping her back to him. "No."

He resisted the urge to correct her with a "no, thank you." He wasn't here to teach her manners. "Maybe some other time, then."

"No." She grabbed one more handful of french fries, then waved goodbye to them all. "I have to go back to work now. We're harvesting the peonies."

"Right. Tell Kate I'll make dinner for her," said Darius. "You too, if you want."

"We have to work all night, then I have to sleep."

"Don't forget to have fun this summer," Nate told her. Her fine eyebrows drew together as if she wasn't sure what he was referring to. But she didn't ask for an explanation, just ran back to the bicycle she'd left on its side next to the drive-through.

The two firemen gave Ethan a sympathetic look. "Sorry that didn't work out." Was Darius trying not to laugh? It sure seemed that way.

"First swing, right? When I tell her I'm working with Maya, she'll relax. This is for her benefit, after all."

"You should have told her that right away. She tends to be

very black and white about things. Now she'll think you weren't straight with her."

"Yup, sorry to say it, but you're screwed," said Nate cheerfully. "It was the fish, man. That was the nail in the coffin. S.G. can't stand any kind of fish. When that girl makes up her mind about something, there's no changing it. Might as well beat your head against this table."

Ethan dragged the last bite of his burger through a puddle of ketchup. "I'm not even surprised," he told the other two. "Didn't I warn you I was bracing for disaster?"

"You did, but I thought you were being dramatic," Nate said. "Can you work this case without talking to her? Maybe do it over the phone? I have her number."

Ethan reached for his phone only to remember that it had disappeared after his last call with Charley. He'd searched all his clothes and pockets and his travel bag. He'd even stripped the bedding off his bed. He'd looked under the bed, through the antique desk, in every bureau drawer. No sign of it. He'd even wondered if Jessica had pulled another of her little jokes.

"On top of everything else, my phone's missing," he told the other two. "The good luck continues."

"Strange things," Darius said ominously. "Strange things."

Ethan looked glumly at his bag of soggy fish burgers. He shoved it farther down the picnic table, only to watch the raven swoop down on it and fly away with the entire thing in his beak.

At least he had a couple of guys around to laugh about it with.

CHAPTER EIGHT

Jessica burst into the waiting room of the Aurora Bay Hospital emergency room. She spotted Maya sitting with her head in her hands, elbows propped on knees. When Jessica reached her side, she saw that her friend had tears dripping onto her hands.

The sight shocked her.

She'd seen Maya cry before, of course; when she'd sprained her wrist, when she'd lost her sweet sixteen necklace, when she'd broken up with Lucas Holt in high school. But it didn't happen often. The sight tore a hole right through her heart. She sat down next to Maya and put a comforting arm around her shoulders.

"Is he—" She was so afraid that Harris might be gone that she couldn't finish the question.

"He's in there right now." Maya lifted her face from her hands and wiped away her tears with the cuff of her sleeve. "He's on IV fluids and they're doing an ultrasound on his heart—" She broke off, her mouth twisting with the effort not to cry again.

"Maya, it's okay to lose it, you know. You don't always have to be calm and collected. You can be a freaked-out daughter."

But her words didn't have the effect she'd expected. Maya

sat up, her spine stiffening. "No, Jess, I *can't* lose it. I need to keep it together right now. If you want to help, help me do that."

Jessica had never seen her so upset. "Of course I want to help. That's why I'm here."

Maya folded her lips together, as if fighting to hold onto her cool. She drummed her fingers on the seat next to her. "It's driving me crazy waiting out here. If I'm not on their asses every second, how do I know they'll do right by Dad?" Her honey-brown eyes flashed with true fear.

"Because they're doctors doing their job. Why wouldn't they?"

"Remember when my cousin was pregnant and she almost died of a blood clot because the doctor didn't believe her?"

Tension sang in every line of Maya's body. Jessica remembered that incident very clearly. It was the first time she'd realized that her beloved Badgers, being black, faced difficulties she didn't know about.

"We won't let anything like that happen," Jessica said firmly. "We'll raise hell, both of us."

Maya gave her a teary smile. "What are you going to do, withhold their cinnamon buns?"

"If that's what it takes."

Her friend's face relaxed, just a bit. Not that her worry had eased; it still lurked behind the smile.

Maya shoved up the sleeves of the bright fuchsia sweater she was wearing. "I'm surprised you're here. Isn't the bakery still open?"

"This is more important. I left Nia to close up. I even told her she could knock off early. You know I hardly ever do that."

"Did you get my message to Ethan?"

"Yes. He's fine."

"He is pretty fine, now that you mention it." Finally, the

normal Maya was coming back. Her smile actually widened to include both corners of her mouth.

"I'm trying not to notice, believe me. Are you thirsty? Do you need some water? A Coke?"

"You're actually volunteering to get me a Coke? Never thought I'd see the day."

Jessica had been trying to get her to quit drinking sodas for years now. The more she tried, the more Maya drank.

"Yup, I'm throwing all my principles aside for you."

"It's okay, I'm good. I might throw up if I drink something." She settled back into the position Jessica had first found her, learning forward, elbows planted on her knee. Her legs jumped restlessly and she gripped her hands together. "Dad told the nurse he hasn't felt like himself for days. But he kept telling me he was fine."

"You know he doesn't want you to worry." Jessica rubbed her shoulder in sympathy. "Harris likes to do the worrying."

Tears sprang back into Maya's eyes. "If anything happens—if he—Jess, my dad is my everything. He's the only one who's always had my back. Without him—" She hunched her shoulders away from Jessica's touch. A wall seemed to have gone up between them, an invisible barrier Jessica could sense but not breach.

The hospital lighting slid across her cheekbones. Maya was so gorgeous, but Jessica knew that she went to great lengths to de-emphasize her looks in order to command respect from her fellow police officers. She kept her hair straight, slicked against her head, and wore minimal jewelry. It didn't work, of course. She was still beautiful. They'd been friends for so long that her features were as familiar as a sister's—but not right now. The dryly funny, loyal-friend side of Maya was nowhere to be seen.

With her highly tuned intuition, Jessica had a sudden flash of what life might be like for her friend. To always have to be on guard. Always watching her back, and that of her father. All the little slights she had to shrug off in order to do her job. Not to mention the big ones, like being scared to death for her father.

How exhausting.

How weary she must be. And scared.

She toyed with the frayed friendship bracelet on her wrist, the one that somehow had survived since they were twelve. Whatever Maya needed right now, she'd do it, she vowed silently.

But Maya surprised her by shaking off her tears. "What was the thing you came to the station about? We were going to talk about it later, remember? After I met with Ethan?"

"Oh, it's not important."

Certainly not compared to Harris Badger being in the hospital.

"You always do that, Jess. You put your own shit on the back burner for everyone else's. Come on. It'll distract me while we wait."

Jessica drew in a breath. She felt silly dumping her problems on Maya when she was dealing with something much more serious. "I'm getting pressure from Mom to sell the bakery."

"Someone wants to buy it?"

"A cruise line." She made a face. "They probably just want the property. It's such a good location."

"So you're not interested."

"I don't know. I can't even think about it. You know me and—"

"Decisions." Maya said the word along with her.

Jessica winced. "I hate them."

"But just the big ones. I mean, you keep that bakery running like nobody's business. You hire people, you sometimes manage to fire people—"

"Just once. He was stealing. Like literally stealing, not just eating too many muffins."

"Yeah, but you did it." The distraction was working. Maya was all fired up now. "I thought you were too softhearted to fire him, but you did. It's not like you can't make *any* decisions."

"I know. I know. But this one's too big. I need help. You're so strong, Maya. What would you do?"

A shadow crossed Maya's face, as if the weight of the moment was sinking down on her again. "Just because I seem strong doesn't mean I always am."

Again, Jessica sensed that flash of exhaustion. It tore at her heart.

"I know that. How can I help, Maya?"

Maya jumped to her feet and twisted her hands together. "Wave a magic wand and make my dad be okay? I'm joking," she added quickly as she started to pace back and forth. "No magic or crystals or any of that. That's your world, not mine."

"My world?"

"You know, the Jessica head-in-the-clouds bubble. Like Glinda the Good Witch floating down from the sky."

Jessica stared at her, at a loss for words. Did Maya really think she lived in a bubble? She'd never said that before. Maybe she was so rattled by her father's condition that some truth had broken loose.

"Hey, it's not a bad thing," Maya said as she passed by in her pacing. "We all love you for it. It works for you, just not for me. I can't afford to live in a bubble."

As Jessica watched her friend pace, her stomach slowly dropped to the soles of her feet.

Did she live in a bubble?

Maybe so. Maya was out there slaying dragons as a police chief, breaking barriers, protecting the town, while Jessica stayed safe in her comfort zone bakery-castle. Frozen in the face of big decisions.

"Listen, there's something you can do for me," Maya said as

she executed another tight turn on the invisible racetrack she was following. "Ethan James."

"What about him?"

"Tell him to go home. I don't have time to deal with a side case. Between my dad and my regular work, I have enough on my hands. S.G. can wait a little longer. Tell him to send me an invoice for his flight and other costs."

Jessica hid her shock. Maya always held herself to such high standards. To drop this investigation—she must be scared to death for Harris.

"Are you sure? You were so excited about that case. I know that Ethan's already been reading your notes."

"I'm sure, Jess." Maya's voice cracked with exhaustion. "I hate to do it, but I have to be real."

Jessica's heart twisted at the expression on her friend's face. She looked so disappointed in herself. "I'll tell him. No problem."

A young male doctor in blue scrubs emerged from the door that led to the exam rooms. Maya abandoned her pacing and hurried toward him. Jessica got up and followed after her.

"Your father is stable," the doctor told Maya. Even though he kept talking, Maya burst into such a storm of tears that Jessica could barely hear him. He was relatively young, bronze-skinned, with a slight accent—perhaps from India. She'd never seen him before, but he radiated competence and enthusiasm. "We must Medevac him to Anchorage for the surgery as we don't have a cardiac unit here. But he's in good shape and his prognosis is excellent. It may not be necessary to perform the surgery open-heart. There's a new technology that enables them to operate through his artery. It's incredible, really, and far less invasive. Are you okay, Miss?"

Maya couldn't manage an answer, so Jessica stepped forward. She listened closely to what the doctor was saying, in case Maya missed it while she sobbed.

The ultrasound had revealed that he had a badly damaged aortic valve. It would have to be replaced with an artificial valve. The surgery would take place tomorrow. He would probably be in the hospital for up to a week, and then full recovery might take several weeks to months until he felt normal again. Diet and life-style changes were highly recommended. He would need to follow up with a cardiologist on a regular basis.

Jessica kept careful mental notes until finally the doctor finished. "Any questions?"

Maya wiped away her tears as she steeled her spine. "Can I go with him on the helicopter?"

"No, I'm very sorry, but there isn't enough space."

"That's okay, I'll drive up. Can I see him?"

"That should be fine, but you'll need to make it quick. The helicopter is already on the roof, waiting for him. Do you have Medevac insurance?"

"Yes."

Really? Jessica did a double-take. She herself had never given a thought to Medevac insurance. Maybe Maya had been more worried about her father, and for a longer time, than she knew.

Which explained why she'd asked Ethan to come up in the first place.

"Matt will take things from here." A nurse hurried over, while the doctor nodded to them both and prepared to leave.

Maya surprised everyone by flinging her arms around the doctor. "Thank you, Doctor. Thank you for taking care of him. If you ever need a favor from the police depart—"

"Ahem, Maya." Jessica tugged her away before she crossed any ethical lines and promised to cancel the doctor's parking tickets. "She's been very worried," she explained to the doctor.

"Most understandable." He gave a little formal bow to them and backed away.

Matt, the nurse, took over and explained that they would

need to take an inventory of the possessions Harris had on him before they loaded him onto the helicopter.

Maya's crying fit had passed, and she seemed to finally focus as the nurse walked her through the Medevac process. Once the helicopter landed in Anchorage, Harris would be taken directly to the cardiac unit where the hospital's top cardiologist was standing by.

Jessica lingered nearby. Now that Maya had a mission, she was back to her usual self. Strong, practical, decisive. Completely caught up in the task before her—getting her dad on that chopper. Her tears were behind her.

Jessica should probably go find Ethan and pass along Maya's message. She took a few steps away, then a few more. Maya was so wrapped up she didn't seem to notice.

When she was halfway to the exit, Maya called out to her. "Jess, wait."

Maya dashed across the room, and apparently she was still in a hugging mood, because she threw her arms around Jessica.

"Thanks for being here," she murmured.

"Always."

"You're such a good friend. I'm sorry we didn't get more time to talk about the bakery sale. Maybe when I get back?"

"Sure."

Maya squeezed her hard. "I'll call you tonight from Anchorage."

As she pulled away from the embrace, regret flashed across her face. "I wish I didn't have to let S.G. down. That's the worst part. I know she's counting on me. I was so sure with Ethan around, we could make it happen. I dragged him all the way to Alaska for no reason. I feel bad about that, but I guess you can't plan for everything."

"True that." Jessica squeezed her hand. "You're doing your

best, Maya. You already have a full-time job, don't forget that part."

"Right. My job. I gotta give the station a call." She pulled out her phone, her hands trembling. That sight struck Jessica right through the heart. Her cool, unflappable friend, the one who arrested brawling fishermen without a blink, was still really shaken up.

Phone still in her hand, Maya paused. "One more favor, Jess. I don't want to break it to S.G. over a phone call. Will you go see her and tell her what's going on? Make sure she knows I'm not forgetting about her. It's just gonna have to wait."

"I'll tell her. Don't worry about S.G., she'll be fine. I think all that hunting she did in the wilderness trained her to be patient. I've seen her wait in line for a walnut-cinnamon bun for an hour without complaining."

Finally Maya flashed a genuine smile. "You're going to have to hold town-wide grief sessions if you sell the bakery, you know."

After one last hug, and a request to give one to Harris as well, Jessica left the hospital and headed for her car. She blinked away tears as she went over everything that had taken place in that waiting room.

Her sense of how exhausted Maya was from fighting all her battles. How worried she was about Harris. What she'd said about Jessica living in a bubble. That thing about Glinda the Good Witch. Why had she never said any of those things before?

Jessica knew why. Because Maya loved her and didn't want to hurt her. She was probably tiptoeing around her feelings. Maybe she didn't believe Jessica could handle it. Maybe Maya thought of her as someone who preferred pleasant fantasy over tough reality.

It works for you, not for me. I can't afford to live in a bubble.

Bubbles burst when they collided with anything hard. Like a big decision.

Jessica got into her Subaru and stuck the key into the ignition. Ugh, maybe she *did* live in a bubble. But that didn't mean she had to stay there.

A wild idea flashed into her brain.

Her friendships were the cornerstone of her life. Her romantic relationships came and went—she always managed to screw those up—but when it came to her friends, she was always there. Especially for Maya.

What if there was a way she could have Maya's back—*and* step out of her bubble?

CHAPTER NINE

"Celebrating something?"

The bartender at the Olde Salt—a lithe woman in a tight ribbed top with a graphic design of a raised middle finger on it—poured him another cherry soda.

"Yup. The end of my first day in Lost Harbor. Wasn't sure I'd make it, but here we are."

To tell the truth, it was hard to believe he'd only been here about twenty-four hours. A lot had happened in that time. Most of it, he'd rather forget.

"Uh...congratulations?" She lifted an eyebrow as she slid him a plastic dish of peanuts. "We don't usually off our visitors on the first day. We like to wait until a bear comes along, or an orca. Mosquitoes, black flies, that sort of thing."

"Great." He lifted his glass in a toast. "Something to look forward to." He downed it with a jaunty smile.

"You here on business or fishing?"

He couldn't tell if she was flirting with him or just being bartender-friendly. Even though she was very attractive, with a short pixie cut emphasizing her cheekbones, he didn't find himself drawn to her. Maybe the fact that he was engaged was finally sinking in.

"I guess you'd call it business."

"Wait." She narrowed her eyes at him. "I recognize you. You're Padric's friend. You were here for the volunteer auction last year."

"Good memory."

"It's a curse. I never forget a face, and with the faces I see in this place..." She gestured at the motley crew of weatherbeaten fishermen holding down the stools at the other end of the bar, "that's unfortunate. Anyway, I'm Toni, just holler if you need a refill."

He nodded and relaxed with his drink. The Olde Salt sat nearly at the end of the boardwalk, the long curving arm of the harbor filled with shops and restaurants that were open only in the summer. Most of them were shack-like storefronts, some on stilts planted in the mudflats below. But the Olde Salt had been built nearly a century ago, the oldest surviving structure around. With its weathered cedar siding and foundation sinking unevenly with the frost heaves, it looked every one of its eighty years.

Inside, very little light filtered through the small windows, which were darkened by years of smoke. Old ships' lanterns hung from the low ceilings, occasionally bonking someone on the head if they stood up without looking. Vintage newspaper articles and sepia pioneer-era photos decorated the walls. He could just imagine the stories that had been told here over the years.

Old Crow, freshly showered and barely recognizable, waved at him from one of the tables, where he was playing chess with another elderly local.

Ethan signaled to Toni, and ordered Old Crow another of whatever he was drinking.

"Don't bother," she told him. "He hasn't paid for a drink here in twenty years. It's like a tourist attraction to buy Old Crow a drink."

He chuckled at that. Apparently he'd gotten his own private viewing of one of Lost Harbor's tourist attractions. Yes another thing he'd rather forget about today.

He swung around on the stool, facing the tables, and rested his elbows on the slightly sticky bar top. Might as well take in the local color while he had the chance. He planned to be hard at work on this case by six am tomorrow morning. The quicker he wrapped it up, the sooner he could fly back to LA and sort out things with Charley.

His stomach knotted at the thought. He had to find a way to communicate better with his future wife. He didn't know much about marriage, but he was fairly sure communication was important. Olivia and Jake didn't always agree, but they knew how to work things out. Then again, they were madly in love. He and Charley were more...practical.

The door of the Olde Salt opened, spilling a brief splash of light across the floor. A woman stood in the doorway, her curvy body backlit by the setting sun, outlining her figure in golden light. He blinked at the sight. It reminded him of something, but he couldn't put his finger on it.

And then the door slammed shut—it was an oak door with fancy forged hinges, heavy as hell—and Jessica Dixon from Sweet Harbor hurried toward the bar. He watched her approach, bemused by the fact that she seemed to be everywhere. One day in Lost Harbor, and he'd now seen her what, five or six times?

She'd changed into long buckled boots and tight jeans, with a fuzzy angora conductor's hat perched on her head. Her hair hung loose over her shoulders, and several pendants and necklace chains adorned her neck.

She didn't wait for her eyes to adjust to the relative darkness inside the saloon. In her headlong rush to the bar, she didn't seem to notice him at first.

"Toni." She cupped her hands together to project over the noise of the bar. "I have to talk to you. It's urgent."

But Toni was all the way at the other end of the bar, serving a crowd of excited charter boat passengers. She waved at Jessica, clearly unable to hear her.

"Mother-fu—" Jessica caught herself, finally glancing around her and noticing Ethan. "Mother fun day is tomorrow," she finished with a sweet smile. "Just planning how to celebrate."

"Mother fun day is an important day," he said gravely. "It's one of the best holidays, almost as good as Groundhog Day."

She rolled her eyes at him and plopped her butt onto the stool next to him. "So you made it to Happy Hour."

"I missed Happy Hour, but it's okay, I got here in plenty of time for the rest of them. You know, the more miserable ones. To go with the rest of the day."

She glanced at his fizzy soda. "What are you drinking? Looks delicious."

"A very masculine cherry soda."

"Right, you said that you don't drink. I won't either, then." She lowered her voice to a confidential murmur. "Toni always makes me try the most disgusting bottles, things that probably came from some shipwreck or something. This is the perfect excuse to take a pass."

"Happy to help out." He took a sip and noticed new lines of stress on her face since the last time he'd seen her at the B&B. "Everything okay?"

"Well, not entirely. I wanted to tell Toni first, but I might as well start with you. Maya's father has to have heart surgery, so she's on her way to Anchorage right now. She wanted me to tell you that she has to cancel the job."

He cocked his head, certain that he'd heard that wrong. "Say what again?"

"The job, the search for S.G.'s family, it's going to have to wait. You're free. You can go back to LA. She said to send her an invoice."

Back to LA? Already? An empty feeling stole over him. It didn't feel right, canceling the investigation. His head was already in it. He had questions, he had lines of investigation to pursue. He was *interested*.

Face it. He didn't want to go back yet.

Jessica was watching him curiously, her eyes the color of whisky in the low light. "I thought you'd be thrilled at this news. You didn't seem to be enjoying your time here in Lost Harbor."

"It's had its challenges," he admitted. "But I don't like walking away from a job. How long does Maya think she'll be in Anchorage?" Maybe he could take a few days to do some fishing here. A vacation. He'd told Charley he'd be gone for a week, after all.

"She doesn't know, obviously. But even after the surgery, she's going to have her hands full taking care of Harris." She shook her head sadly. "I really hope that goes well. Maya has no patience for being sick. She's never called in sick at the station in her entire career."

"Heart surgery is a little past 'sick,'" he pointed out.

"That's true. And we're talking about Harris Badger, and she'd do anything for him. Anyway, the point is, the case is closed, at least for now. At least..."

She hesitated, eyeing him sideways.

"What?"

"I had an idea. I wanted to talk to Toni about it first, but..."

Uh oh. Jessica seemed like someone whose ideas could easily lead to trouble. Case in point, her "prank" involving Old Crow and the shower.

Though with time, he could now see that it was pretty funny.

He sighed. "Go ahead. What's your idea and does it involve me getting drenched or jailed?"

She screwed up her face and looked up at the ceiling. "I hope not?"

That made him laugh. "Okay, let's hear it. What are you thinking?"

"Just promise me you won't say 'no' right off the bat." She rushed ahead before he could answer that. "Never mind, you probably will say no, but maybe you'll think about it and that 'no' will magically transform into a 'what a fabulous idea, Jess, let's do it.'"

If nothing else, she had him intrigued. "This is going to be crazy, isn't it?"

"There's a good chance," she admitted. "Toni would probably tell me to jump in the harbor instead of proposing this, but since she's busy, here goes."

"Go for it."

She toyed with the bracelets on her wrist. "Here's the thing. I just got a truth bomb dropped on me and it opened my eyes to some of my own personality flaws. I realized that I want to change a few things."

"Such as?"

"I don't want to list all my flaws, but basically it comes down to not being so head-in-the-clouds. I need to be more boots-on-the-ground."

"Like an army?"

"What?"

"Boots on the ground, that usually means an army. Ground troops."

She shuddered. "I don't like that comparison. I'm a pacifist. But yes, I want to become more ground-based. A little more realist, a little less optimist."

That thought made him a little sad, surprisingly. He liked her sunny personality. He hoped she didn't want to change that as well.

"Okay, but I don't see what any of this has to do with me. You're going through some kind of personal transformation, good for you. Where do I come in?"

She inhaled a long breath, her chest rising and falling, bringing his attention to the deep V of her cleavage. *No flirting. No ogling.*

"I want to fill in for Maya. Just because she's dealing with a medical crisis she shouldn't have to abandon everything else."

He stared at her blankly. "Fill in for her?"

"With the S.G. investigation. I've heard Maya talk about it enough times and I've heard all the gossip about S.G. That's one thing about running a bakery, you hear all the juicy stuff. And to fill in the gaps, there's the homework she gave you. I can be up to speed on the whole case in no time, and then we can get to work." That bright smile of hers lit up the dank atmosphere of the bar. It made him slightly dizzy, as if someone had blindfolded him and whirled him around and around.

Every instinct told him this was a bad idea. She was a baker, not a detective. And she was too appealing for him to spend that much time with.

"Not happening," he said flatly. "Maya's the one who hired me. Now she wants me to go home, so I'm going home. Without her, there is no job."

His rejection didn't dim her enthusiasm at all. "I thought about this. I expected you to react this way. Don't worry, I can pay you. I'll pay you even more than what Maya offered."

"My day rate is pretty high."

He hadn't actually planned to charge his full day rate, since he doubted that anyone in Lost Harbor could afford it, and he didn't really need the money.

"I'm not worried about the cost. I'm doing this for Maya. She feels terrible about letting S.G. down. What harm could it do to let me help?"

"What if she wants to solve the mystery herself? Are you sure this is what she wants?"

Her shoulders slumped and for the first time she looked unsure of herself. "That's a good point. She was really excited when S.G. asked her to find her family. I wouldn't want to case-block her. That's like cock-block, except with case," she explained.

"Yeah, I got it." He'd gotten it a little too quickly. Seeing her pretty, merrily curved lips form the word "cock" was like a direct message right to that part of his body.

She fell silent, tracing a pattern on the bar as she thought it over. Finally she shook her head. "She told me that she feels bad for S.G. and for wasting your time. That's it. I don't think she really cares who investigates the case. That's why she called you in. Besides, we'll simply be continuing what she started."

"Why can't you just ask her first?"

"I don't want to bother her. She's got enough to deal with. For once in Maya's life, I want something to be taken care of without *her* having to manage it. If she knows I'm doing this, she'll just worry and that's the last thing she needs."

This sounded like big trouble...so why was he so tempted to go along with it? Was it because of Jessica? That bright, hopeful smile and the way she always smelled like something delicious? Right now it was crystallized ginger.

Damn his improved sense of smell. It was making this more complicated than it needed to be.

"So you want me to not only continue this investigation but allow you to be part of it, even though you have no investigative experience or relevant skills and have a good chance of getting in my way and fucking it up."

A flush came in a wave across her face. "That was mean."

"Yeah, it was. We don't know where this investigation is going to lead. Do you think everyone's going to be watching out for your feelings along the way? Toughen up, buttercup." He downed the last of his extremely masculine cherry soda.

For a long moment she gazed at him with an expression he couldn't quite read. "You said 'we,'" she said finally.

"Figure of speech. Means nothing."

Still, a smile was dawning on her face, like the sun peeking over the horizon. "I think it does. You're in, aren't you?"

"Let me sleep on it. It's been a long day. I'm in no shape to make decisions right now."

"That's fair." Her amber eyes gleamed with amusement. "Has it occurred to you that I could try to investigate on my own? I read all the Nancy Drew books, every single one. I've helped Maya with a couple of cases. I'm pretty resourceful."

"Then why'd you come to me?"

She lifted her chin. "Simple courtesy. But if you refuse, I might just go ahead on my own."

"You think you're that tough, huh?"

"Hmm, I don't know." She gave his drink a pointed glance. "If I drink cherry soda will I be as tough as you?"

He snorted. "Maybe someday I'll tell you the real secret of my toughness." Lord, he was talking as if this was going to continue for a while. What was up with that?

She must have caught on to that too, because the energy between them shifted into a different gear. Something fresh and exciting vibrated between them. He felt it all the way down to his gut. Not to mention his cock.

Jessica swallowed, sleek muscles moving in her throat. He wanted to touch that creamy skin.

The tension between them was broken by the arrival of Toni, who reached over the bar to give Jessica a hug. "What's up, girl?"

"Ethan doesn't think I'm tough. That's what's up."

Toni looked between the two of them as she folded her arms across her chest. "Have you arm-wrestled him yet?"

"No, because I don't want to injure a Sweet Harbor guest." She planted one elbow on the bar and beckoned to Toni. "But I can challenge you. I know you can take it. You are a black belt, after all."

With Toni's lithe frame and general badass manner, Ethan would definitely put his money on her. How could a baker compete with a bartender for toughness?

As the two women got into position for their arm-wrestling match, murmurs of "Toni ... Jessica ... ten bucks on Jess...twenty on Toni..." spread through the bar and the other customers gathered close.

"If I win, will you promise to seriously consider my proposal?" Jessica asked him. With her legs braced apart, one arm planted on the bar, the other resting on her hip, her auburn hair flowing down her back, fire in her eyes, he found her stance wildly arousing.

"And if you lose, will you drop it and let me go home?"

She cocked her head, narrowing her eyes at him. "Why do I get the sense you don't really want to go home?"

Damn her and her "intuition." "Just wrestle. Three, two, one..."

She must have been right, because after two minutes of muscle-straining struggle, when Jessica slammed Toni's arm onto the bar to the raucous hollers of the crowd...he cheered right along with the rest of them.

CHAPTER TEN

Ethan finally located his missing phone the next morning. Somehow he'd managed to kick it under the four-poster bed, all the way into the farthest shadowy corner. The battery on his old flip phone had jarred loose and it was completely dead, so it took a while for him to get it operational again.

He spent the time doing the stretches that kept his leg limber. If he forgot them for even a day, the damaged muscles would tighten up. At least he could enjoy the view of Seafarer's Beach at low tide as he worked out. The wet sand reflected silver light in the misty morning. Exposed underwater boulders shone dark against the wet sand. The occasional dog walker picked their way through clumps of seaweed and driftwood.

Finally his phone came back on with a flurry of beeps. He'd missed ten calls altogether—two from Maya, seven from Charley, and one just this morning from Dr. McGee.

Great. More pressure to go along with the virtual wedding, no doubt.

He clicked on the message from McGee.

"Good morning, Ethan. I'm sure by now you've spoken to

Charlotte. If you need support in processing this shift, I encourage you to call on me. We can set up a video call if you check with my assistant."

What shift? What was he talking about? Why did McGee know more about his life than he did?

He scrolled back to the last call from Charley.

"Since you've been ignoring my calls all day, I scheduled an emergency session with Dr. McGee. He's helped me realize that this marriage is not a good idea. If you can't even summon the bare minimum of excitement about my mentor, we're simply not suited to each other. Somehow I don't think you'll mind that I'm breaking things off before we go any further. Maybe you should think things through a little more the next time you propose. I bear some responsibility too, of course. Not even a life coach always gets it right. Goodbye, Ethan. I wish you nothing but good things."

He laughed out loud in the empty room. The sound startled a raven that had landed on a willow branch outside his window. It lifted both its wings, ready to fly off, then cocked a beady eye at him and settled back down.

"The next time I propose? Not making that mistake again," he told the raven. "And just for the record, she's absolutely right. I don't mind."

That did it—apparently the raven wasn't enjoying the conversation. He took off in a whir of black feathers.

He shouldn't be talking to birds anyway. He was a cynical detective.

Ethan didn't listen to the other messages from Charley. If their relationship could be derailed by one misplaced cell phone, they'd never had much chance anyway. And if getting dumped left him feeling like this—so relieved he could sing—they *really* didn't stand a chance.

That would teach him to pay attention to "visions." It had all been a lie. The meadow, the bride, the handholding—all a bunch of crap.

What an idiot he'd been. He didn't even *want* to marry Charley. He never had—or he wouldn't be feeling so free right now.

On the other hand, now there was nothing stopping him from sticking around Lost Harbor and finishing what he'd started.

He'd tell Jessica the good news over whatever freshly baked pastries were filling his room with that incredible mouthwatering aroma.

MAYA TEXTED Jessica with the news that Harris' surgery had gone well, but that they'd be in Anchorage for at least another week.

Don't forget to tell S.G. how sorry I am.

I got you covered, she texted back. *Don't worry about anything here. You take care of Harris.*

She texted Denaina to set up a meeting with S.G. Denaina told her that S.G. was so busy with the peony harvest at Petal to the Metal that she rarely had time for anything other than work, eat, and sleep.

Well, she could definitely help with the eating part. And maybe she could ask S.G. a few questions while she was at it.

Whether or not Ethan joined in, she was doing this.

She packed her largest-size bakery box with enough walnut-cinnamon rolls and scones and muffins to feed the entire Petal to the Metal crew, including Kate Robinson.

She hadn't seen much of Kate since she'd come back to Lost Harbor. She popped in an extra raspberry brownie just for her. Kate loved anything with chocolate.

Balancing the box on one hip, she was headed for the side

exit door when she nearly collided with Ethan, who was trotting down the stairs from the guest quarters. Freshly shaven, wearing a blue Henley that made his hazel eyes look extra clear and penetrating, he made her breath hitch.

"Good morning."

Something was different about him. She didn't know what it was, but it gave her an awkward feeling. Or maybe that was from last night and those surprising new sparks she'd noticed.

"Good morning," he answered politely enough. Still, her intuition told her something was up.

"What's wrong?"

One eyebrow lifted. "What makes you think something's wrong?"

"Something's definitely wrong if you can't answer the question."

He snorted. "Fine. Charley just dumped me. My fiancée. Ex."

Something perked up inside her, but she stomped it down. He was probably crushed and heartbroken. Grieving. Wondering what had gone wrong. At least that was how she always reacted to a breakup.

"Oh. I'm sorry to hear that."

Ethan folded his arms across his chest, looking impassive. He didn't seem to want any sympathy, at least not from her. But he could probably use some coffee.

"Help yourself to whatever you like from the bakery cases. It's all included in your stay. The coffee is Zimbabwe Dark Roast this morning. Highly recommended."

He didn't budge. "Where are you off to?"

"Taking some treats to some hardworking farmers."

"You're going to see S.G." He didn't say it as a question.

"Goodness, you really are a good investigator." She tried to step around him, but he blocked her.

"I want to come with you."

"This is more of a personal visit." A step to her left got her nowhere. The guy moved quickly.

"I don't believe you. I think you're planning to investigate on your own. You're using baked goods to pave the way, just like you did at the jail."

"Very insightful. You might even say intuitive."

"It's just logic. Let me come with you."

She narrowed her eyes at him. "Does that mean you've come to an official decision?"

"It might."

Exasperating man.

That mental comment must have showed on her face, because he gave in with a jaunty smile. "I decided yes, that I'll continue the investigation without Maya."

"And *with* me?"

"We'll see. We have to discuss parameters. I don't want you to be in any danger. You're not trained for it."

"Did you learn nothing from last night?" She lifted her right arm and showed off her biceps. Her sleeve fell back from her flesh, which felt oddly intimate under his gaze. "Turns out that kneading dough for two decades makes some pretty strong muscles."

"There's a lot more to it than that," he said gravely. "It's about being alert and prepared for anything. Do you know how many times I've been physically attacked while pursuing a case? I know for damn sure that Maya wouldn't want you to get hurt. I don't either."

She regarded him for a long moment, testing his seriousness. Every line of his face showed how strongly he felt about this particular issue.

Personally, she thought he was being too cautious, since this was Lost Harbor and she knew many of the people in town, even those who'd committed crimes. She didn't believe that either of them would be in any danger. They weren't trying to apprehend drug dealers or hardened criminals. They'd just be trying to find answers for S.G.

But if they were going to work together, she had to acknowledge that he had more experience than she did. Reading the entire Nancy Drew series in middle school didn't really count.

"Fine. Grab yourself some coffee and we'll discuss parameters on the way to the farm."

"Excellent plan." He finally stepped out of her way and headed for the counter.

"Maybe you should grab those notes so you can fill me in," she called after him.

"No need." He tapped the side of his head. "It's all in here."

She sighed as she watched him chat with her morning server, Annie from Louisiana. One of the many twenty-somethings who drifted through Lost Harbor seeking adventure. Just like Mom had done, thirty years ago.

He said something that made Annie laugh. Ethan could be so charming when he wanted to be. So far he hadn't bothered with her. He'd been mostly pretty grumpy.

Not that it mattered in the least, since he was heading back to LA as soon as they wrapped up this case. Or maybe even before— he hadn't committed to any kind of timeframe.

Anyway, she didn't need him to be charming. She just needed him to share the information and knowledge that he possessed. That was all he was to her. A kind of guide to investigating and being "boots on the ground." Nothing more.

It would be smart of her to keep that in mind and stop noticing things like the strong line of his back as he bent over her bakery case.

CHAPTER ELEVEN

The peony farm was a glorious sea of color, from vibrant scarlet to delicate oyster-pink, with dashes of sunny lemon and pure cream. And the fragrance! Carried by the light breeze coming over the bay, up the bluffs and across the peony fields—it teased her senses and tugged a smile to her lips. Bliss. Sheer bliss.

Ethan kept sniffing like a wolf, inhaling the air as if it was water. "This is incredible. They ought to bottle this up and sell it."

"I thought you were the tough hard-boiled investigator," she teased. "Since when are you so into fragrance?"

He shrugged. "Just a tool in the toolbox." He shaded his eyes and scanned the fields. "Do you see S.G.?"

Next to one of the long Typar-covered beds of peony bushes, Kate straightened up and waved to them. With a bag slung over her shoulder and clippers in one hand, she was collecting the stems of the still unopened buds. Jessica knew they were destined for a cooler, where they'd be kept from blooming until they could be shipped out to the distributors who supplied florists around the world. This time of year, midsummer, the only source for peonies was right here in Alaska.

The other blooms would be sold at the farmers market or be used to fill local orders.

"Is that a raspberry brownie I smell?" Kate called.

Jessica laughed as she stepped across the mown grass toward the edge of the peony field. "How can you smell anything over these peonies? It's like heaven here."

"To me that's like white noise by now. Chocolate on the other hand…" She set down her clippers and gave Jessica a brief hug. Then she cocked her head at Ethan. "Please tell me you aren't looking for me again."

Ethan grinned. "Depends. Are you staying out of trouble?"

"Always. I mean, never."

Jessica snorted, since Kate was always getting into one kind of trouble or another.

"We're actually here to talk to S.G. Is she around?"

"Somewhere. She might be feeding the chickens." Kate waved toward the old homestead farmhouse where her grand-mother lived.

"Thanks. Mind if we go up?"

"A bribe might help."

Smirking, Jessica opened the bakery box and offered Kate her pick of pastries. Truly it was amazing how she was always welcomed whenever she brought breakfast. It was like a magic skeleton key into every locked space.

"Welcome back to Lost Harbor, Ethan," Kate called as they headed for the farmhouse. "I knew you'd be back."

"Why does everyone keep saying that?" Ethan murmured to Jessica as they walked. "Also, I need that cinnamon roll recipe of yours. Works like a charm. I want to try it out next time I'm buttering up a cop for information."

"*'Butter'* them up?" With an exaggerated wink, she held up a croissant that had so much butter the paper was greasy.

"Cute."

She smiled sassily at him, half-wishing that "cute" referred to her.

This attraction was so very inconvenient.

S.G. came skipping over to them from the enclosed pen where chickens pecked at the ground and squabbled. "Something smells so good!"

Jessica waved the croissant at her. "Could be this, or it could be the gigantic walnut-cinnamon roll I also brought. Or both," she added, as S.G. plucked the croissant from her hands. "Take all you want."

In mid-bite, S.G. froze as she noticed Ethan. "Why is *he* here?"

"It's annoying, isn't it?" She shared a complicit smile with S.G. "But there's actually something we wanted to talk to you about."

"Him too? He tried to give me fish."

"Well, he's not the brightest bulb in the pack, is he?" She winked at Ethan, enjoying the chance to get in a dig at him. "But he's harmless."

"He's not harmless," the girl said through her last mouthful of croissant.

Jessica paused in surprise. What did S.G. have against Ethan, other than the fish incident? "Do you think he's dangerous? I really don't think so. I've gotten to know him a little and I think he's fine."

S.G. swept him up and down with her pale eyes. Jessica wondered what she was picking up on. Even though her education had been lacking in a lot of ways, she was very sharp about certain things. Mostly they involved wilderness survival skills, but you never knew what else might pop up.

"He can fight," she finally declared.

Ethan flung up both his hands in a no-threat-here gesture. "I'm not here to fight. Besides, have you seen Jessica arm-wrestle? She might have the edge on me."

"Arm-wrestle?" Curious gray eyes swung her way.

"I'll show you some time." Jessica dug around for the stickiest, most caramel-drenched walnut-cinnamon roll in the bunch. "How about we take this somewhere and sit down and talk?"

"I still have to feed the chickens." But she happily took the sweet roll in one hand while she used the other to grab another handful of chicken feed from her sling.

Jessica and Ethan exchanged a glance. Apparently Ethan was in—or enough "in" so that they could discuss the situation with her.

"Maya had to go to Anchorage and she wanted me to tell you that she has to pause her investigation into your family origins."

S.G.'s shoulders slumped as she tossed feed into the pen. "Okay."

The fatalistic tone in her voice broke Jessica's heart a little. That was the voice of someone who rarely got what she wanted. Someone who always had to defer her own wishes.

"But Ethan and I had an idea." She ignored Ethan's soft snort at the suggestion that it wasn't just her idea. "How would you feel if *we* took over the case until Maya gets back? Ethan is a private investigator, in fact Maya asked him to come help. And I'd like to do what I can too."

"What can you do?"

Another soft snort from Ethan.

"Good question. I can...talk to people. I know just about everyone, and I've even met some trappers who have come through here. I've spent time in Lost Souls Wilderness. Did you know that I own a part-share in a float plane?"

"You do?"

"Yes, some friends and I went in on it together. We used to spend weeks every summer hiking around Lost Souls. I know some people there who might know something. Connections, it's called." She made a little face at Ethan, since that sounded like more of a big-city term than something anyone used in Lost Harbor. Here, almost everyone was connected some way or other.

"Also, there's my biggest strength."

"What?"

"I know a little bit about how you feel. I have no idea where my father is. He isn't in touch with me."

"Why not?"

Ugh, now that she'd brought it up, she should explain the entire story. "When I was eight, my father showed up here with a sailboat. He wanted me to live with him on it. He was going to sail from here to Hawaii, then live in the islands, maybe sail to Tahiti. He thought it would be a great adventure for me. My mom left it up to me, and I chose to stay here. I guess that hurt his feelings. I only heard from him a few times after that. I don't even know where he lives anymore."

She caught herself as all the old guilt and confusion rolled over her. She rarely thought about that time anymore. But it had been terrible, having to make that choice.

"That's sad." A marmalade hen pecked at the ground by S.G.'s feet, making her jump.

"Yes. Anyway, I know it's not the same as for you, but I understand why you want to find out about your parents."

S.G. scattered the last of her feed, then wiped her hand on the bag. "Maybe Ethan can help you find your dad."

"Hm." She shrugged, but that wasn't in the cards. If her father wanted to make contact, he knew where she lived. "Maybe if he does a good job with your case, I will."

S.G. nodded her agreement. "Okay."

Now she looked Ethan's way. They shared a cautious glance. "Do you mean you're okay with us continuing the investigation?"

"Yes. Every night I have a dream about it." She fiddled with her sling. "In the dream my parents are drowning. Someone keeps pushing them down. They're going to die if I don't find them."

"Sweetie." Jessica touched her on the hand. "It's just a nightmare. It doesn't mean they're actually drowning." Or even alive, but she didn't say that. S.G. understood perfectly well that her family might be dead.

But Ethan took a different tack. He took out his phone and opened a recording app. "S.G., would you mind telling the entire dream to my phone? It could be just a dream, but it's also possible you remember something on a subconscious level."

S.G. sent a cautious glance in Jessica's direction. She nodded encouragingly. "That's a great idea."

The girl took the phone from Ethan's hand and spoke into it. "My parents are drowning and someone keeps pushing them down."

She tried to hand it back to Ethan, but he refused to take it. The corner of his mouth quivered with repressed laughter. "Can you see what they look like?"

"No. They're under water. Wait. Yes, my mother has long hair. I think it's blond."

"And your father?"

She screwed up her face. "He's almost bald."

"And what about the water they're in? Is it a lake? A river? The ocean?"

She thought for a while, then shook her head. "Not a river. It's not moving like a river."

"Big waves, like the ocean?"

"No."

"And where are you in the dream? Are you in a boat? Or watching from the shore?"

Her eyes, so light they were almost ethereal, lit with respect. "These are very good questions."

"Thank you," he said gravely. "I appreciate that."

And just like that, Ethan had won her over.

Jessica wasn't sure how she felt about that. Ethan might decide he didn't need her anymore and continue the investigate on his own. She had to find a way to prove that she could contribute.

"I think it's a boat. But I'm not sure," S.G. said in answer to his last question. She looked across the property at the peony fields. "I have to start working."

"Of course."

She handed Ethan his phone, then shook his hand.

Apparently, they had a deal.

"One more thing," he asked casually. "Do you still have the clothes and other items you had with you when you arrived in Lost Harbor?"

"I saved everything in a box."

"Can we look at that box?"

S.G. pointed at Jessica. "She can. It's in my room at Denaina's." As she took an enormous bite of her walnut-cinnamon bun, she skipped off toward the brilliantly colored peony fields.

Ethan and Jessica headed back to the driveway where Jessica had parked her old Subaru. "I guess we have a case," he said.

"You could sound a little more enthusiastic about the 'we' part."

"I'm not used to working with untrained civilians." He opened the passenger side door with a jerk.

"And I'm not used to working with patronizing cheechakos. But here we are."

"Chee what?"

"See? You don't even know the Alaska basics. You need me, that's what's really bugging you." Wagging a triumphant finger at him, she opened the driver's side door. "Right now you need me to check out S.G.'s box. I think she trusts women more than men."

"Yeah, there might be something to that," he agreed thoughtfully. "No wonder, considering her history."

They both got into her car and seamlessly continued the conversation. "Did I imagine it, or are you relying on a dream that may or may not have anything to do with reality?" she asked him.

"I wouldn't say 'relying.' But a good investigator looks at all possible clues."

"Maybe I should pull out my crystal then."

"Your what?"

Oops. She'd let that slip out without proper preparation. She started up her car, which had a hole in the muffler and therefore conveniently kept conversation to a minimum. It had been very handy during their shouted discussion of "parameters," which seemed to mostly involve her letting him handle anything that reeked of danger.

Fine with her.

"What now?" she shouted over the roar.

"Let's go see that box she kept."

She nodded cheerfully and backed into the turnaround to exit, startling a pair of geese that were wandering across the grass. "Sorry, ladies!" she called to them. "I didn't see you there. My bad."

They honked back, clearly irritated by the metal intruder.

She noticed that Ethan was rubbing his forehead with an expression of pain.

"So you talk to birds. And you like crystals."

"And?"

He didn't answer, just shook his head. He'd mussed up his hair with his rubbing, so she reached over and straightened out an especially unruly lock.

He allowed it, though he shot her an incredulous glance.

She returned it with a sunny smile. Such a grouchy bear.

"You're probably extra crabby because your fiancée just dumped you."

"Thanks for reminding me."

"If you'd forgotten, it probably wasn't meant to be."

"Obviously it wasn't meant to be, or we would still be together. Watch out for that—"

She veered around a rooster who'd gotten loose from the pen. Rolling down her window, she scolded him. "You should know better. You're going to get yourself killed like that."

As she rolled up the window, Ethan sighed deeply. "What would it take for you to let me drive?"

"Well, I suppose you'd have to be okay with me telling you where to go."

"I can live with that."

She hit the brakes, and they switched seats. Maybe it was petty, but she thoroughly enjoyed the rest of the drive to Denaina's, because her instructions went mostly like this: "Right at the next road. Not there, that's a driveway, can't you see the difference, cheechako? There, see that crab trap in the weeds? Take a right there. You mean you've never seen a crab trap, city boy? It has a raven perched on it. Hello, my beauty, do you mind if we pass?"

Yes, she definitely enjoyed herself. Ethan? Probably not so much.

CHAPTER TWELVE

Jessica spent an absurd amount of time chatting with Denaina, a Native Alaska woman with the kindest smile Ethan had ever seen. She left the rest of her pastries with Denaina, and came back to the car with a large cardboard box in its place.

"She says the only thing that's missing is S.G's knife. She confiscated that when she moved in. No weapons in the home."

He moved to take the box from her, but she held it away. "S.G. wanted me to look through it, remember?" She slid into the passenger seat and plopped it on her lap. "I'll do it while you drive."

He gritted his teeth, reaching for his patience. Back when he'd worked closely with his sister Olivia, it hadn't been like this. Olivia was a meticulous, careful investigator who loved solving puzzles. They'd brainstormed cases, backed each other up, divided the work peacefully. Jessica, on the other hand, seemed to fly by the seat of her pants, operating on instinct and pastries.

"How about we go somewhere and look through the box together," he suggested. "Since we're apparently a team now."

She smiled brightly. "That sounds fair. Oh, I know a great

place. You take the first left after the second curve in the—"

"I got this," he told her. He forced his jaw to relax. "No need to be a human MapQuest." He started up her car, wincing at the hoarse rattle from the rear. "Have you considered fixing that muffler?"

"I did consider it. But I decided fixing the hot water heater was more important. You're welcome."

Lord give him patience.

He drove to an overlook he happened to know about. The first time he'd come to Lost Harbor, he'd had extra time on his hands because Padric was in the process of reconnecting with Zoe Bellini, his childhood best friend. He'd discreetly given them time together when he knew it was safe. During those off times, he'd driven around Lost Harbor to get a feel for the town.

He'd discovered the overlook when he'd stopped to take a photo and nearly tumbled off the cliff. The view was so entrancing he'd forgotten to watch his steps carefully enough. Understandable, once you saw the full vision of jagged mountains and the blue-tinted glaciers wedged between them.

At the end of a path that wound through grass and wildflowers, a bench had been installed on the very edge of the bluff. A memorial plaque announced that it was in honor of Jack "Hammer" Holt. The bench offered a view of the mountains across the bay, where sun glinted on the snow that still lingered on the highest peaks. Clouds of mist clung to the steep green slopes. It was such a dramatic vista that he'd sat for an hour, just watching the play of light and clouds.

"Good choice," said Jessica approvingly. "This is my favorite patch of wild strawberries. We put them in muffins later in the summer."

Now that she mentioned it, he did detect the scent of strawberries. Every time their legs brushed against the plants growing alongside the path, a heady fragrance rose into the air. He found it nearly overwhelming—sweet perfumy scents mingling with fresh sun-warmed grass. It made him both dizzy and almost deliriously happy.

Jessica looked at him oddly as they reached the bench. "Are you okay?"

"Yeah, it's just the smell here is incredible. I think it's making me drunk. I don't remember it smelling so good last time. But that's because—" He broke off as he sat down on the little wooden bench. "Put that box in the middle so we can both see it. I want to take photos and a video of every item."

"Because why?" she asked curiously as she took the other end of the bench, the box on her lap. "What were you about to say?"

"What are you waiting for? Let's open that box."

She lifted her eyebrows meaningfully.

"You're holding the box hostage until I answer your question?"

"Aren't you just dying to see what's in here?"

He shook his head. This was definitely nothing like working with Olivia. "Fine. I had an accident and ever since then I've had a more acute sense of smell."

"Really!" Her eyes widened, catching dazzle from the golden morning sunlight. "That's amazing. What sort of accident would do that?"

"Well, I was clinically dead for a minute, so that might have done it. Now can you hand over that goddamn box? Honestly, you are the most aggravating—"

She scooted over and planted the box between them. "Here you go, but I want to hear more about this incredible new gift you have. Do you promise to tell me more about it later?"

"It's not a gift. It's an anomaly. It probably means I have brain damage." He took out his pocket knife and slit open the tape that held the box closed.

"Technically, I should be doing this," she pointed out. "S.G.

said so explicitly. We should respect her wishes."

Silently, he handed her the knife. He appreciated her scruples. Not many people had such things anymore, in his jaded experience.

Perfectly comfortable with handling his knife, she quickly sliced open the box. Obviously baking involved unexpected skills like knife-handling and arm-wrestling prowess.

The box was filled with animal hides. No, not hides, he realized as Jessica drew them out one by one. Clothes made from animal hides.

"This must be what she was wearing when Nate found her," Jessica explained. "I remember hearing about her handmade wardrobe." They examined each item in turn. He took photos of the tunic, the trousers, the boots.

"Is there any chance we could learn anything based on the animals these hides came from?"

She shrugged. "Maybe, but I doubt it. These all look like fox and lynx to me. Pretty standard skins."

Of course she would know something like that. Maybe working with a local would be helpful after all.

"What about the pockets? Anything there?"

Gingerly, she reached inside the pocket of the trousers. He didn't blame her for being wary; a strong rank odor hovered over the box. The first pocket was empty, but the second one held a small piece of fabric.

Real fabric, not animal skin.

She turned it over and rubbed it between her fingers. "It's very soft and silky."

"It looks almost threadbare. All the color has been leached out of it. Can I feel it?"

She handed it over. It was a scrap, nothing more, but it didn't fit with the rest of the clothes.

"Maybe the trapper got hold of a length of silk at some point,"

Jessica suggested. "As a present for S.G."

"Hmm." He grunted, turning it over and over in his hands. "I don't get the impression that he cared that much about her. She was like a servant. Why would he get her a present?"

"We can ask her."

"Do you have her phone number?"

Jessica nodded and pulled out her phone to dial it. "Hi there, S.G. We have a quick question for you. We found a super-pretty piece of fabric in one of your pockets. It's so deliciously soft, I want to curl up in it. What is it, do you know?"

After a moment, she nodded and ended the call.

"She says it's something she's always had, but she doesn't know where it came from."

"Always had." Thoughtfully, he ran his finger across it. "That might mean it was with her when the trapper found her."

"Like a baby blanket or something?"

"Or part of what she was wearing. She obviously wasn't naked, or she wouldn't have survived long enough for Murchison to find her."

"Good theory. But how does it help?"

"I might be able to get a buddy of mine at the FBI to analyze it."

"That would be cool. Do you think it's silk?" She reached out to feel it again, and somehow their fingers managed to brush against each other. A spark literally arced between them, and she quickly drew her hand away.

"Weird static electricity," she said with an awkward chuckle.

He didn't think it was static, but he didn't want to discuss the alternative—that it was sheer chemistry.

"I don't know much about fabrics."

"Oh!" Her eyes lit up and she clapped her hands together. "Before we send this off to the FBI, maybe we should talk to someone who does know about fabrics."

"Who's that?"

"We happen to have an amazing tailor in town. She's an Old Believer Russian who can craft the most incredible clothes out of the most random thrift store fabrics you can imagine."

"Old Believer?"

"Yes, we have quite a few here in Lost Harbor. Have you seen the women around town wearing full-length dresses and head scarves? The men in tunics?"

He nodded, since they were hard to miss, with their unique throwback outfits—like the Russian version of the Amish.

"I always thought they kept to themselves."

"Yes and no. Olga has a shop right in town. She mostly makes clothes for the Russians, but not exclusively. And she knows everything about textiles. Let's go!" She put the trousers back in the box and closed it up. "At least let's give it a try before we hand it over to the feds."

"My buddy would be doing us a huge favor," he pointed out. "It's not like he's dying to get his hands on a fifteen-year-old bit of cloth."

"Are you arguing just to argue, or do you really think this is a waste of time?"

He cocked his head and thought it over. "That first one."

"Thought so. Come on!"

She grabbed his hand to tug him to his feet. The same jolt of energy they'd experienced earlier jumped between them.

This time there was no ignoring it or pretending it was anything other than "sparks."

Caught off guard, he met her confused gaze and they looked at each other for a moment, blinking in the sunshine. Neither spoke. In his case, that was because he didn't know what to say. So what if there was an attraction between them? They were all wrong for each other. Crystals? Intuition? Talking to geese?

There was another problem. If she was really planning to pay his fee, she was technically his employer. And if that wasn't enough, twelve hours ago, he'd been engaged.

For all those reasons, sparks between them were a bad thing. Solve this case, go home. No stops in between.

She must have come to the same conclusion, because she dropped his hand at the same moment that he pulled his away.

He carried the box while she led the way back up the path to the road. The way she moved—light and sensual, like someone aware of the wind on her skin and the sun on her hair—kept his eyes riveted on her.

He didn't have to take this job, he reminded himself. His commitment was to Maya, and she'd told him the job was off. S.G. didn't need answers about her family right away. She'd waited fifteen years, she could wait some more.

But if anyone knew the urgency of "don't wait," it was him. You never knew when death might take a swing at you. S.G. had survived so much. She deserved to find the truth. If he could help, he should.

He watched a butterfly flutter past Jessica's hair, which gleamed copper in the sunlight. Who was he trying to kid? One big reason he wanted to continue working this case was walking right in front of him. Jessica kept surprising him. He wanted to see what other skills she had up her sleeve beyond plumbing and arm-wrestling.

Like that sad story about her father. The look on her face while she'd shared it had tugged at his jaded heart. It made him want to shield little eight-year-old Jessica from that pain. Of course he couldn't do that, but he could do his best for S.G.

He'd just have to ignore those inconvenient sparks.

After all, they probably just meant that he and Jessica were polar opposites—even magnetically speaking.

CHAPTER THIRTEEN

Olga, the tailor, twisted the scrap of fabric this way and that, rubbing it between her fingers and even sniffing it. "Very fine silk," she finally announced. "Expensive. Thousand dollars a yard."

"Do you have any idea where it was produced?" Jessica asked her.

"There is no way for me to know. This kind of luxury fabric is rare to see."

"Could it have been made in Alaska?"

"Oh no." She laughed as she waved that off. "No one creates fabric so expensive here."

"One other thing," Ethan interjected. "Can you tell what color it used to be?"

She took out a magnifying glass from under her work counter and studied it for a long time. "Rose pink," she finally announced.

"You're sure?"

"Mostly sure. But it's very old."

Jessica let out a long sigh as they left her little shop, which was overflowing with bolts of fabric. "I guess I was wrong."

"About what?"

"About her being helpful. That was a total waste of time."

Ethan shot her an astonished look. "Are you kidding? It's a huge clue. The fabric is pink and expensive and S.G. has had it forever. It must be something that dates from her early life. That tells me that her family is most likely wealthy."

"But if we don't know anything about where the cloth came from, what difference does it make?"

"The first rule of investigating is persistence. Most leads don't go anywhere. Chin up, Tasty Cakes."

She gave a double take as they strolled along Lost Harbor's main downtown street, where they'd parked her car. "Is that your idea of a nickname?"

"It's a tribute to your sweet rolls. Why, does it bother you?"

She pondered it, rolling the term over her tongue. "Well, I don't see how anything with the word 'cake' could be a problem. Cake is one of humankind's best inventions. I suppose it's better than my other nickname."

"What's your other one?"

"Jessica." She laughed at his confused expression. "It's, uh, short for Japonica. That's what my mother named me."

"Japonica..."

"It's an edible flower. My mother was kind of a hippie flower child."

"Was? I'm sorry—"

"Oh no, she's still very much alive. But now she's more interested in her retirement fund than edible flowers."

He chuckled as they reached her car. "Should we grab some lunch, Tasty Cakes? The second rule of investigating is to keep your blood sugar up so you don't fall asleep during a stakeout."

"Sure, I could eat." Even though she said it casually, her heart warmed at his friendly tone. Maybe he was finally starting to take her seriously, like a fellow detective, practically.

Her cell phone rang. Nia didn't even wait for her to answer before she began talking.

"There's a man here looking for you. He's large and kind of scary. He says he has the right to shut down the bakery."

She stopped in her tracks. "*What?* Is it someone from the DEC?" The state health department came through every year or so for an inspection, but they'd never failed one—so far.

"He says he's working for Gary Phelps and that you need to come sign something immediately or we'll have to shut down. What should I do?"

"I'll be right there. Don't do anything. Tell him I'm on my way."

Ethan was watching her with worry in his eyes.

"I have to go. My mom's husband is up to something." She turned first one way, then the other, forgetting what she was even doing on Main Street on a sunny afternoon.

"Here." Ethan placed his hands on her shoulders and guided her toward her car. "I'll drive."

"No, it's fine—"

"I'll drive," he repeated firmly. "You're too upset. It's not safe."

"It's like five blocks. There's no need to drive."

He opened the passenger door and pointed. "Sit."

Too freaked out to argue anymore, she sat, and he whisked her to the Sweet Harbor Bakery as if on a magic carpet.

He did even more than that. As soon as he caught sight of the beefy man in the badly fitting blazer, he told her, "I recognize him. Not specifically him, but his type. He's here to intimidate you. Don't sign anything. In fact, I have an idea. Introduce me as your lawyer. I know how to handle him."

Worked for her. She had no idea if Gary had any right to shut down the bakery. If she was smart, she would have already contacted a lawyer instead of waiting for the peony harvest to end.

Ethan walked briskly up to the stranger, while she held back. Stubble covered the lower part of his face and his bushy eyebrows made for a permanent frown. She didn't recognize him; he probably came from Rocky Gulch or even Anchorage.

The bakery had already closed for the day, and the stranger had interrupted Nia in mid-cleanup. The floor was half-mopped and the chairs were upside down on the tabletops. The only people in the shop were Nia and the intruder. At least no customers were here to witness this.

Ethan gestured for her to go ahead and address the man.

Calling on all her nerve, she stuck out her hand. "Hi, I'm Jessica Dixon, and this is my lawyer, Ethan James."

His expression shifted as he took in the sight of Ethan's set jaw and general air of competence. "I'm Hutch Brinker. I'm working for Gary Phelps on the development of this property. Seems we've run into a situation here."

He handed her a document, which she held so that Ethan could read it too. She couldn't get her eyes to focus on it; all the words blurred. Luckily, Ethan wasn't paralyzed with fear the way she was, and he was able to read it.

"This is nothing but an empty threat," he said with reassuring confidence. "If you really want to take legal action, feel free."

"Wha—" she gasped.

He squeezed her hand and she snapped her mouth shut.

"We don't want to do that," Brinker said. "Mrs. Phelps wants to avoid it. They just want a decision."

Well, that was good news. At least her mother didn't want to sue her.

"Do what you need to do," Ethan told him. "This piece of paper is meaningless." He crumpled it up and handed it to

Jessica. "I'm recommending strongly that my client toss it in that beautiful stonework oven over there."

His air of complete authority sent a wave of relief over her. She could handle this. She could even play along with Ethan's bravado.

"Isn't that oven gorgeous?" she said. "A stonemason from Italy made it. He was dating my mother at the time. He was one of the *good* boyfriends."

"You mean the kind that doesn't send a goon to your place of business to try to browbeat you?"

She clapped her hands together in applause. "Exactly! I do love the word 'browbeat,' by the way. It's so descriptive, especially when you're talking about someone with such impressive eyebrows."

Hutch Brinker glanced between the two of them and shrugged his big shoulders. "No point in dragging this out. I know Gary Phelps and he doesn't let a deal slip away. He'll win in the end. Best to sign now before things get ugly."

"Is that a threat?" Ethan shouldered past Jessica to face off with him. They were almost equal in height, but Brinker had quite a few pounds on him. On the other hand, Ethan looked much more fit. Overall, Jessica gave Ethan the advantage, but she hoped this didn't get physical. Her glass bakery display cases had cost a pretty penny. "Why don't you be more specific. What's gonna happen if she doesn't sign?"

Brinker held up both hands. "Can't predict the future. All I know is Gary's a good businessman. This chick is in over her head." He didn't even glance at Jessica as he made his scornful comment.

"I wouldn't be so sure."

That sounded almost like a compliment, if you squinted hard and looked at it from different angles.

"Jessica, what do you say? You're the owner around here. Do you want this man on your property?"

"You know my motto. No shirt, no smile, no service."

Brinker shifted his shoulders, adjusting his blazer on his beefy frame. She wondered if he'd rented it for the day to look extra-impressive.

"You heard her, my man. Please report back to your boss that we will not be signing anything today."

He didn't budge and Jessica got a horrid sinking sensation that even if he left now, this man was still going to be a problem. Was she going to have to deal with incidents like this until she agreed to sell the bakery?

"Should we call your best friend, the police chief?" Ethan cocked his head toward Jessica.

The man smirked. "Good luck with that. Heard she's in Anchorage at a hospital."

Ethan continued as if he hadn't just hit a speed bump. "Luckily there's a whole police department working under her."

"Yeah. Too bad they're all morons except her."

"Believe me, they're perfectly capable of executing an arrest for trespassing. The jail is tiny. Extremely uncomfortable, nothing good to eat. One and a half stars at the most."

As he spoke, Ethan maneuvered the man toward the door. He did it so smoothly that the intruder barely seemed to realize it was happening.

But Brinker did have one more thing to say before he stepped out the door onto the porch. "You better think, Japonica Dixon. Think hard about how you want this to go down."

As soon as he was gone, the breath rushed out of Jessica's body. Ethan shut the door and returned to Jessica's side. Without thinking, she leaned her forehead against his chest. Her heart raced from the aftermath of adrenaline. His arm came around her and settled firmly on her back.

It felt good. Insanely good.

"I can't believe that just happened," she choked. "It was like an episode of *The Sopranos*. Did he really threaten me?"

"Sure sounded like it to me."

"Me too," Nia piped up. She'd been so quiet that Jessica had forgotten she was there. "I'm going to take off now, if it's okay. I have a date with a dip net and a very fit fisherman. The salmon are running."

Jessica lifted her head from Ethan's jacket. Wow, he smelled good. Clean and spicy, like a barbershop and a field of strawberries. "Sure, Nia. Sorry you had to deal with that guy."

"It was fun watching him get shut down. Nice work, dude." Nia tossed her apron in the hamper and hurried toward the kitchen's back door.

In the sudden quiet, Jessica lifted her gaze to Ethan's, her face flushing. How embarrassing that she'd automatically turned to him for comfort, when he was essentially still a stranger.

He kept his arm around her. "You okay?"

"Yes, I'm fine. Of course. Tougher than I look." As his arm dropped, she gave a shaky laugh. "I should have arm-wrestled him, that would have taught him a lesson. So what does that piece of paper say?"

"I'm no lawyer, but I've seen enough legal docs to play translator. Basically they want you to sign off on selling this location to Prince Cruise Lines. If you don't, they're threatening to sue you for breach of contract."

"Breach of contract? What contract?"

"Your contract with your mother, apparently."

Oh for heaven's sake. "The only contract we have is a piece of watercolor paper. She dumped the bakery on me because she got bored and wanted to travel to Big Sur. Every once in a while I send her some money, whatever I can afford. But since she got married she hasn't asked for any. *Gary* is loaded."

"Do you think she knows about Brinker coming here?"

"I don't know. I don't even want to ask her. We'll just get into a fight."

Ethan frowned as he scanned the document the man had left. "If there isn't much in the way of a contract, I recommend you hire a lawyer."

"I—" She bit her lip. Lost Harbor had a shortage of good lawyers, and Kate was the only one she trusted. She wouldn't be available until after the peony harvest. "You're right. I was hoping if I ignored the whole thing my mom would drop it. I guess I called that wrong. Now it's escalating."

He scanned her face with those perceptive eyes of his. "Maybe this is a silly question, but do you want to sell it? You could probably make a good profit."

"I don't know. I don't know! I mean, of course I don't. Or maybe I do?"

He cocked his head at her with a curious frown. "Okay."

How could she articulate this? "I love this bakery. It's my home. Literally, because I live in one of the rooms upstairs. It's my work too, and I love that. I love making people smile when they bite into one of my sticky buns. I love looking out my window and seeing mountains and mudflats and wild roses. All my friends are here. This," she spread her arms wide, "this is all I've ever known. I've never been outside of Alaska. I rarely even leave Lost Harbor."

"So then it's a flat 'no'."

"Maybe? But then I think maybe I'm stuck in a rut. Or not even a rut, because that means you were going somewhere before you got stuck. Me, I'm always here. So it's more of a...barnacle situation. I'm stuck like a barnacle. My mother thinks it's bad that I never go anywhere. I can see her point. So..." She threw up her hands. "I can't decide."

"Fair enough."

She folded her arms across her chest, feeling exposed and shaken up. A long bath with some rose petals and yarrow would be helpful right now.

"Do you think that man, Hutch Brinker, is going to come back?"

"Possibly. They might flesh out that legal threat first."

"You rattled him. Thank you."

"My pleasure." He seemed to mean that sincerely. "I'm not a fan of threats and intimidation."

She stepped behind the counter and opened the refrigerator where the leftover baked goods were stored. "I think that deserves a reward. How about a spinach and feta croissant sandwich? For some reason those never sell out."

"The word 'spinach' might have something to do with that," he grumbled as he took a seat at a table and stretched out his legs. "But sure, I'd love one."

As she took out the covered tray, a sense of dread filled her. Big life decisions were the *worst*. Why was her mother putting her in this situation? What would Kate advise? What would Maya do? She'd never gotten a chance to consult with Maya before Harris got sick. Now Maya had much more important things to worry about.

All her friends were wrapped up right now. She was on her own with this decision. And she had no idea how to make it. All she wanted to do was hide under her covers until it all went away. So ridiculous.

But of course she couldn't do that. For one thing, S.G. was counting on her.

Another crazy idea formed.

She hit the button on the microwave to heat up the sandwich. "If Gary really wants to sue me, don't they have to deliver the paperwork to me?"

"Yeah, that's what he has Hutch Brinker for."

"What if he can't find me?"

"What are you going to do, disappear?"

"I'm thinking about it."

She brought him a plate with the steaming croissant. He sniffed at the spinach croissant like a wolf. She wondered how detailed his enhanced sense of smell was. Could he tell that she'd used whole wheat flour for the croissants? And a boatload of butter?

"Looks great, thanks. I'm missing something, though. How are you going to avoid a process server? They're experts at locating people and this is a small town. Not many places to hide."

"This town might be small. But out there—" She gestured at the window and the bright vista outside. Past the wild roses and the towering delphiniums was the pebble beach, then the wind-ruffled bay, and finally the immoveable backdrop of the mountain range. "There's plenty of room."

It took only a second for Ethan to get her drift. "You want to hide out in Lost Souls Wilderness."

"I wouldn't call it hiding out. I'd call it investigating. The hiding is a side benefit."

"You're talking about S.G.?"

"Exactly. The best way to make progress is to find the trapper's cabin where she grew up. I'm betting we could find more clues like that pink cloth."

"There's a chance." He nodded in agreement. "But we don't exactly have GPS coordinates for that cabin. Maya printed out some Google Earth maps with possible locations, but that's about it. S.G. made a drawing of the cabin, but that's no use until we find something to compare it to."

Jessica paced back and forth next to the table. The more she thought about this plan, the more she liked it. She could avoid Hutch Brinker, investigate for Maya, and put off making a decision all in one swoop. It was perfect. "But Maya hadn't heard about S.G.'s drowning dream. That could be a clue, you said so yourself. And didn't S.G. tell Maya some details about the route she took to get here? I bet you anything that if we put all that information together we can find that cabin."

"Very optimistic."

"You bet I am. We can do this." Now she was on fire with the possibility. "Are you up for a wilderness experience? I can get us there with my float plane. But I can't go alone. The buddy system saves lives."

"So you want me to be your buddy?" He spoke through a mouthful of spinach pastry.

"Yes. I'll pay you whatever your day rate is."

"Plus hazard pay?"

She bit her lip, thinking about her dwindling savings and how much it might cost to pay a lawyer. "How much extra is that?"

"Depends. Will you be providing the food? Because I can take a few bucks off if this is how we'll be eating."

She thought about it. Planning a trip into the wilderness was a big deal. She usually spent a few days gathering together all the necessary gear. "I suppose if we use the float plane as a kind of base camp, we can store some food there. But we have to be careful because of bears."

"I don't know if I should be more worried about the float plane or the bears."

"You don't have to worry about any of it. I got this." She gave him her most confident smile. "You deal with the goons. I'll deal with the wild beasts. You could think of it as a vacation. People actually pay a lot of money for guided trips to Lost Souls Wilderness. Technically, I could actually charge you for my time instead of the other way around."

He finished the sandwich and brushed crumbs off his fingers.

"Yeah, that's not happening. My vacations usually involve a lot of sleeping and eating."

"Okay, then think of it as an adventure. A story to tell."

"Assuming we live to tell it," he murmured.

"Of course we will. It's not that dangerous if you know what you're doing. Honestly. City boys."

Her goading had exactly the right effect. He shrugged his wide shoulders and gave in.

"Fine. I'll be your wilderness buddy. But just so you know, I nearly died recently and I have no intention of doing that again any time soon."

"Noted."

CHAPTER FOURTEEN

Ethan had come to a conclusion sometime between his show-down with Hutch Brinker and Jessica's brainwave about Lost Souls Wilderness. He had no intention of charging her for this investigation.

He wouldn't feel right about it. He was eating well, staying at her B&B for free, getting a break from LA traffic and the usual grind. And now there was a float plane involved.

Ever since he'd first seen the wild peaks of Lost Souls Wilderness, he'd wondered what it was like over there. Every story he heard intrigued him even more. Like the one about the tribe of Native Alaskans that had disappeared into a glacier a hundred years ago. No one knew where they'd gone or why they'd vanished. Some people said that spirits lived in the forests; others just talked about the bears.

Padric had told him about some of his experiences in Lost Souls, hiking there with Zoe when they were teenagers. Now he was going to see it for himself, and the adventure of it thrilled him.

The preparations took a solid day, during which he kept a

careful eye out for anyone who might be a process server. At the firehouse, Nate Prudhoe lent him a backpack and an already broken-in pair of hiking boots. His fiancée, Bethany, tucked a first-aid kit into the pack.

"Jessica's probably already packed one," he told her.

"Then you'll have an extra. No arguing. Doctor's orders. And make sure you're back for the wedding."

Nate handed him an invitation. "Two weeks. At our house on the hill. Pray for sun."

"If we're not back in two weeks, we'll have bigger problems than missing your wedding."

Nate clapped a hand on his back. "Any trouble, we got you. We're used to pulling people out of the sea around here. Summer storms, winter storms, we're on it. And you know how to handle a bear encounter, right?"

He'd planned to completely avoid the bears. Failing that, he'd follow Jessica's lead.

"I'm going to rely on my expert guide."

Nate nodded, looking reassured. "Jessica knows what she's doing. You'll be in good hands."

The preparations for the trip showed him another side of the girl he'd first thought was just a pretty baker. Jessica knew exactly what to pack for the trip and made efficient work of the process. Tent, ground cloth, sleeping bags, Therm-a-Rests, water filter, dry bags for matches and toilet paper, cooking gear, food, head lamps—it was dizzying.

Not only did she have to pack, but she had to entrust the bakery to a rotating shift of twenty-somethings with countless different scheduling demands.

"What if Hutch Brinker comes back?" he asked.

"I told them to shut down if that happens. Hutch Brinker can deal with the wrath of hungry Lost Harbor-ites craving their sticky buns."

Understandable, he had to admit.

Finally, they loaded everything into Jessica's Subaru and headed for Trumpeter Lake just outside of town. "I came here earlier for the preflight," she told him as they pulled up next to a small shed next to a dock. "I had to drain water from the floats, that sort of things. We just have to load up and go."

The lake's marshy shoreline was punctuated with several docks that stretched into the tranquil water. Jessica parked her car near the head of one of the docks. Tethered to the end of it, a sporty red plane perched atop two gleaming white pontoons, floating almost surreally on the water's surface.

"This is my plane, it's a single-engine 208 Caravan," Jessica said proudly as they hauled their backpacks, a cooler, and two extra duffel bags down the dock. "Five friends and I bought her used and fixed her up. It's a good thing no one had dibs on this week. We make up a schedule at the start of summer." When she reached the plane, she dropped her gear and caressed its shiny curved fuselage. "You wouldn't believe how much this lovely lady costs me every year. But she's worth it."

"Are planes always ladies, just like boats?"

"Just like humans, they're on a spectrum." She winked as she opened up the hatch and climbed onboard. Her long hair was tamed into a braid that she'd pulled through the opening of a Lost Harbor Puffins baseball cap. She wore spandex jogging pants tucked into hiking boots that laced up the front. Her excitement about the trip to Lost Souls shone in her bright eyes and eager movements.

"How many times have you flown it?"

"I have to fly a certain number of hours a year to keep my rating. Don't you worry your pretty head. I got this." She beckoned to him to hand up their gear. One by one, he swung the duffels and backpacks into her grasp so she could stow them in the storage compartment.

Faster than he was really prepared for, they were tucked into the tiny cockpit. She handed him headphones for ear protection and started up the ignition.

"Do a lot of Alaskans have their own planes?" he asked curiously.

"It's not uncommon." She spoke absently as she checked gauges and flicked toggle switches. "So many places are inaccessible except by plane. And the regional airlines don't fly everywhere."

As soon as she started the engine, they began gliding across the water. "No brakes on these planes," she explained as she steered toward the center of the lake. "I'm positioning us so we can take off into the wind, though it's so glassy today there's hardly any. One of my mom's boyfriends owned a float plane sightseeing operation. He taught me how to fly. We had some great family trips across the bay."

"Was he one of the good ones?"

A shadow crossed her face. "He was. I prayed he and my mom would stay together. I could never understand why they didn't. I still don't."

"Relationships." He shrugged. "It's hard to make them last. Jaded detective here."

"Yeah, it's amazing that I'm not more cynical. My friends laugh at me for being optimistic, but they don't understand that if I weren't, I'd be—" She broke off and used the distraction of piloting the plane to avoid finishing her sentence.

At least that was how he saw it.

He also knew where that sentence was heading. If she wasn't able to stay optimistic, she'd be mired in bitterness. She might be just as cynical and jaded as he was.

Thank God she wasn't. Her optimism was so refreshing. He liked her just the way she was, even though she was apparently determined to scare the crap out of him as they picked up speed and skimmed across the surface of the lake.

"We're on the step now," she shouted over the drone of the engine. "In a second we'll be airborne. There isn't a process server chasing down the dock after us, is there?"

He tried to laugh as he dug his hands into his seat. No armrests here. "All clear."

"Come and find us, asshole!" With a maniacal laugh, she worked the controls so the nose tilted into the air. With a stomach-dropping lurch, they lifted off the surface and headed straight for the treetops on the other end of the lake. "Up, up, up, come on," she muttered. "You can do it, beauty."

Was she kidding? Was it too late to jump off this thing? He looked wildly down at the lake, only to see it disappearing from beneath him, replaced by treetops so close they seemed to brush against the float plane's pontoons.

"Wooooooohoooo!" shouted Jessica as they cleared the woods and aimed for the sky. "Yeah baby."

Ethan unclenched his jaw and peeled his fingers off the vinyl seat cover. At least he'd kept his cool outwardly. Jessica didn't have to ever know that he'd just about crapped his pants in her float plane.

Once they were fully airborne, he was able to relax enough to enjoy the magnificent spectacle unfurling all around them. Little powderpuff clouds flirted with the plane as they passed. Seabirds tilted and wheeled nearby, as if intrigued by this new breed of fellow airborne being. Way below, the Misty Bay waves turned into little wrinkles on the water's surface.

It was a short trip across the bay, and soon a massive upwelling of rock and trees loomed up ahead. The mighty and ancient Lost Souls Wilderness, part cold-climate rainforest, part glacial overflow from the endless ice fields beyond.

Jessica ascended another thousand feet so they could comfortably clear the closer slopes. Last night, they'd spent some time poring over S.G.'s account of her solo trip from her cabin to the cove where she'd stowed away on a fishing boat. They'd studied topo maps in order to match her descriptions with the geography of the area. And then they'd factored in her dream about the lake.

Only three locations really made sense, and all three were close enough so that they could hike from one to the other. They'd selected the largest lake—none of them were named—and decided to make that their base of operations. It was located in a long and gently sloping valley that would be easy to navigate through.

As the bay disappeared behind them and they entered the territory of wooded slopes and high snow-topped peaks, a kind of awe crept over him. The forbidding wilderness encircled them, as if checking out the encroachers into its realm. *Strange things happen around Lost Souls Wilderness.*

"We come in peace," he muttered to himself.

"What?"

He shook his head, embarrassed.

"Talking to the wilderness? I totally get it," she shouted over the engine noise. "I always ask permission before I fly in here."

"What if you get a 'no'?"

"I have. I turned back once. A big forest fire came through right after that. I could have been trapped."

That sounded like a fairy story. But as he gazed out at the enigmatic cliff faces and spruce trees so tall they caught clouds of mist in their tops, he realized he wouldn't be surprised if ancient magic lurked in this wilderness.

Maybe Jessica was right after all. Maybe some things went beyond "common sense."

The little plane chugged steadily through the curving valley that would lead them to their destination. Even though he'd studied the topo map until his eyes blurred, everything looked so different in real life.

"Keep an eye out for that lake," she told him. "You'll have a clearer view than me."

He gave her a thumbs up and scanned the valley for a lake shaped like a lopsided heart, with one lobe dwarfing the other. At first he worried that the summer growth of vegetation would mask its shape, but when it finally came into view, he recognized it immediately.

"There." He pointed ahead of them.

"Yup, that's it." Jessica worked the controls and they went into a descent.

The more elevation they lost, the faster the trees seemed to be rushing toward them. *Jesus.* Were they breaking the laws of physics trying to land a plane on a fucking body of water? The flat expanse of the lake came at them like a brick wall. He flung up his arm to shield himself as the pontoons splashed onto the water. She pulled back on the controls to bring the nose up, and the plane skimmed across the lake like a dragonfly.

It felt like forever that they raced across the water, but it was probably only a matter of seconds until she throttled down. They sloshed to a halt pretty much in the center of the lake.

"Holy Mary mother of God, we're alive." He peeked out from under his arm.

"So far," she corrected with a grin.

"You did it. You landed a plane on a puddle of water. You're a goddess."

Her lips curved in a funny little smile. "Technically, we didn't land, we alighted. Hardly anyone says that though."

He lifted up her hand and pressed his lips to her warm skin. "Whatever you call it, you did that with your bare hands."

"Tougher than you thought, right?"

"You're a goddess," he repeated.

She cleared her throat and took back her hand. "Let's pick a beach and anchor as close as we can to it. That will minimize the rowing. Can you reach that yellow oilskin bag back there? It has a blowup dinghy inside."

Okay. Back to business. Obviously he'd embarrassed her with his overflow of compliments.

The after-landing checklist, unloading the gear and rowing to shore in the inflatable dinghy took about an hour. They left some of the gear—most of the food and the cooler—on the plane to keep it out of the reach of wildlife. Once they were safely onshore, with the float plane securely anchored, it was time to set up camp.

All of it was hard physical work, and his leg was aching when they finally relaxed onto a driftwood log next to the small campfire Jessica made on the beach.

"Good work, buddy," he murmured to his leg. He rubbed it absently as he gazed at the deep green of the lake and the dark reflections of the spruce on the surface. The quiet was immense. There were sounds—a squirrel chirp, the lap of water on the pebbled shore, the comforting crackle of the fire. But those sounds only emphasized the lack of manmade noise. Compared to West Covina, silence ruled here in Lost Souls Wilderness.

So did the cold. Even in midsummer, a chill set in as the sun made its leisurely way across the sky. Nate had also given him a thick fleece-lined rain jacket with a hood. He hadn't thought he'd need it, but damn it felt good against the cool touch of the evening air.

Jessica waved away black flies as she fed driftwood sticks into the fire. "The smoke will chase away the bugs," she explained. "I did bring head nets in case the mosquitoes get out of control. But these flies will bite right through your clothes. They can drive you insane. I remember once I was out here with my friends and we spent the whole time whacking flies off each other. We were black and blue by the time we got home."

She brought him a mug of instant soup, which he accepted eagerly. The scent of chicken and salt went right to his head. "Wow, that smells good."

"Everything tastes better in the wilderness. Try it. You'll see." She smiled encouragingly at him as he took a sip.

"Can't argue," he agreed. "Left field kind of question, but is that why you like it out here? Because things taste good while you're defending yourself from hordes of insects?"

"I like it out here because it's magical." She knelt by the campfire to feed more driftwood into it. "Don't you feel it?"

He cocked his head, going along with her delusion because she knew this place better than he did. An eddy of a breeze off the lake touched his neck. Silver flashed under the surface; maybe a fish on the hunt. An uneasy chill went down his back. He recognized that feeling. The same sensation crawled across his neck when someone spotted him during a stakeout. But this was the wilderness and no one was around for miles. And he certainly wouldn't call that feeling "magical."

"Hm," he grunted, not wanting to let her down. He swallowed more of his instant soup. So basic, and yet it was really hitting the spot.

She rolled her eyes. "You think I'm imagining it."

"Didn't say that." His leg spasmed and he adjusted its position.

From her spot by the fire, she handed him one of the turkey sandwiches she'd brought for the night's meal. "What's going on with your leg?"

"Nothing to worry about." He hated talking about it; it was his problem and no one else's. He didn't even like being asked about it.

Jessica sat back onto the driftwood log and fixed him with

eyes that looked like pure gold in the misty light. "I need to know," she said gently. "It's just the two of us out here in the wilderness. If you have any physical limitations, it's better if I know."

"It's not a limit—" He gritted his teeth. She was right. They were relying on each other out here. She had a right to know. "It's just something I work with. I had bone cancer when I was a kid. Childhood osteosarcoma. It's gone now, but I still feel some effects from the surgeries. I've spent months of my life doing PT and my functionality is almost a hundred percent. Maybe ninety-six percent. But it does ache sometimes. You don't have to worry, though, I'll be able to keep up."

He braced himself for the usual responses. Pity. Fear—as if cancer was contagious. Medical advice—have you tried such-and-such for the pain? That was why he didn't like talking about it. It was a lot of fucking work.

But she just nodded. "Okay. Thanks for telling me. The important thing out here is communication. I'm going to trust that you'll tell me if you need anything, like a break or a change of pace."

"I will," he assured her. Could he actually do that? Would he? He thought about it, and realized that yes, he would. Jessica had an accepting way about her that put him at ease.

"Let's come up with a plan for tomorrow, yeah?"

And he didn't even have to change the subject. God love this woman.

She unfurled the laminated topo map of the area and they pinned down the corners with rocks. As they ate and waved away flies, they studied the lines that indicated ridges and trails and waterways.

"S.G. said she followed a trail from the cabin to a creek bed, then turned east along the creek." Jessica pointed to a spot on the map not far from them. "Should we try that one?"

Ethan pulled out Maya's notes, which he'd packed into a Ziploc bag in his backpack. He scanned the section about her journey to Lost Harbor. "She said it took her three days. Is that the right distance?"

"But it was in winter. Travel is easier in winter because she had a dog sled for part of the time."

"But then the dogs ran away. She said she thinks they knew that Murchison was back. She was on her own after that. I think we should try this other one." He pointed at another trail that had caught his eye.

Jessica traced a line with one finger. Her nails were cut short and he noticed several burn scars and nicks on her skin. Baking had its own dangers, apparently.

He resisted the impulse to put his hand on hers. To caress it. His respect for her kept growing, and along with it, his attraction.

"I could ask my crystal," she murmured.

And...back to reality.

"Are you telling me you brought a crystal with you to Lost Souls Wilderness?"

"I bring it everywhere." She shot him an annoyed glance as she dropped her hand from the map. "Why are people so weird about crystals? Mine helps me tune into my intuition."

"Maybe because logic is more important. Intuition is just... emotion. It can be biased. You can't really trust it."

She reached into her pocket and drew out a felt drawstring bag. "In my experience, it's more trustworthy than people are." A sparkling cut crystal on a delicate chain tumbled into her palm. Even though it was clear, it refracted golden light across her skin.

"You're going to do it right now?"

She gave a disappointed sigh. "I knew you'd be like this. Are you really so close-minded?"

"Close-minded because I don't want a rock telling me where to go?"

"You don't have to watch if you don't want to."

"Oh, I'm watching. I gotta see this."

Rolling her eyes again, she sat next to him on the log and let the crystal dangle from her fingers. After a moment of silent communion with it, she asked out loud, "Should we try the northern trail to find S.G.'s old cabin?"

The crystal quivered and swung in a side to side motion. "That's a no," she explained. "Should we try the trail Ethan suggested?"

This time the crystal moved the other direction. "That's a 'yes.' I guess you win."

He laughed at the sheer absurdity. "You made it move that way so I'd warm up to your crystal."

"Then if you don't accept what it says, let's take my route."

"Just because your crystal agrees with me doesn't mean I'm wrong."

She addressed the crystal again. "Should Ethan open his mind a little?"

The crystal moved in the "yes" direction.

He shifted closer to her and addressed the crystal himself. His leg brushed against hers, but he didn't move it. "Should Jessica use her own damn common sense to figure out the best route?"

The crystal shivered, then swung up and down—"yes."

Jessica looked at him strangely. "The crystal only answers to me, you know."

"It seemed to answer me just fine. Right answer, too. Thank you, crystal."

Her eyebrows drew together, her expression perplexed. Her skin looked so soft in this light. He noticed a spray of freckles across her nose. A curl of hair loose from her baseball cap. How had they gotten so close together? It would be weird if he changed position now, so he didn't.

"You're right, it did answer you. That doesn't usually happen. Ask it something else," she demanded.

"This is silly."

"Please. Something we both agree on. Let's see what it says."

"It doesn't say any—oh fine." He spoke to the sparkling crystal again. It was pretty, if nothing else. "Should we go to sleep early tonight?" That was already the plan they'd agreed to.

But the crystal swung the other direction—"no."

They exchanged a glance. "Maybe we should reconsider," Jessica said. "Or maybe it's confused because you're the one asking."

"Or it might be just a rock."

"Ask it something else. Something completely out of the blue. Something that we haven't discussed at all."

"Okay." He cast around for the strangest thing he could think of. Nothing came to mind.

"Something completely random right off the top of your head!" she urged.

Various possibilities flitted through his brain. He stared at the crystal, feeling almost hypnotized.

"Come on! Whatever you're thinking, right now," said Jessica. "Just say it!"

Words blurted from him before he could stop them. "Should we kiss?"

CHAPTER FIFTEEN

Jessica felt her face flame. She'd *just* been thinking about what it would be like to kiss Ethan. He just looked so...yummy sitting on the log next to her, firelight playing across his face. Sure, he was laughing at her crystal—usually a black mark against a guy—but her crystal seemed to like him.

And now it was swinging strongly in the "yes" direction to his question about kissing. She quickly dropped it into its bag and yanked the drawstring closed. "That's enough of that."

But Ethan wasn't so quick to dismiss it this time. "You really need to respect your crystal more," he teased.

"Of course I respect my crystal. That doesn't mean I do everything it says. It might just be picking up on—" She broke off abruptly.

"Hmm, picking up on what? The fact that you want to kiss me?" His hazel eyes danced with amusement, but they held more than laughter. There was heat there too, and behind that, seriousness.

"You're the one who asked the question. Maybe you're the one who wants to kiss."

The space between them flared with awareness. Her throat went tight. She swallowed hard. He lowered his head toward her, a slow journey that gave her plenty of time to move away, or object.

She did neither.

"Maybe I do," he said in a gruff voice. Maybe the same tightening thing was happening to his throat as to hers.

As he came closer, his clean scent enveloped her. Her eyelids fluttered, always a sure sign that she desired someone. Her lips parted on their own as her eyes dropped to his mouth. His firm lips curved in a slight smile. Light stubble darkened his jaw. There was a groove to the left of his mouth but not the right.

And then he was too close to examine and she lifted her eyes just as his mouth claimed hers.

They stepped into the kiss as if they were jumping into a summer lake together. His lips were warm and steady, brushing fire against her sensitive flesh. Tingles flickered across her nerve endings and she opened her mouth for more. His hand moved to the back of her head to bring her closer.

Oh yes. More of that.

She made a sound deep in her throat and turned fully toward him. He deepened the kiss, finding the tender inner skin of her mouth and setting it aflame. One of his hands still held her head, and the other came around her back. Her body relaxed in his hold as if turning liquid under his touch. Heat expanded from her lower belly all the way to her fingertips. She wanted to meld her body with his, climb into his lap and claw his jacket out of the way.

A fly bumped against her cheek and she waved it away. Even so, it broke the moment. Ethan relaxed his hold and gently drew his mouth away from hers.

She blinked at him in shock. She and Ethan had *kissed*. Not just a casual kiss either. A real kiss. One that reached right into her heart and planted a seed. She didn't want it to stop. She wanted to keep kissing him all night. She wanted to lose herself in his warmth and strength.

Disoriented, she touched her lips, which felt plumper than normal. Swollen and sexy.

"Jessica."

"Yes." She swung her head to meet his serious gaze.

"That was quite a kiss."

"I noticed."

"I'd like to do that again sometime. Like, soon."

Heat rolled across her face. Was this actually happening? Was her attraction to Ethan being brought into the light and turned into something real? They were so different, her and Ethan. She was head-in-the-clouds. He was boots-on-the-ground.

And yet...that kiss.

She ran her tongue across her lips, still tasting him.

"But we should probably talk first," he continued in a sober tone.

Right. *Words.* Not sensations. Not feelings. Not images. Verbal communication. "About your breakup?"

"No, it's more than that." He swiped the back of his hand across his forehead, where a mosquito had landed. "There's a thing I need to say to anyone I get involved with."

Her stomach tightened. Whatever this "thing" was, she knew already that she wasn't going to like it. The tone of his voice told her that. "It was just a kiss. We really don't have to overthink it."

He cracked his neck to relieve some tension. Wow, he really did look uncomfortable. "You're right. We can leave it at that if you want."

She scrubbed her hands down her thighs. That wasn't what she wanted at all. She'd rather kiss him again and again, then maybe get naked and kiss some more. "Go ahead, say your thing. Even if we don't go any further, I'd like to know what it is."

"Okay." He cleared his throat. "I made a mistake getting engaged to Charley."

That was the thing? She'd sensed all along that there was something off with his engagement. "Because you broke up?"

"No. Because I never intended to get engaged to anyone. I don't intend to have children. I don't believe that I have a future."

Puzzled, she waved away another insect. "No future? At all? I don't understand."

He shifted on the log and stretched out his leg. And then it clicked.

"Because of your cancer. But didn't you say it's gone now?"

"Yes, I hope it's gone for good. I believe it is. I'm down to yearly biopsies now. But I'll always have a chance of recurrence. I'll always have some pain. I may develop other problems. I don't know if I can have children. It's too much to ask of someone."

She picked up a willow branch and poked at an ember that had escaped the campfire. She didn't have an easy response to his confession, but her heart ached for him.

They sat in silence for a moment, both of them watching the flicker and glow of the fire.

When he spoke again, his tone was lighter. "Besides, more things than cancer have tried to kill me. I've nearly died a few times in my life. I told you about the most recent."

"The one that left you with a better sense of smell?"

"Yes. It also caused me to make a mistake and propose to Charley. That was something I swore I'd never do. And obviously, it didn't end well."

A bird flapped overhead, something with long wings that passed too fast for her to identify. Possibly an eagle returning to its aerie for the night. A chill tickled her back—a sad sensation.

"So you believe that because you've had all these experiences that you're going to die young?"

"You can only dodge it so many times." He gave a jaunty shrug, making a joke out of it.

Some joke.

"We're all going to die," she pointed out.

"True. But it's generally a pretty abstract concept. It's something out there," he waved his hand at the forest that marched in dark stands toward the lake. "Something you don't have to think about much. I've had to think about it a few times now. Death has its eye on me."

"Okay, but even if that's true... Why don't you think of it the opposite way? You're hard to catch. You're a champion when it comes to evading the Grim Reaper."

He chuckled and rested his elbows on his knees. "Maybe you're right. I could think of it that way. But it doesn't matter how I think of it. I don't want someone else—a woman or a child—to suffer because of me. What if I don't escape the next time? I decided early on that it wouldn't be fair to have a family."

With her stick, Jessica traced a pattern in the cinders in the campfire. What a momentous decision to have to make at a young age. "It's perfectly fine not to want a family. I know others who don't."

"I know. But thank you," he added.

"How old were you when you decided that?"

"I don't really remember. I've always thought that way. I've never really questioned it—except when I proposed to Charley, and I was under the influence of who-knows-what when that happened."

She nodded thoughtfully. "So was it a conscious decision or more of a life-just-keeps-happening decision?"

"Excuse me?"

She laughed at his confusion. "Since decisions are so hard for me, I've thought about this a lot. It seems to me that some decisions happen without really thinking. Like me and the bakery. I never *chose* to run it forever. But here I am. It's the difference between conscious and unconscious decisions."

He gave her an arrested look. "Interesting. Very perceptive."

With a flush, she turned back to the fire. "Thanks. And thanks for telling me about all that."

"Moving on to you...would you still want to kiss me again? Knowing that?"

She concentrated on the ashes she was stirring. Embers leaped into the air in bright arcs, then sputtered out.

Probably exactly what was happening to this fragile thing between them.

"You probably assume that I do want a family," she said softly.

"Do you?"

"Do you want my honest complete answer?"

"Yes." He tilted his head toward her. She read genuine interest on his face, something she didn't see very often on the dates she'd been on.

"Out of all my friends, I've always been Team Romance. I assumed I'd find a good man and get married. I want that—I want someone to love me, someone to go through life with. Someone to snuggle with, laugh with, fight with. All of that. You know. A soul mate. But someone like that hasn't appeared."

"Maybe that's your problem." He rubbed his right leg, which was stretched out nearly to the fire. She wondered if it was still paining him.

"What is?"

"Believing there's such a thing as a soul mate." His dry tone would have offended her if it wasn't also gentle.

"Maybe. My friends say that too," she admitted. "They think I should just let it go and be more practical. But I'm an optimist so I keep hoping."

And hoping. And dating. And getting disappointed. But she

didn't have to detail all that to Ethan. He was just the newest non-soul mate to cross her path.

"What is a soul mate?" he was asking. "How would you know if you met one?"

"*How* would I know?" She stared at him in disbelief. How could he not understand such a simple concept? "We would just...fit. We'd understand each other. We'd want the same things. I'd sense it."

"Got it. Intuition."

"Don't knock it, city boy. Especially out here." She tugged her jacket around her and shivered. "Intuition could save your life."

"As could common sense," he pointed out. Which left them right where they'd started—at opposite ends of everything.

It was getting late; the sun was only visible in flashes behind the very tops of the trees on the slope to the west. It was probably about ten by now, judging by the degree of light remaining in the sky.

"Well, now that we've confessed our deep dark secrets, should we hit the hay?" she said lightly.

"Oh honey." His voice rumbled across her nerve endings in the most delicious way. "I have more deep dark secrets where those came from."

She shivered lightly. "How do you know I don't too?"

"With that angelic face of yours? I assume you do. It's always the innocent-looking ones who turn out to be trouble."

She laughed at that. "You should talk to my friends. They would tell you how right you are." She got to her feet and collected their sandwich wrappers and the instant soup package, then dropped them in the fire. "Common sense says that we should rinse our mugs out in the lake. Any little scrap of food smell could draw a bear."

He rose instantly to his feet. "I'll do that."

"Aw, you're offering to wash dishes? What a man." She meant that with all sincerity.

"Somehow it feels more manly when it involves bears."

"Hopefully it won't involve bears. That's kind of the whole point."

He gathered up their two stainless steel travel mugs and trekked them down to the shoreline.

As soon as he was gone, she gave in to the sadness that had gathered in her heart while he'd told her his "thing." Just as she'd suspected, Ethan wasn't for her. She couldn't be with someone who didn't want to think about a future. That sounded terrible. It was guaranteed to end in a broken heart. Hers, specifically. She didn't have the ability to be involved without putting her whole self into it. That was why she was Team Romance.

Toni always told her she should stop looking for someone who fit her perfectly because no one like that existed. Kate maintained she should just have fun and not worry about things like soul mates. Easy for her to say, now that she was in love with the Hottie Fire Chief.

Maya was the only one who didn't lecture her about holding out for a soul mate; probably because she knew it was pointless. Maya knew she was a hopeless romantic and didn't judge her for it. All she said was, "Honestly, I don't think you have it in you to hook up. That's not how you're built. Why lie to yourself?"

But how would she know if she didn't try it?

Maybe Kate and Toni—who were both Team Sex—were right. Maybe she was going about this the wrong way.

Maybe being with someone like Ethan would be a good way to step out of her comfort zone. She wouldn't be tempted to figure out if he was her soul mate because he couldn't possibly be, despite their sparks.

As she kicked cinders into the fire, she surreptitiously watched Ethan down by the shore. He squatted next to the rippling water, all lean lines and wide shoulders. It must have taken so much work and dedication to come back from his surgeries. That was impressive. She'd done physical therapy once for a sprained ankle; after two weeks she'd been bored out her mind. But Ethan had kept at it and now you'd hardly know there was anything different about that leg.

And if you thought about it, his decision not to have a family could be seen as thoughtful. He didn't want to bring anyone else into his doomed circle.

Under his jaded surface, he had deeper layers than she would have expected.

But that didn't mean she should get involved with him. In fact, she was almost a hundred percent sure she shouldn't. Even if it was just for a few days, he had the ability to throw her heart into chaos. If that one kiss had such an impact on her, what would sex do?

Don't think about sex with Ethan.

Too late. Images were already flipping through her head. Bare skin, straining muscles, thrusting hips, hazel eyes drilling into hers.

She shook it off. They were sharing a tent tonight—though in separate sleeping bags—and she didn't need to be teasing herself with something that would never happen. Team Sex, she was not and never wanted to be. She never had sex with anyone unless she thought they had a chance at forever.

And how has that worked so far?

Not well, okay? I've been wrong every single time. Get off my back.

Too bad there wasn't a bird nearby with whom she could talk this over. Never a goose around when you needed one. The flies weren't at all a good substitute; they simply didn't know how to listen.

By the time she and Ethan had finished cleaning up the

campsite and tucked themselves into their ten-below-zero sleeping bags, her decision was made.

"I can't, Ethan," she whispered as they both stared up at the roof of her little tent. "We're just too different. I'm not built for hook-ups. I wish I could. But I can't."

CHAPTER SIXTEEN

It was for the best. Ethan knew that. Literally two days after his engagement had ended, he had no business getting involved with someone else.

And he and Jessica had no business being together anyway.

Well, they had *business*. Investigative business. Best to keep it that way.

But that kiss...it was no exaggeration at all to say that it had shaken him down to the soles of his borrowed hiking boots. Her lips were so soft and *wondering*...as if every moment of contact was a step into a magical new world. Jessica saw magic everywhere, even in him. And while they'd kissed, he could almost imagine he saw it too.

It was intoxicating.

He shifted his head on his makeshift pillow, which was nothing but a fleece jacket rolled up under his head. Outside the reinforced nylon of the tent, the mosquitoes hadn't forgotten about them. They kept dive-bombing the mesh window. He scratched at a bite on his neck, lightly so as not to disturb Jessica.

Her sleeping form curled next to him, so cozy in her fluffy

bag. He turned carefully onto his side so he could look at her. Her lips were parted, rosy and soft. *Don't look. Don't remember.* Her auburn hair fanned across her sleeping bag in waves, curlier than normal since she'd unbraided her hair. He spotted a scattering of spruce needles caught in her curls and smiled affectionately.

Out here she was different, like some kind of dryad, part forest creature, part girl. One hundred percent fascinating.

Those needles might be uncomfortable if she turned over and they poked her. He should extract them. Gently, so as not to wake her.

His hand hovered over her hair, but then he thought better of it. She'd told him clearly that she didn't want to get closer. Cleaning spruce needles out of her hair would probably cross that line.

Regretfully, he withdrew his hand and rolled onto his back. He should get some sleep, dammit. That was why they'd turned in early, despite what Jessica's crystal had indicated. Which just proved that crystals were full of crap.

They needed their sleep because tomorrow they'd be hiking for a good twelve miles round trip. In LA he worked out, lifted weights, and swam laps to stay in shape, but hiking in the wilderness was a different kind of challenge.

He closed his eyes. *Go to sleep, city boy.* Usually he was able to sleep on command. It was a skill that had served him well in his work—when he got a break on a stakeout, or when he only had brief moments to rest during a case.

His work.

Now that he no longer had to please Charley, should he reopen the James Agency? Closing it down hadn't amounted to much. He'd given notice to his landlord, posted the news on his website and informed the clients who kept him on retainer. Put a message on his voicemail. It could all be undone, though he'd probably already lost some of his regulars.

Once he got back to LA, he could be back in business within a week.

The prospect didn't excite him. As a PI, he saw the worst side of humanity. The cheating, selfish, greedy, violent, sociopathic side. It was nice to get a break. Nice to sleep in a tiny tent in a vast wilderness, with a sleeping beauty at his side. A beauty who believed in the best of people. Who believed in magic.

So ridiculous and yet endearing at the same time.

Thinking of Jessica and her crystal, he finally drifted into a half-sleep. Out of ingrained habit, part of him still kept watch as if he was on a stakeout. The wilderness sounds melded into a gentle lullaby—wind whispers, sleepy squirrel chirps, mosquito drones.

Which was why the first hint of an unfamiliar sound brought his eyes wide open. The rustle of underbrush—but heavier than the scurry of a mouse would produce. Something large was out there. Bear? Intruder?

He reached under his makeshift pillow for his weapon. He hadn't told Jessica that he was bringing his Ruger. It came with him on every case. Standard gear. He lifted himself up on his elbow and peered out the screen at the back of the tent. Nothing. No movement, no out-of-place figure.

Silent and immobile, he waited and watched. The sound didn't return.

He must have imagined it.

After that, it took hours for him to finally fall asleep. When Jessica shook him awake, he felt as if he'd only slept at most a few minutes.

Bright-eyed, she crawled into the tent and waved a mug of coffee at him. "If you get your butt out of this tent, this hot caffeinated beverage can be yours."

"Good God," he groaned. "You're perky in the morning. Because of course you are."

"That's what a lifetime of getting up at five to bake scones will do to you. Also I'm excited about our first day of detective work. I'm reliving all my Nancy Drew fantasies." She thrust the coffee mug at him. "Come on. Doesn't this smell deliiiiicious?"

But not even the coffee could chase the grogginess away. Nor could the breakfast of instant apple-cinnamon oatmeal. Not even the six-mile hike to their first potential cabin location brought him fully alert. When the area turned out to be empty of anything remotely resembling a cabin, he gave up.

He slumped down to the ground in a sunny glade bursting with fuchsia fireweed. "I need fifteen minutes of shuteye, Nancy Drew. Will you keep watch?"

"Are you still thinking about that noise you heard last night?"

"Yeah."

He'd told her about it over breakfast, but she didn't have any answers. Maybe a bear had prowled through their campsite. They'd searched the area around the tent and found no scat or other bear sign.

"Don't worry," she said. "It was probably a vole or a shrew, something little. At night in the wilderness everything sounds louder because it's so quiet."

"You're the expert." He interlaced his hands behind his head and let his eyes drift shut. The sun, now directly overhead, shone straight onto his face. Sitting next to him, arms wrapped loosely around her knees, Jessica scooted over so her body blocked the sun.

"Is that better?"

"Yes, much better. You're an angel."

"That's only because you don't know me," she murmured. "I'm not always an angel."

"Got any evidence for that?" Half asleep, teasing her, he

wasn't really expecting a response. So when she bent down and bit him on the chin, his entire body jerked in response. It didn't hurt—her teeth gently settled around the point of his chin, while her warm breath heated his skin. But it shocked him.

"You bit me."

"You're just so yummy with all that two-day beard growth." Her lips were so close to his as she made her laughing comment. The midday sun haloed her hair and his blood turned thick in his veins.

"You aren't teasing me, are you?" The roughness in his voice accurately reflected the urges running through him at her touch. "Because that wouldn't be fair at all."

"You're an investigator who asked for evidence, that's all." Her merry lips curved as she straightened up. Their flavor rushed back to him—strawberries and wild honey. "Now take your nap, city boy."

"You're a devil."

She tilted her head back with a laugh, her throat a creamy arch of exposed flesh. A bolt of lust shot through him, so powerful it took his breath away.

He gritted his teeth until it passed. Maybe she'd bitten him because she was tempted to take things further. But her reasons for saying no were still valid. He agreed with them, in fact. There were too many gulfs between them to risk getting involved.

She'd set down the boundary. He intended to stick to it.

He forced his eyes shut so he wouldn't be distracted by the pure sunshine that was Jessica Dixon. A nap, that was all he needed. A few minutes of rest would restore his willpower, then he could go back to blocking out her sensual appeal.

If he managed to do that, he'd deserve a gold medal in denial.

He heard the rustling of the topo map and knew she was studying other options for the cabin location. He enjoyed being on this adventure with Jessica. He couldn't remember ever having more fun on a case.

What if he didn't have to leave Lost Harbor? What could he do here that would take the place of following cheating spouses? Spouses cheated here too, of course. But no one needed an investigator to figure it out. The good old town grapevine did that job just fine.

He could work for Maya Badger. Except he'd never wanted to join a police department. That sort of environment didn't suit him. He didn't like chains of command and so forth. He preferred working for himself on his own timetable. There was his tech work, of course. He could do that from here. He could do that anywhere. He could do it from a float plane if he had to. A tent. A dinghy.

A distant report stopped his aimless thoughts in their tracks. He sat bolt upright.

"That was a gunshot. Probably a rifle."

"I know." Jessica sat on her heels, head cocked to listen. "I can't tell where it came from, can you?"

Another shot rang out.

He shook his head. "I can't. Is hunting allowed out here?"

"No. But the forest service people aren't here enough to notice. Someone might have shot at a bear, I suppose. Bad idea, but it happens." Two worried lines creased her forehead. "I hate to end your nap, but we should probably get back to our camp."

He didn't argue with that. Those gunshots had burst the illusion that they had this remote wilderness to themselves. Apparently there was someone wandering around with a rifle.

He pushed himself upright and brushed off his pants. His gun was tucked into its usual spot, strapped against his chest. He patted it just to be sure. "Let's go."

Jessica slid the straps of her backpack over her shoulders and they trekked silently back toward the lake. They'd spent the

morning hike debating what to call the lake, since no one had officially named it. They'd landed on Twisted Heart Lake, inspired
by its elongated shape. But now they didn't talk at all. Those
gunshots seemed to haunt their steps.

But they didn't hear anything else suspicious, or run into any
hunters. By the time they made it to camp, he'd almost convinced
himself the gunshots were entirely innocent.

But one look at the lake told him otherwise.

Jessica gasped in shock as she came to a stumbling stop beside
him. "Oh my God. My plane!"

It was mostly submerged beneath the surface of the water,
with only one pontoon still visible. They could see a flash of red
just under the waves; perhaps still mostly intact, perhaps not.

She ran toward the driftwood log where they'd beached the
inflatable dinghy. All the air had leaked from it, leaving nothing
but a shriveled pile of rubber.

She knelt next to it. "We can blow it back up. The pump's in
the tent."

Silently, he crouched next to her and held up one end of the
dinghy. Someone had slashed it with a knife.

She reared back, shuddering, and he caught her against him.
"Let's go back into the forest," he whispered. "We're too exposed
out here."

"What do you—" Her eyes went wide as she got his meaning.
They rose to their feet. He kept her close to him as they stepped
back into the shelter of the tall spruce.

He found a safe position behind a large boulder covered with
moss and lichen. Indicating silence with a finger on his lips, he
tuned into the sounds around them. Water dripped from the
tallest branches overhead; it must have rained here a bit. Wings
flapped as a bird launched into the air somewhere. He heard
nothing human. Nothing that didn't belong.

Finally he relaxed.

"I don't think anyone's here, do you?"

"No." Her face was still pale with shock, her freckles like bits of gold scattered across her nose. "Those gunshots...they sank my plane. Why would someone do that?"

"I don't know. But we can't hang around to find out. They might come back."

"What should we do?"

"Get the hell out of here. We need to get to a place with cell service. We don't have a way to get home without your plane."

She drew in a sobbing gulp of breath. "That plane has been in my life for six years. It's like a friend."

He knew she was on the verge of losing it, but he couldn't let that happen right now. He had to keep her on task. She could mourn her lost plane later.

He didn't think anyone wanted to hurt them—if they'd really wanted to, they would have stuck around and ambushed them as soon as they got back. It was a message. A "get out of here and don't come back" message from the kind of cowards who didn't want to show their faces.

"You stay here, I'll pack up the tent," he whispered.

"No. We'll both go. It'll be faster."

He nodded. Holding her hand to keep her nice and close, he led the way toward the sheltered spot where they'd set up the tent.

"Let me check inside first. Stay by that tree."

"But—"

"Parameters, remember? If something's dangerous, I go first."

She nodded reluctantly and dropped his hand so he could go. He stole toward the tent, then crouched at the opening.

It was a mess.

Slash marks on the sleeping bags bled with white stuffing. Their extra clothes were scattered in all corners of the tent. Even the air mattresses had been knifed.

Definitely a message.

He pulled his head out of the entrance flap and rested his hands on his thighs. "I have a better idea," he told her. Jessica was holding onto the tree as if it was the only thing keeping her upright. "Let's leave the camp just how it is. If they come back they'll think we haven't returned yet."

"Okay, but how are we going to sleep?"

"We'll take turns. It'll be fine. Only one of us at a time will get to be cozy, but hey, isn't camping supposed to be uncomfortable?"

He saw the muscles of her throat move as she swallowed. She was handling this pretty well, all things considered. Probably because she was still in shock.

"Is there anything you need from the tent? All we left was our sleeping gear and extra clothes."

She ran her tongue rapidly across her lips. "Underwear."

"Good thinking. I'll grab it."

He crawled into the tent and rummaged through the mess for her undies. He finally found two pairs of panties that he never would have imagined were hers. One had bright red lipstick kisses printed all over it. The other was made of very luxurious-looking leopard print silk.

"Do you always dress like this when you camp?" He tossed her the two pairs as he made his way out the tent flap. She caught them in midair and tucked them into her backpack.

"Awfully personal question." Her sassy tone made him breathe a sigh of relief. Apparently she'd gotten ahold of herself while he'd been poking around in the tent.

"Well, you can't get more personal than stranded together in the wilderness, can you?"

"I suppose not." She drew in a long breath and gave her tent a sad last look. "I've had a lot of good times in that tent." Tucking her thumbs under her straps, she straightened her shoulders. "Let's get going. I know where we should head."

"Where's that?"

"I was studying the map while you were napping and it's actually only twenty-five miles or so to Aurora Lodge. We could do that in two days if we go hard."

Aurora Lodge was the opposite direction from where they'd planned to search. Several ridges loomed between them and the lodge.

"Is there a trail?" he asked.

"Sort of. It won't be an easy hike. But I think we can do it. We'll have to ration our food just in case it takes longer. Most of the food was still on the plane, so all we have are the snacks I brought for today. Luckily I brought my water filter so we won't run out of water."

He adjusted his own pack, tightening the belt around his hips. "Lead the way."

Her woebegone nod conveyed so much—fear, courage, sadness. His heart went out to her, and he took a moment to draw her in close to his chest. "We got this, sweetheart. I'm not going to let anything happen to you."

Inhaling the scent of her hair, he repeated that vow to himself. His mission had changed. It no longer had anything to do with a mysterious orphaned runaway. It was about keeping Jessica safe.

And him too, of course, if that worked out. Given his history, the chances weren't good at all.

CHAPTER SEVENTEEN

Jessica led the way toward the switchback trail that would eventually bring them to Aurora Lodge. They'd have to hike around the lake and up a ridge to connect with the old logging trail that she'd located on the map. It had the dotted lines that meant it wasn't used anymore.

But maybe that was incorrect. Maybe someone *was* using it for nefarious things that required shooting people's float planes.

The grief over her murdered plane lurked just under the surface, but she refused to let it out. First they had to survive. The plane was insured, but she had no idea if this kind of thing was covered. How was she going to break it to her fellow owners that it was gone?

And how was she going to get over the fact that someone in Lost Souls Wilderness wished her harm? Lost Souls had always been a refuge, an escape into another world. The idea that something so terrible could happen here—she'd be struggling with that for a long time.

A bear attack would have been easier to deal with, to be honest.

The steady presence of Ethan right behind her gave her a lot of reassurance, but still, she found herself scanning the forest at every curve in the path. Was someone up there on that crag, flat on their belly with a sniper rifle? Was a knife going to come whizzing through the air at their heads?

Increasingly gray clouds chased each other across the sky. On top of everything else, it would likely rain tonight and her beloved tent was gone. They'd have to sleep curled under a tree. In the deepening shadows, the thick moss growing on the tree branches took on eerie shapes, like sloths or misshapen snowmen. They kept brushing past enormous stands of devils club with their prickly stems and leaves as big as elephant ears.

For a long time they didn't speak. Every so often Ethan would tap her on the shoulder and they'd stop and listen for telltale sounds of another human being. But they didn't hear anything suspicious.

They took care not to leave any footprints, though an expert tracker would probably find them easily enough. Occasionally Ethan would stop and use a spruce branch to brush away a mark in the path behind them.

After about an hour, once they'd reached the other side of the first hogback ridge beyond the lake, she relaxed enough to speak out loud.

"When do you think it'll be safe to stop for the night?"

"Let's go until just before nightfall. How much longer is that? I'm not good at Alaska time-telling."

Already the sun was winking from behind the trees to the west. "Another hour, maybe. How's your leg?"

He hesitated just long enough for her to realize he was probably hurting.

"Let's stop now. That way we can get up at first light and hit the trail again."

"Good call." With a sigh of relief, he slid off his backpack and dropped it to the ground. After scanning the area, he pointed to a grove of young hemlock trees whose long branches swept the ground with their graceful tips.

"We'll be out of sight and safe from rain under there."

"Looks good to me."

Wearily, they stepped off the trail and made their way into the grove of hemlocks. She chose the tree with the longest branches and dropped down to her hands and knees to crawl under them. A relatively clear—though dim—space welcomed her. Dead branches bristled from the trunk.

"We'll have to break these off," she told Ethan as he joined her. "Otherwise we'll get stabbed every time we move around."

"I'll do that if you want to figure out dinner."

He set himself to his task, while she eased her backpack off her back.

"It's going to be a cold dinner," she told him. "We can't risk a fire under here, not with all these dead branches. *Especially* not with a gun-wielding plane murderer out there."

"Agreed."

"Do you think we did a good enough job not leaving any tracks?"

He shrugged. "I don't know. Just in case, I'll be standing guard tonight."

"No. We'll take turns. You need sleep too." That sexy groove next to his mouth had already deepened with fatigue. Given the fact that he hadn't slept much last night, she was amazed by his stamina on the trail.

"Okay, but do you know how to shoot a gun?"

Her eyes went wide. "You brought a gun with you?"

"Sure. Standard equipment for a PI."

She chewed at her bottom lip. On the one hand, she wished guns didn't exist at all. On the other hand, if someone was chasing them with a gun, she didn't mind having one of their own. "Yes, I know how to shoot a gun. One of my mom's boyfriends taught me. He liked to hunt. He took me hunting once and it was the most horrible experience of my life. Well, until now, I suppose."

"Hey, hey." He reached for her and massaged the tendon between her neck and her shoulder, the exact spot that was sore from her backpack. "We'll be fine."

"You don't know that." The fear she'd been pushing back since the sound of those gunshots welled up. "This was such a stupid idea. I have no business trying to fill Maya's shoes. I should never have dragged you out here. If we die it will be my fault and I'm so so sorry, Ethan."

"Hey." He cupped his hand around her cheek. The rough warm comfort of his touch sang through her. "Remember what you told me yesterday? I'm hard to kill. Champion of evading the Reaper. And you're with me, so that makes two of us."

"Or you're a magnet for disaster," she pointed out. "It's hard to argue with that right now."

He chuckled. The way he was working so hard to keep her spirits up...well, it melted her heart, frankly. "Look, if you don't believe we'll be fine, let's ask your crystal."

"My crystal." The blood drained from her face as she realized that she'd left it in the tent that morning. "Oh my God. My crystal's gone too. They probably stole it...they...they..." She couldn't catch her breath. Everything she loved was being snatched from her. Her bakery, her plane, her tent, her crystal, everything was crumbling around her and falling apart...

Ethan tilted her head up so she was staring into her eyes. "Jessica," he said sharply. "Take a breath. I got your crystal."

"Wha...wha..." she stuttered.

"When I went back in the tent to grab your cute little panties, I saw your crystal too. I knew you'd want it with you. Here." With the hand that wasn't holding her cheek, he nestled the familiar felt bag into her hand and curled her fingers around it.

She looked down at her hand, at the irreplaceable gift he'd just given her. No million-dollar diamond could mean more to her than her beloved crystal. "You don't know what this means to me," she whispered.

"I'm getting a pretty good idea." His dry tone acted like a tonic on her rattled nerves.

"No, you really don't. I know you think it's just a ridiculous quirky habit. But it's a lot more than that. Maybe I'll tell you sometime."

As relief flooded through her, she kissed the little bag, then drew out the crystal just to make sure it was still there. Like her own personal North Star, it twinkled back at her, radiant in the shadowed shelter of the hemlock.

She beamed at Ethan, so grateful she wanted to throw him down and kiss him into tomorrow.

"Tell me now," he said. "Why is it so important to you?"

She bit her lip again. Even her friends didn't really understand why she needed her crystal. But Ethan had saved it for her, even though he didn't think much of crystals, and that meant so much to her.

"When I was a kid I went through a phase when I got kind of paralyzed when it came to decisions, even simple ones. Like if I wanted peanut butter and jelly or tuna for lunch. It drove my mother absolutely nuts."

She dangled her crystal from her fingers. Even in the dimness under the tree, it sparkled like cold fire. "Then I was browsing at a craft fair one summer. This woman was selling all kinds of beautiful crystals and agates. I couldn't stop staring at this one. She asked if I wanted to try it, and I was like, for what? What do they do? So she talked about how they can heal and focus different energies, and that sort of thing. Then she mentioned that she used hers to help her make decisions, and I was like... sold! I used my entire life savings to buy it."

"You had a life savings already?"

"It was about fifty dollars, mostly from mopping the floor at the bakery."

She carefully put her crystal back into its bag. "Anyway, it really helped me pull out of my decision-making paralysis. I still have trouble with certain decisions, but I know I'm not completely on my own, if that makes sense."

Ethan had been snapping off branches as she told him that story, and now he brushed his hands on his pants. "It actually does. I'll never mock your little friend again."

He flashed a grin at her. Probably still trying to cheer her up. She'd take it.

"Thank you."

"How'd you manage to make that decision about your father?"

"Excuse me?" She blinked at him.

"The one you told S.G. about. You said he wanted you to live with him, and your mother left it up to you."

Staring at him, her throat tightened. He had a good memory for detail; probably went with being an investigator. "It was. It was terrible. It was the worst thing I ever had to do."

"Did your crystal help?"

"No, I—I didn't have it then." She frowned, thinking back through hazy memories. "I chose to stay with my mom because— honestly, I was afraid that if I wasn't there she'd vanish into thin air. She was always itching to travel. But I did love my father. It broke my heart when he didn't come back after that."

"Seems like a big decision for an eight-year-old. No wonder you got freaked out by decisions after that."

She opened her mouth to object, then closed it. Was that when she'd first experienced her decision-paralysis? Was it *why*?

She'd never really put it together before. She'd always assumed her indecisiveness was just a personality flaw. But *of course* it must be connected.

Holy shit. This was big. This meant that she wasn't just a coward when it came to decisions. She was...scarred. It was different.

Turning away, she searched through her backpack for the crackers and plastic jar of peanut butter that would be their dinner. Right now, survival was the only thing that mattered. All the delicious treats she'd packed into the cooler—they were all probably at the bottom of the lake by now.

Who would do such a thing?

"Do you think all of this is related to S.G.? Maybe someone doesn't want us to find the cabin?"

"It's one theory. But the first rule of investigating is don't get stuck on one particular theory. Keep an open mind."

"Wasn't something else the first rule? Persistence or something?"

"The first rule of investigating is don't correct the lead investigator," he said sternly.

She laughed. "Okay, if my plane wasn't sunk because of S.G., what else could it be?"

He shrugged one shoulder as he accepted a handful of crackers. She handed him a spoon for the peanut butter. "Maybe someone's doing something illegal out here. Smuggling or drug running."

She paused as a shiver passed through her. "I didn't think about that. It's a good thing I'm not a professional at this. I don't have a mind for crime."

"And I hope you never change." His surprisingly tender smile swept the breath from her lungs. Did he really mean such a lovely statement? Or was he still just trying to keep her spirits up?

"That's nice of you to say, considering that you think I'm kind of a flake."

If he weren't a cynical PI, she would have sworn that was a blush she spotted on his face.

"Maybe I did jump to some conclusions," he murmured. "I was off-base."

"Extra credit for admitting it." She handed him an empty mug.

He peered into it with such a disappointed expression she had to laugh. "Am I supposed to imagine a hot drink in here?"

"Nope. I have a surprise for you." She reached into her backpack and whipped out her favorite piece of camping gear. "Never leave home without your portable hot water heater. Battery powered for those times when you're out of fuel and can't make a fire." She beamed at him as she showed off the gadget, which looked like a shoe horn with an extra hook on it. She poured water into his mug and fit the heater onto the rim. "The light will go off when it's hot."

He gazed at her as if she'd just descended from the sky on a beam of heavenly light. "You angel."

"Back to angel, is it? Make up your mind."

Cocking his head, he swept her with one of those up-and-down surveys that sent shivers across her skin. "I'm thinking a little bit of both."

"And I'm thinking you're not wrong."

She pulled out several packets—instant coffee, tea, hot chocolate. He chose hot chocolate, which earned him even more extra credit points in her book. Chocolate was always a plus.

Once they both held steaming mugs of hot chocolate, they settled onto the ground. The forest floor was a thick bed of needles, surprisingly soft under her butt.

"You should probably sit next to me to conserve body heat." He patted the ground right next to him. "We're talking survival."

Was that an invitation or a safety tip? Did it matter?

"I am a big fan of survival," she told him as she moved to his side.

He gathered her against him with one arm and she snuggled close with a sigh. Between the warmth from his body and the hot sweetness of chocolate on her tongue, she could almost imagine that she wasn't chilled and stranded and afraid.

CHAPTER EIGHTEEN

They sat together, sipping their hot chocolate and munching on crackers, letting the sounds of the forest take over.

Moisture dripped steadily from the outer tips of the hemlock branches. But where they were sitting, propped against the trunk —so close to the heart of the tree—it stayed dry. Almost cozy, or it would have been if they still had their sleeping bags.

At least she wasn't out here alone. The presence of Ethan right now was the difference between terror and hope. She didn't really doubt that they'd make it out of here, and that was because of Ethan.

In a very short time, he'd become extremely important to her.

She chased away that thought, because of course he was important to her right now. Her survival depended on him. Once they got out of this situation, they'd go right back to being incompatible opposites.

Or were they?

"I've been wondering about something," she murmured as she nestled even closer against his chest.

"Hm?" He sounded just as sleepy and content as she felt.

"I know you don't believe in my crystal, and that's fine. I get it. But with your near-death experiences, did you ever think of those as a kind of magic? Something you can't entirely explain away with facts and logic?"

He lifted his arm away from her shoulder and she whimpered as the chill immediately invaded. "I take it back! Don't leave. Come back, arm! I'll skip the awkward questions."

With a chuckle, he knocked away a twig that had been poking at him. "I'm not leaving. Here." He spread his legs apart, the farthest knee bent up, and patted the ground between his legs. "If you really want to be warm, sit here."

It seemed so intimate. Like how you would sit with a boyfriend. But she really did want to stay as warm as possible, so she climbed over his leg and settled between his thighs. His other knee came up, like a door closing, and she was surrounded by his body. He nudged her to relax against his chest.

She could have cried from the heavenly feeling of so much body heat flowing into her. When he lightly encircled her with his arms, her happiness was complete. "I could sleep here," she murmured. "This is heaven."

"You should sleep. Consider me your sleeping bag."

"Mmmm." Her eyes half closed as she hummed contently. "But what about you?"

"I'm good. Don't worry about me." A certain strain in his voice caught her attention. So did a certain swell against her lower back.

Adrenaline raced through her. He was getting turned on. Or was she just imagining it?

Testing, she shifted her butt back and forth. The bulge against her back grew in response.

"Sorry," he muttered. "Ignore that. Basic physiological reaction. I know where you stand."

"Maybe, but I'm not standing," she pointed out.

"That's...not exactly..." She smiled to herself as he searched for the right words.

"Besides, a girl can change her mind. Isn't that the first rule of investigations, to keep an open mind?"

The swelling grew even more. From behind her, he stroked his fingers through her hair, as if he'd been holding himself back from touching her.

"That's true. It helps to explore all possibilities."

"Explore. I like that word." Her breath hitched as he divided her hair so it flowed over both her shoulders. He blew hot air against the back of her neck. She shivered deliciously.

"So when you say that you've changed your mind..."

"I said a girl *can* change her mind."

"Right. I might need a translator here." He picked up the bulk of her hair and moved it all to one side, exposing the side of her neck. Next thing she knew, his warm mouth was chasing away the chill with a kiss. "Have you changed your mind? Can I convince you to change your mind?" He nibbled lightly on the flesh over her tendon. She gave a soft moan. "Should I talk to your crystal and make my case?"

"Trying to go behind my back with my crystal? Get your own, city boy."

"Maybe I have my own. It's built in. Sometimes I even listen to it." He draped her hair back around her neck, so it was no longer exposed to the cold. "To answer the question you asked, something did happen to me when I nearly drowned. I had a vision. I guess you could call that 'magic.'"

She twisted around to gaze up at him. This was fascinating new information. "Really! What did the vision tell you?"

"It told me to get engaged to Charley. So much for visions." The groove along one side of his mouth flashed as he smiled briefly. "Big mistake. Even my sister warned me."

"Oh." She settled back, disappointed. There went any

chance of finding common ground on that topic. "My crystal isn't always 'right,' because I don't always ask the right questions. Like when we asked if we should go to sleep early last night. It said 'no,' but obviously that was wrong because—" She sat upright again. "Wait, maybe it wasn't wrong! If we hadn't gone to bed early, maybe we would have spotted the intruder you heard."

"And maybe he would have shot us instead of your plane. It's pointless to speculate. That's why it's better to rely on logic."

The vibration of his chest whenever he spoke was doing something spectacular to her nerve endings. Heat pooled in her belly and her nipples chafed against her several layers of clothing. So inconvenient, the way her body responded to someone *so different* from her.

"Logically speaking, we shouldn't be attracted to each other," she pointed out. "If we went only by logic, we wouldn't go one step further."

"Ah ha." He wound a lock of her hair around his index finger and tugged lightly. Tingles spread from her scalp right to the intimate place between her legs. "So you do rely on logic sometimes. That's why you said no to us. Maybe you should have checked with your crystal. Maybe your intuition speaks more than one language. Attraction, for instance."

How dare he use her own beliefs against her like this? And why was he making so much sense? "Some things are just obvious," she said. "I didn't have to consult my crystal to know we shouldn't have sex. Oooh, do that again." She arched her chest as the sensations from her scalp made her nipples zing with arousal.

"The word 'sex' covers a lot of territory," he murmured. His lips brushed her ear. Lord almighty that felt good. "Would you consider this 'sex'?" With his teeth he tugged lightly on her earlobe. With one hand still playing with her hair, he used the other to squeeze her upper thigh. *Verrrry* close to the spot that was throbbing underneath her clothes.

"No," she managed. "Not sex."

"How about this?" He ran his strong hand up and down her thigh, from her knee to the juncture with her hip. At the same time, he set the flat of his tongue against the sensitive skin just behind the point of her jaw.

She bit back a moan. "Not quite."

"All right then. Good to know I'm safely in the no-sex zone." As he spoke, he pressed kisses along the flesh of her neck, all the way to her collarbone. He pushed aside the fabric of her jacket to bare her shoulder and continue his kissing. When the jacket got in his way, he moved his other hand to her zipper and slowly slid it down. Not all the way, just enough to expose her shoulder. In the process, he brushed against the tip of her breast. Intentional or not, that brief touch sizzled across her nerve endings.

She shifted restlessly against him. If this was the no-sex zone, it was both amazing and maddening at the same time. She pressed her butt back, searching for that press of flesh. Yup, there it was. Even bigger now, more prominent. More tempting.

She shifted forward to give herself some space and slid her hand behind her back to touch his bulge.

He hissed a breath through his teeth. "Hey now."

"That's not sex, is it? I'm not even touching your penis."

The organ in question jumped as she mentioned it.

"That's true." He spoke in a strangled voice. "Sort of. Ahhh." A groan as she pressed the heel of her hand against him. "Fuck, Jessica. We're in the middle of the woods and—gr-ah-mmm-hmm." His words collapsed into an inarticulate mumble as she continued to caress him.

The satisfaction of seeing him so affected was practically orgasmic in and of itself. She felt quite proud of herself for finding a way to get all his so-called logic out of his head.

Until he turned the tables on her and snuck his hand between her legs. With her own arousal already in a state of high tension, she had no defense against that touch. She let out a whimper as her legs fell open. Still completely clothed, of course.

Still not sex.

Just mind-melting, pleasure-center-exploding, nerve-tingling mutual stimulation. That was all.

She certainly didn't need to ask her crystal about *that*, and she had no intention of checking in with her own better judgment. Screw that. If she followed that bitch, she wouldn't be experiencing this exquisitely delicious moment with the wildly intriguing Ethan James.

She tilted her pelvis to get more contact with his hand. Even through her clothes, she felt its strength and skill. No messing around searching for the right spot. He clamped his hand right where it felt best—or close, anyway. She ground her groin against it to guide him to the exact location where her craving was centered. He adjusted immediately, which was a hundred times better than guessing right the first time.

Ethan was an investigator, after all, someone who believed in exploring possibilities. He sure was a good explorer, judging by the way he fingered her mound through her clothes—stroking, testing, adjusting.

His mouth came back to her neck. The way he licked and suckled had her twisting against him. Her nipples tingled even though his flesh wasn't even touching hers. It was like some kind of secondhand arousal stoked by his lips on her neck, his hand between her legs.

Then it all stopped. She was left on the edge of a precipice, gasping for air. He put his hand over her mouth and whispered, "Shh. I hear something."

She went still and held her breath. A few endless moments later, quiet footfalls sounded on the trail. Neither of them moved a muscle as the slow, deliberate footsteps passed by their location.

Someone was walking right past them. The hemlock tree did

a great job of hiding them, but it also kept her from seeing what was going on out there.

What if it was someone who could help them?

She pulled Ethan's head down to whisper as much in his ear. He shook his head but didn't speak out loud. Smart—his voice had a much higher chance of carrying.

They waited until they couldn't hear any trace of those footfalls. Then he finally spoke.

"I think we should get out of here."

"Why? He didn't see us here. It's a great hiding place."

"It's a trail he uses often."

"How do you know that?"

CHAPTER NINETEEN

How could he explain something that was so obvious to him?

"It was the way he walked. It was definitely a man by the length of his stride. He wasn't paying close attention to his steps, the way you would if it was unfamiliar territory. That's why he didn't notice that we'd been through here. I'm sure we left some traces behind us."

Jessica blinked at the roughness of his tone. He knew that his irritation stemmed from being ruthlessly booted out of a near-sex experience. With her lips still parted and her cheeks rosy from arousal, he wanted to throw her down right there on the forest floor. Not even a bit of bark in her disheveled hair or the smudge of sap on her cheek took away from her appeal.

Sexual frustration could really mess with your mood.

"But isn't that a good thing?" she asked. "He didn't notice us and now we're safe."

"But we can't continue down this trail. We don't know how far he's going. We don't know when he'll be headed back this way."

"But if we follow him, maybe we'll find out why he's shooting up planes—if he's the one who did."

He'd already considered that option and rejected it. "We have no cell service. We have one weapon between the two of us and no idea how many people we're dealing with. This is a job for law enforcement. We're here for S.G., that's all."

"But what if this is connected to her somehow?"

"Then we walk away and let Maya handle this. Remember the parameters we set? I make the call if things are getting too dangerous? I'm making it. We're not going after that guy."

She nodded, crestfallen. "You're right. I didn't think about all that."

"Let's look at the map and find some other options."

It was so dark by now that they had to use a headlamp to scan the laminated map. She kept it on the dimmest setting possible. He noticed that his mug of hot chocolate had gotten knocked over. He cursed inwardly at how careless they'd been. The smell of hot cocoa could easily have given them away. Either that man out there didn't have a good sense of smell or the wind had been blowing in their favor; under the hemlock it was hard to tell.

"There." Jessica pointed to a meandering line near their location. "I bet no one uses that one because it's a pain in the ass."

"Why?" Just what he needed, a more difficult trail.

"Very steep, lots of switchbacks. It's not maintained by the Forest Service or any of the volunteer groups, as far as I can tell. It might not even exist anymore. This map is a few years old."

He gazed at the map in the low light. "Well. I'm game. At least it heads in a completely different direction."

"And we can still reach Aurora Lodge, it'll just take longer."

His leg twinged at the thought of even more hiking. He rubbed out the cramp before it got too tight. "No problem here."

She didn't argue, which he appreciated. He'd do whatever he had to do.

They quietly packed everything back up. Just in case, he took out his gun and went first. When he saw that it was clear, he gestured to Jessica. The under-branches grabbed at her hair as she crawled out. Once she was free of the hemlock, she brushed forest debris off her clothes. He helped by picking the biggest twigs from her hair; really it was just an excuse to touch her again.

"By the way," he said softly. "About before, I have just three words to say."

She glanced up, eyebrows lifting. "What?"

"To be continued."

With a sassy smile, she picked up her backpack. "We'll see. I might have to check with my crystal first."

MORE HIKING. More throbbing in his leg. More silent words of encouragement—*let's go, buddy.*

More watching Jessica's rounded ass three feet ahead of him.

As darkness settled into the forest, they had to slow their pace. But neither one suggested stopping. They located the abandoned trail only with the help of Jessica's GPS. Otherwise they never would have known it existed. Once they were on it, things got a little easier.

It occurred to him that maybe someone had deliberately left the entrance overgrown to hide it.

"Jessica," he hissed. She stopped so abruptly that he bumped into her. He steadied her with one hand, while enjoying the sweet thrill that went along with touching her. "Do you see any sign that this trail's been used?"

"I can barely see the trail itself," she whispered. "But I don't think so. It feels very lush and overgrown. These alders can take over very quickly if you don't cut them back."

"Okay. Just checking. I want to make sure we're not walking into a trap."

"Like a bear trap? No one uses those anymore."

"No. Just—" He shook his head, amused by her innocence when it came to evil-doers. "It's all good. Let's keep going."

They forged ahead.

More prickly branches hitting him in the face. More night mosquitoes whining in his ear. More aching deep in his scarred tibia.

He couldn't go too much longer, he knew. His body wouldn't let him. As much as he wanted to be invulnerable and immune to pain, he knew better.

"I'm gonna have to stop soon." He said it quietly, an admission that went very much against the grain. But they had more hiking ahead the next day, and the next, and he didn't want to injure himself.

She glanced behind her. "I'm more than ready. Do you think it's safe?"

"Not sure I care at this point," he said lightly, making a joke of it.

But from her expression, she knew perfectly well he wasn't joking.

"These alders aren't very good shelter. I think I see some taller trees up ahead. Can you make it another quarter mile or so?"

"Of course," he gritted. "Lead on."

He limped after her. He hadn't worked his leg this hard in a long time, and he was paying for that. Too many stakeouts. Too many hours at the computer doing research. Meanwhile, Jessica still moved with the same easy stride, though clearly just as tired as he was.

They grew them tough here in Alaska.

Ethan doesn't think I'm tough, he remembered her saying. The joke was on him.

A grouping of spruce trees loomed up ahead. "Almost there."

He laughed grimly. "You make it sound like we're about to reach our hotel. Like they're holding a room for us."

"Welcome to Chez Spruce," she joked. "Your home away from home in the wilderness. Come on in and rest your head on a pillow of spruce needles. Awaken to the weird and creepy sound of branches in the wind."

He smiled at her effort to distract him from how fricking fatigued he was. Sweet of her. She was a good wilderness guide, the perfect companion on this wild adventure.

Veering right, she ducked under the arching branch of a bush that blocked the path to the spruce trees. He followed suit, using his arm to shield his face from the wet leaves.

He was still blinking raindrops out of his eyes when he emerged from the bushes into a clearing.

"Holy guacamole," Jessica breathed. She was staring at a structure tucked under the spruce trees. It was barely visible in the not-quite-dark Alaska night. It seemed to be abandoned. Tall grass and clover grew thick around it.

"It's not Chez Spruce. It's Chez Spruce Grouse," she said.

"We don't know that."

"I know. I just thought it was funny that I'd just made that joke about Chez Spruce, and now... Come on, let's check it out."

"No." He grabbed her arm before she could take off across the clearing. "Someone could be in there. Possibly armed."

"No one's been in there for ages. It's falling apart."

"Please. Let's just watch it for a while. Just to be safe. Barging into a suspicious building in the middle of the night is—"

"Against one of your investigation rules?"

"Horror movie 101, I was going to say."

She laughed and allowed him to tug her behind a boulder

that sat near the edge of the clearing. From here, they could peek around the boulder to check on the cabin, but remain out of sight.

He hoped.

Jessica spread out a ground cloth for them to sit on. Seriously, if he had to pick someone to get lost in the wilderness with, he couldn't choose better than her.

"You know this fits every single bit of description S.G. gave Maya about the cabin," she whispered as she plopped her butt down on the cloth. "Homemade log cabin. Rotting roof. Hidden in the forest. Doesn't it look like the drawing S.G. made?"

He lowered himself next to her, keeping his aching leg stretched out. "It's hard to tell, it's too dark. And that description probably fits most of the old cabins in this wilderness."

"You're such a pessimist."

"To an optimist, everyone looks like a pessimist. Even a realist."

"Oh, whatever. We can wait." She set her backpack between the boulder and her back and leaned against it. He did the same. They propped each other up, shoulder to shoulder.

"You should sleep," she whispered. "I'll keep watch."

"No way."

"Yes. You need some rest. I can tell. You're very grumpy."

He laughed silently, but he couldn't disagree. "That's not what's making me grumpy."

"What is?"

"The fact that I was so close to making you come," he growled in her ear. "We got interrupted right when it was getting good."

Muffled laughter from her direction. "Same, city boy. Same. Now hand me that gun you keep fondling and close your eyes. I got this."

He must have slept longer than the fifteen minutes he'd planned. Because when he woke up the color of the sky had shifted from stormy charcoal to fog gray. His eyes dragged open.

They felt gritty, as if he'd slept on a sandy beach instead of a boggy clearing.

Jessica was snoring softly next to him. His gun, still safely in its holster, was tucked under her backpack.

He smiled wryly. So much for keeping watch. He wasn't too worried about it, though. If anyone had come anywhere close to them, he would have woken up. She'd probably spent a couple of hours watching an empty house, needed some sleep, and decided that it wasn't worth waking him up to take over.

Good call.

He rolled his neck, feeling the inevitable cracks and pops from an uncomfortable night. Jessica stirred. He went still, hoping he hadn't woken her up, but it was too late.

Her eyelashes slowly lifted. She blinked at him with sleepy dark-gold eyes. "Is it morning?"

"I don't know what time it is, but the light's changing."

They both spoke in hushed tones. Solemn mist drifted through the clearing. Moisture clung to every spruce needle and tall blade of grass. No wind disturbed this spot, but that didn't make it peaceful. Instead, it felt heavy.

"Sorry I fell asleep," she whispered.

"It's okay. We both needed it." He shifted so he could look around the boulder at the cabin. "Looks the same as it did last night, except rattier."

"Literally nothing happened while I was watching. The biggest excitement was when a mosquito landed on my nose. It was bigger than a hummingbird."

"Sorry it was boring, but that's good news. Should we go check it out?"

She nodded eagerly. "I just have a feeling this is it. Now that it's getting lighter outside, it looks exactly like S.G.'s drawing. Even down to the crooked door."

He had to agree. Adrenaline trickled through his veins the same way it did when he was close to cracking a case.

A finger of sunlight brightened the eastern end of thick spruce grove.

"Look, the sun's coming out," he whispered.

"First light." Awe softened her voice.

"What does that mean?"

"It means we live another day."

He smiled at that. With his history, another day was always a bonus.

The sunbeam lengthened until it touched the cabin, bathing it in gold. Even with its tumbledown appearance, its windows glowed with reflected light.

"Ready?" he murmured.

But just as they were about to emerge from behind the boulder, the front door flung open. A figure stood in the doorway.

CHAPTER TWENTY

"Get back!"

Ethan's hiss made her stumble back behind the boulder. She nearly tripped over her backpack but he caught her before she could make a sound. He snatched up his holster and drew out his weapon.

Perfectly still, barely breathing, they watched the dark figure step forward and resolve into a person standing in the sunlight. A man, she saw. Not at all the type of man she would have expected to run into out here.

He was very well-groomed, first of all. The general "mountain man" look involved lots of unkempt facial hair and clothes that rarely saw a washing machine. Then there were the wilderness scientist types who wore expensive Patagonia rain pants and fleece vests.

This man didn't fit either of those categories. He wore an Irish cable-knit sweater and ribbed corduroy trousers. His beard was trimmed, his hair only an overnight degree of mussed, as opposed to uncombed for the last week.

He was maybe in his late thirties and really quite attractive.

She stole a glance at Ethan, who was also studying him closely.

"Armed?" she breathed.

He shook his head. "Don't think so. Stay here."

"*What?*"

But before she could object, he stepped forward into the clearing, gun aimed at the man. "Don't move," he called. "Keep your hands where I can see them."

The man froze, arms by his side, hands open.

"Who are you?" he called. "What do you want? I'm not looking for trouble."

He had a pleasant accent—like a brogue, Scottish or Irish, Jessica couldn't really tell the difference.

"Is this your cabin?" Ethan stalked toward him.

"Who's asking?"

Ethan flashed his investigator ID.

"I can't see that."

That didn't seem to bother Ethan. "I'm investigating a crime that may have happened in this cabin. Kidnapping, possible trafficking. Know anything about that?"

Ethan stopped about twenty yards from the man, whose face went grim.

"No."

"Are you the one who's been shooting things up out here?"

"What 'things' are you referring to?" the man asked cautiously. "I fired at a skunk once but that didn't go well for me."

"What are you doing here?"

"I'm not inclined to have a chat with someone aiming a weapon at me. Let me see that ID again."

Peering from behind the boulder, Jessica shook her head. This man was no more a plane-murdering criminal than she was. Her intuition *and* her common sense agreed about that.

She abandoned her spot behind the boulder and hurried after Ethan. "Put that down," she murmured. "We don't need it."

Ethan frowned at her, but he must have agreed with her because he let the weapon drop as she came to his side.

"Sorry, sir," she called to the strange man as she stepped toward him. "We've had a rough night, getting shot at and all."

"Aye, that sounds like a trial indeed."

"What are you doing?" Ethan grabbed her by the arm. "I told you to stay back. Remember the parameters?"

She shook him off. "They don't apply because there's no danger here."

"You don't know that."

She planted her hands on her hips. "Actually, you're right. There's a grumpy guy with a gun around, making me nervous."

"I'm not *grumpy*. I'm protective."

"Can you just point it somewhere else so we can have a conversation with this fellow? He's not even from here. Is that any way to treat a visitor?"

She turned back to face the stranger.

He'd tucked his hands into his pockets and was watching them with amusement. "How long have you two been married? I'm guessing it's at least ten years."

"Oh, we're not married at all. In fact we only just met a few days ago when I brought cardamom cherry scones to the jail and—"

Ethan interrupted. "We're from Lost Harbor. We're looking for a cabin that fits this description. Would you mind if we look inside?"

"Are you police officers?"

"No. I'm a private investigator and my associate here is—"

"Best friends with the police chief," Jessica said. "And a baker."

"Your scones do sound tempting." The lilt in his voice made

him sound constantly amused. "I have no problem with you touring this cabin, but would it be too much to ask you to holster your gun?"

Ethan didn't look happy about that request, but he complied. He tucked it back under his jacket.

"Jessica." Keeping his voice low, he touched her arm. "Be careful. Criminals can seem like normal people on the surface. We don't know this man."

"Well, is threatening him with a gun the best way to get to know him?"

"Just. Be careful." He ran a hand through his hopelessly mussed hair. "You're going to be the death of me, I swear."

"Oh, so after all those near-death experiences *I'm* going to be the final straw?"

"Are you coming in?" the man called. "It's perfectly fine with me if you don't, you know."

She turned away from Ethan and marched toward the cabin. "I'm Jessica Dixon, and this is Ethan James."

"Alastair Dougal."

"Where are you from, Alastair?"

"New York. Scotland before that."

He stepped back to allow them into the dark cabin. Jessica shivered as she stepped inside. A dank and gloomy atmosphere clung to the stained logs and rickety old furniture. A sleeping bag and foam mat were set out on the floor. On the table sat a water jug and a pile of canned goods—pinto beans and chicken soup, corn Niblets and beef chili. The smell of must and ancient ashes prickled her nose.

As she gazed around at the dingy space, her heart sank. Other than the man's belongings, everything else had been cleared out. Nothing remotely "personal" remained.

"Lovely place you have." Might as well be polite.

"Truthfully, it's not mine. I found it empty and I've been using it as a base for a few days."

"A base for what?" Ethan ducked his head under the beam over the doorway as he stepped in. Immediately his nostrils twitched. Right now she was glad her sense of smell wasn't super-charged.

"Oh no," said Alastair. "I'd like a little more reciprocity before I share any more. What is your interest in this cabin?"

Ethan scrutinized him for a long moment. Jessica decided that the investigation parameters applied here—he was in charge of information flow. So she held her tongue while he pondered.

"We think that a young girl was held captive here by a trapper. We're investigating the case."

Alastair's eyebrows rose. Jessica liked his eyes, which were a very pure green, like spring grass—not a color she saw very often. "A young girl, eh? What age?"

"Why is that relevant?"

"Is she about fifteen now?"

Jessica nodded eagerly. Could this possibly be their first clue? "Roughly, as far as she knows. She doesn't know her birthday."

Alastair scratched at his overnight growth of black stubble. "Interesting indeed."

"Why?" Ethan demanded. "Why is this interesting to you? What are you doing out here, all the way from New York, or Scotland or whatever?"

He didn't answer immediately and the two men engaged in a stubborn stare-down. Finally Jessica stepped in between them.

"This is getting us nowhere. Alastair, we're trying to find the girl's family. That's all we want. We don't want to get in the way of whatever you're trying to do. We just wanted to look around and see if we could find any clues. Honestly, I don't see anything, though. Do you, Ethan?"

He didn't answer, but she detected the same disappointment in his face.

"And you?" he asked Alastair. "You're obviously looking for something too. What is it?"

Alastair eyed him carefully. "You said you're a private investigator?"

"Yes. Hired by the Lost Harbor police chief."

"Then maybe you can help me too."

Finally the tension in Ethan's shoulders released. "This is supposed to be my last job."

"Then your schedule is clear after this."

"That depends. What are you after?"

Alastair stepped to the table, which was just a piece of plywood on an old cable spool, and picked up an expensive-looking leather binder. He pulled out a photograph and handed it to Ethan. Ethan tilted it so Jessica could see it too. A couple smiled back at them. The woman was at least twenty years younger than the man, with a fragile, beautiful air about her.

"This is my sister and her husband. They had trouble getting pregnant, so they decided to adopt a newborn. They came here to Alaska because there was a teenage girl who'd decided to give up her baby for adoption. They'd been in communication with her through a private broker. I'm not privy to those details, though I know it was an expensive process. My brother-in-law was quite wealthy so he didn't care how much it cost them."

"Was he Anthony Berenson?" Ethan asked.

Alastair's head jerked up. "So you know his story."

"Not all of it, but I know the end. I'm sorry."

Of course. Jessica drew in a breath of the musty air. Anthony and Carole Berenson were the couple who had died in the crash of a small private plane. That was one of Maya's theories, that they were S.G.'s parents.

Alastair's face tightened, as if he didn't want condolences.

"Thank you. But I don't consider it the end. The last message I got from my sister was that something had gone wrong with the transfer of the baby and they hadn't been able to get her. They were flying somewhere else to sort it out. I knew there was more that she wasn't saying, but she didn't answer any of my texts after that."

Jessica exchanged a glance with Ethan. "Was it S.G., do you think?" If so, this information didn't solve the mystery of S.G.'s family. The Berensons would have been her potential adoptive family, not her birth parents.

"Very likely." He turned back to Alastair. "Do you know who the baby's mother was?"

He shook his head. "They were pretty secretive about the whole thing. It was all a bit on the sketchy side."

"Did they ever mention anything about her that might be a clue? A starting point for a search?"

"All I remember is that she was very young, but that she had a good reason to give up her baby beyond being young. But they never said what. It was something other than the usual family issues."

Jessica's heart ached for the poor young woman whose pregnancy had set in motion such a tragic chain of events.

Good thing Ethan was there to keep them focused.

"Do you know if they sent her a baby blanket?" he asked Alastair. "Pink silk? Expensive?"

He startled. "Indeed they did. Family heirloom. Carole wanted her baby to be embraced by the Dougal family from her first moment."

Jessica felt a physical jolt of excitement. Their first real clue! "That proves it, then. The girl we know is the baby your sister was going to adopt. She still has a little scrap of that blanket."

A surge of emotion washed across Alastair's face. He turned away for a moment to wrestle himself back to normal.

Jessica gave Ethan's hand a squeeze. This was their first real progress, but she felt bad that it had brought Alastair to tears.

"Is that why you're here? To look for her?" she asked gently.

"No, though I'd be glad to meet her." He turned back to face them. "I've never believed that crash was an accident. But until now, I haven't had the time to poke around. That's why I'm here. I want to know what really happened to my sister and Anthony." He nodded at Ethan. "If you agree to work with me, that's what we'll be trying to find out."

"I'll think about it. There might not be much to find, fifteen years later."

"Believe me, I'm aware," he said dryly. "Every law enforcement official I've met with has said the same thing."

"Back to the case I'm already on, is there anything more you can tell us?"

Alastair flashed a grin through black stubble. "The quicker you solve it, the quicker I get help?"

"Something like that. Their plane took off from the airstrip at Aurora Lodge. Is that where the transfer of the baby was supposed to take place?"

"Yes."

"Do you know why they chose that location? It's very pricey for a teenage mother."

"Because she worked there, of course."

Ethan and Jessica exchanged another glance. Talk about a clue! This was a huge one.

"What did she do there?"

"That I can't tell you. I do know that Carole and Tony paid for a midwife to stay at the lodge for the last week of the girl's pregnancy."

That was another clue. The midwife must know the identity of the teenage mother. Jessica felt a surge of excitement at how close they were getting to solving this.

But Alastair crushed that hope with his next statement. "However, there's no record of this midwife. I already tried to find her and came up empty-handed."

Ethan handed the photo of the Berensons back to Alastair. "Thanks for sharing all this. We were already headed for Aurora Lodge anyway. Good to know we're on the right track."

"Why were you headed there? It's quite a distance, though I can point you toward a shortcut that isn't on the map."

"Someone sank our float plane," Jessica explained. "We're stranded until we can find cell service."

Oddly, Alastair perked up when he heard that. "Another plane destroyed. I don't think that's a coincidence. I think that's a clue. Tell me where it is, I want to go there."

Jessica exchanged another glance with Ethan. This man was taking all kinds of risks out here.

"Look, man," said Ethan. "Why don't you come with us to the lodge, and after we wrap things up I'll come back here with you. Whatever's going on, it's dangerous. I'm talking people out here with guns trying to chase us away. Don't know who or why or how many."

But Alastair shook his head firmly. "Thanks for the warning. I'll be careful. I've already waited fifteen years. I'm here and I'm not leaving. Show me on your map where you were."

Jessica reached over her shoulder to pull the topo map from her backpack. Alastair shoved aside the canned goods to clear a space for her to spread it out. They all bent over it while she located the Twisted Heart Lake. "This is the lake where my plane is, but it's probably completely sunk by now." She traced the stop-and-start route they'd taken. "This cabin must be here." So she didn't lose track of it, she dug her fingernail into the laminate to mark it.

Alastair took out his phone to snap a picture of the map.

"Thank you. I'll hike out there today. Very carefully," he added, after a glance from Ethan.

Jessica rolled up the map and stuck it back in her pack. "I have one more question. Do you know anything about a drowning?"

"A drowning? What do you mean?"

"S.G has a maybe-memory about two people being drowned. That's why we were looking for a cabin near a lake."

"I don't know anything about that."

"Is it possible the drowning couple were her real parents and that was the problem that came up with the transfer?" Ethan asked.

Jessica's heart twisted for S.G. How many sets of parents could one girl lose?

"I dinna know. Carole mentioned nothing about a drowning or any other details about what had gone wrong. I wish I could be more help to you." He gestured at his stockpile of cans. "I can feed you, however."

Ethan waved off that offer. "We're just going to hit the trail. Wouldn't want to horn in on your corn Niblets and beans."

The man chuckled. "Aye, mate. When I get home, I'm never touching another canned bean."

"I LIKED HIM," Jessica declared as they headed for the shortcut trail Alastair had pointed them toward. It would shave half a day off the trip to Aurora Lodge. Since they were getting such an early start, they might be able to make it in one day. They'd decided to try it, and stop if they got too tired.

"You're so trusting," Ethan scolded. "You really need to learn to be more cautious around people. Everything he told us could be designed to throw us off."

"For what purpose? He wants to hire you! Are you going to take the job?"

If he did, he'd be around for a little while longer. She liked that idea.

No. She didn't. It made no difference to her because they weren't going to get involved. Or have sex.

Okay, she wasn't so sure about that part anymore. Even though she was Team Romance, she could pinch hit for Team Sex, couldn't she?

If ever there was a perfect opportunity to try the Team Sex approach, it would be now. Ethan would be leaving so soon there would be no chance for her to get her heart broken.

A little twisted, maybe, but not broken.

"What do you know about Aurora Lodge?" he asked as they hit the first switchback.

"It's very expensive to stay there. The only way to reach it is by private plane. Maybe by boat, if you're willing to hike a couple days. A Japanese chef who retired from a five-star restaurant is in charge of the kitchen. Honestly, that's about all I know. I've never been there. I believe a billionaire built it as a private retreat in the seventies, and it was turned into a lodge about twenty years ago."

"Do you know any of the people who work there? Where do they get their supplies?"

She shrugged, adjusting the straps of her pack. After their long hike yesterday, her shoulders ached. "I assume they fly everything in from Anchorage. One of my servers worked there as a dishwasher before she came to Sweet Harbor. She said they paid well and that it's a beautiful location. She said it's like a palace in the middle of the wilderness."

The thought of her bakery brought a sharp pang of emotion. Could she really sell the only home she'd ever had? What about her staff, her customers? Her roses and delphiniums?

"I hope you brought your credit card." Ethan was saying.

She bit her lip. Of course paying for their lodgings would be her responsibility. And then there was the fact that they had no ride back to Lost Harbor. Booking a plane to take them home would be another expense.

But this was for Maya, so whatever it cost, she'd pay it.

"I did bring a credit card." Her lungs pumped as the incline grew steeper. She spotted blueberry bushes along the trail and wished they had time to stop and graze. "There's probably enough on it for a night in a broom closet."

"Beats another night in the woods."

"Yes, it does. See those blueberries?" She pointed off the trail.

"I'll take your word for it. What about them?"

"Bears love blueberries. We have to keep talking and stay loud. They avoid people if they can."

"Got it. You'll be sick of my voice by the time we get there."

She doubted that. His voice got sexier and sexier to her. It made her remember last night under the hemlock. Images kept flashing through her at odd moments—like when she became mesmerized with Ethan's long legs and the slight hitch in his stride up the slope.

She shifted her focus away from his fine ass. "Do you think someone at Aurora Lodge might remember S.G.'s mother?"

"It's possible. Hopefully we can find out which staff members have been around for that long."

"Fifteen years is a long time. They may not remember a pregnant teenage staffer."

His breath came fast as he rounded the next curve in the trail. "Still worth trying, since we're headed there anyway."

"Maybe we should just look for a woman in her thirties who resembles S.G."

He made a sound that was half-laugh, half-pant.

"Why are you laughing? Alastair said that the mother was a

teenager. Let's say she was nineteen at the most. That means she'd be thirty-four-ish today."

"But there's no reason she would still be at the lodge. Why would she stay? Besides, we don't even know if she's still alive. She could have drowned, like in S.G.'s dream. Don't get your hopes up, that's all I'm saying."

"See, that's the difference between you and me." She brushed aside an elderberry branch. "I like to be hopeful. It works for me. It's good for general overall health and well-being. Good for the skin. You should try it."

"Alright, I'll try it now. How do I look?" He made a weird face over his shoulder at her.

She narrowed her eyes at him. "Like you're making fun of me."

"So cynical. So jaded. So pessimistic."

"Oh god, you're right." She let out a long groan. "You're rubbing off on me. Two days in the wilderness with you and look at me."

He swept his gaze up and down her body. "You don't look so bad to me. Smell, on the other hand..." He waved his hand in front of his nose.

She lunged at him, laughing, but he evaded her and jogged down the trail.

"You can run but you can't hide," she called after him. "I'm right behind you, getting stinkier every second."

Laughing, he broke into a half-jog. "Dibs on the first hot shower at the lodge."

"Are you trying to run into a bear?"

He stopped so abruptly she nearly crashed into him. She slid past him and took the lead. "Eat my trail dust. First shower is mine."

CHAPTER TWENTY-ONE

Talking loudly to scare away the bears had another benefit. It distracted Ethan from his leg, and it made the journey pass faster that he could have imagined.

The sky cleared and they were treated to the kind of sparkling vistas that belonged in a travel brochure. Hidden lakes dotted with pristine islands studded with spruce. Immense tangles of moss dangling from ancient twisted trees. Sudden sweeps of buttercups in a secret clearing.

At first they talked mostly about the case. Ethan was intrigued by Alastair's theory that his sister's plane had been taken down deliberately.

"They never found the Berensons' plane, you know," he told Jessica. "According to Maya's notes, they did an airborne search but never spotted anything."

"I remember when it happened. I was about fifteen at the time. It's not surprising they couldn't find it. Big wilderness, small plane. No one could have survived anyway, so it wasn't worth continuing the search. What about his idea that the crash is connected to my plane getting murdered?"

"Strictly speaking, you can't murder a plane," he pointed out. "And I think it's a stretch, quite honestly. It's fifteen years later. I checked and there haven't been any other plane crashes around Aurora Lodge since then."

"What do you think went wrong with the handoff?"

"No idea. Maybe the girl changed her mind. That happens. And where were they flying to sort it out? Maybe she ran away somewhere and they were going after her to try and change her mind."

"Where would she have gone with a newborn in tow? It's a several-day hike to get anywhere."

"That's a good point," he admitted. "Another possibility is that the story about the young woman was completely made up."

"No. Alastair didn't lie about that. I'm pretty good at detecting lies. He was telling the truth."

"The truth as he knew it." He paused to take in a sweeping view of a valley with a distant creek meandering through it like a silver eel. "There's no guarantee it's the truth."

Face flushed from exertion, she turned wondering eyes on him. "Wow, you really do have to be skeptical in your job."

"Question everything," he said solemnly. "Trust no one. Survive the night."

"I think I've seen that movie. Or at least part of it. I might have walked out."

He laughed. He was starting to really dig her lighthearted, quirky ways. They'd been together nearly constantly for so many hours in a row that it was easy to forget they'd only met a short time ago. The pre-Jessica time might as well be the pre-Jurassic time. She was so easy to talk to, with no trace of judgement other than teasing him about his cynicism.

After they'd finished speculating about the case, they moved onto other topics. More personal ones.

He told her about a few of his brushes with death, starting with the hornet's nest. She listened with wide-eyed fascination.

"Did you have a vision during that one?"

"I don't remember. I was only six."

"Okay, what about the next one? How old were you then?"

"Ten. When I got diagnosed—" He broke off. Talking about his cancer was never at the top of his list of favorite things. "And no, I don't remember any visions. I read a lot of books. Watched a lot of sports on TV. Played a lot of videogames."

"What books did you like to read?"

"Detective novels. Mysteries."

"Crime-solving stories?"

"Exactly." He picked up the pace as they passed through a shaded section of forest humming with mosquitoes. Hopefully that answer would satisfy her, because the full story was a little embarrassing.

She easily kept up with him. Darn her and her hiking prowess. "You're hiding something."

"What would I be hiding? There's nothing wrong with reading detective stories."

"Of course there isn't. I like them too. I told you I read the entire—" She interrupted herself with a burst of laughter. "Wait a minute. Nancy Drew! You liked the Nancy Drew series, didn't you?"

She sure was good with that intuition of hers. "Maybe I did," he admitted.

She shrieked with glee, the sound bouncing off a granite rock face with tree roots wrapped around it. "This is the best thing I've heard in forever! Did Nancy Drew inspire you to become a detective?"

"No, that was Walter Mosley and Easy Rawlins. But Nancy might have given me a nudge too." He laughed at the joy on her face. "I've never seen you so happy. Is it because you're laughing at the idea of a boy fighting cancer by reading Nancy Drew?"

"No! It's because Maya and I were so obsessed with those books and now you're here and you loved them too and I just... can I kiss you?"

"If you must." He planted his feet on the trail and opened his arms to her. Still laughing, she hopped forward and landed a soft peck on his chin.

He glared down at her. "Excuse me, what was that?"

"I warned you I was going to kiss you."

"Then you should *kiss* me." He tugged her back against him and settled one hand on the small of her back, below her backpack. Its graceful curve tempted him to spread his fingers wider, to savor the swell of her ass. After all the time he'd spent watching her move down the trail ahead of him, he couldn't keep his hands off her one more second. "Like this."

Groin to groin, hardness to softness, their bodies met and clung together. Her rosy soft lips opened in surprise. He claimed them with a ferocious hunger that shocked him. He never got carried away like this; he never allowed himself to.

With Jessica, there was no holding it back. He ravaged the sweet flesh of her mouth as if he'd been wandering alone in the wilderness for years. She made a soft keening sound as her mouth surrendered to his silent demands. *Open to me. Trust me. Come with me.*

In a flash, his cock was so hard it was almost painful. He pressed against her, the contact tempting him to the limit. He wanted to strip all those layers of clothing off her and expose the curves he kept imagining. He wanted to taste every inch of her sweet-smelling skin. Even though she was sweaty and grimy from their time on the trail, her scent still went right to his head. Roses and baking spices and pure arousing woman.

He cupped his hand on her breast, picturing how she would

look. Her nipples would be the color of wild roses. Even through her gear, he felt the peak pebble into hardness. She pressed her upper body against him and groaned under his kiss.

She wanted him just as much as he wanted her. But not here. Hell no.

"We can't do this." With an effort, he pulled away from her.

She gave him a dazed look. "What?"

"I mean, we can't do this here." A buzz saw of lust roughened his voice. "It's not safe. Or comfortable."

Awareness returned to her eyes. "Oh. Yeah. This. You mean sex."

"I do. Am I off-base?"

"No." She ran her tongue across her lips. "You're on base. I think you just made it to second base, actually."

Her light comment eased the tension rampaging through his system. *Hear that, cock? It could happen. Just not now.*

They continued down the trail, both breathing even faster than before. "Have you changed your mind, then? About us?"

"I've been thinking about it. It's possible it could be the perfect thing for the new edition of Jessica Dixon."

"Oh yeah?" he asked warily. He wasn't sure he liked where this was headed. He liked the current edition of Jessica just fine.

More than just fine.

"Yup. I've been clinging to my comfort zone for too long. That's one of the reasons I came out here with you. I wanted to shake things up."

"I thought you wanted to avoid the process server," he asked dryly.

"Well, that too. I'd rather run into a bear than see him again."

"She didn't mean that," Ethan called into the woods.

Jessica laughed. "See, you make me laugh."

"That's good, right?"

"Yes, and it's made me realize that being on Team Romance

means I take certain things very seriously. I'm always examining my dates to see if they could be my soul mate. And I still want to find that," she added hastily.

"But in the meantime you want to step out of your comfort zone?"

"Maybe. Maybe I do."

"Well, the welcome mat is down. Hopefully it's next to a bed, not a tree or a boulder."

She giggled as she stepped over a gnarled tree root in the trail. "I have to admit, it's very freeing that you're not interested in a future. I know you're cynical and jaded and don't even believe in soul mates. So I don't have to worry about whether or not you are mine."

"Good point."

He wasn't sure it was, though. He didn't entirely dismiss the idea of "soul mates," though he might use a different term. What about his sister Olivia? She'd extricated herself from a bad marriage and been very guarded with men after that, until she fell in love with Jake Rockwell. Watching that happen had opened his eyes.

Come to think of it, they'd fallen in love when Jake had hired her. They'd worked together, sort of like...

He shook off that thought. It was nothing like him and Jessica. This was a one-time adventure, nothing more.

"So I'm a cynical bastard and that means it's okay to have sex with me?"

She laughed at his bluntness. "Do you have a problem with that?"

"Nope. No problem. I'll prove it the next time we're anywhere near a bed."

"It's a date."

And if he did have a problem, he didn't plan to worry about it. The thought of taking Jessica to bed was too enticing. Every second he spent with her made him want her more. He didn't even mind the crystals and her reliance on intuition instead of logic. Maybe those things had bothered him at first, but he knew her better now. Jessica was about hope and staying positive, and how could that be a bad thing?

And then there was her loyalty to Maya. And her bravery when it came to things like flying float planes into unknown territory. And her persistence. And her kindness—somehow always sensing when he needed a break, and stopping before he requested it. And that didn't even include the lust that kept building as the hours passed.

A thought filtered through, something new that he'd never considered. He'd made a choice not to ever fall in love. But he'd made it with his head, not his heart. Was that even really possible?

Not that he was falling in love. It wasn't like that. It couldn't be. That would be nuts. Right?

It was nearly midnight by the time they crested the final ridge before reaching Aurora Lodge. By then, his leg was trembling badly. The only thing that kept him going was the thought of a hot shower and a night in an actual bed. And the image of Jessica naked next to him in that bed.

Limping and exhausted, he barely took in the magnificent Tudor-style compound as they approached. Solar lights embedded in the grass illuminated the drive that led to the portico-ed front entrance. All the interior lights were off. A place like this didn't have a twenty-four hour registration desk, obviously.

"What if no one's awake?" Jessica whispered. "It is midnight."

"This is the land of the midnight sun."

"Yes, but it's not like they get a lot of last-minute surprise arrivals. Everyone else comes by plane."

"You're supposed to be the hopeful and optimistic one," he hissed as he knocked loudly on the door.

"That was the old Jessica. I'm trying to be realistic now."

"Can you maybe put that on hold until—"

The door swung open. A woman wearing black-rimmed glasses and a fuzzy pink bathrobe stood before them. Her red hair —a few shades darker than Jessica's—hung over her shoulder in a loose braid. The color combination made him blink.

"Who's out here bickering on the porch?"

"Not bickering, just discussing the possibility that you might have a room available tonight." Ethan tried his "charming" smile, but it had no effect on her.

She looked the two of them up and down, eyebrows lifting. "Do you know this is the first time we've ever gotten a walk-in?"

"Is there a prize for that?"

She didn't seem to appreciate his attempt at humor either. "Where are you coming from? Have you been hiking?"

Jessica elbowed Ethan aside. Just as well, since he wasn't getting anywhere. "We flew in on a float plane for a hiking trip. But my plane is now disabled so we had to hike across a few ridges to get here."

"Sorry about your plane."

"I'm Jessica Dixon, by the way. I own the Sweet Harbor Bakery in Lost Harbor."

Recognition spread across the woman's features, and finally she relaxed. "Best walnut-cinnamon rolls in the entire peninsula. I sent a spy to figure out the recipe but no dice. I'm Kelsey Lewis, the manager here." She turned toward Ethan. "And you are?"

"Ethan James. Jessica's partner." He didn't feel like explaining any more than that until he'd gotten some damn sleep. "Do you have any rooms open?"

"We don't have rooms at all. We have suites. And yes, I do have one available, but you're not going to like the price."

Were women in Alaska always so blunt?

"We have credit cards."

"I don't want your money. I want that recipe." She swung back toward Jessica with a grin. "Can we work out a deal?"

"Can you maybe include a mention of Sweet Harbor in your menu?"

"Hmm, I can think about it. Or we could call them Jessica's Sticky Buns and if anyone asks, direct them your way."

"Ooh, I like that idea—"

"The room," Ethan interrupted. "Any chance of actually setting foot in it tonight?"

"He's a bit grumpy," Jessica explained to Kelsey. "He's more of a city boy and it's been a long hike." She squeezed his hand, taking the sting out of her words.

"Well, we get our share of those here. Come on, I'll show you to your suite. We can work out the details later."

She ushered them into a great room that managed to be both stately and cozy at the same time. Massive rafters crossed the soaring space overhead. The biggest cast iron woodstove he'd ever seen took up the center of the room; its stovepipe ran all the way to the roof.

Richly upholstered armchairs and loveseats were arrayed around the space. Shelves filled with games and books lined one wall. Several cozy side nooks offered a place to watch DVDs or play chess. It smelled faintly of woodsmoke and expensive lemon wax polish. It smelled, honestly, like civilization. A haven in the harsh wilderness.

The relief of getting off the trail made him almost light-headed. As they followed Kelsey up the wide-planked staircase to the second floor, he wondered how many trees it took to heat this place in the winter. Or maybe it was only open in the summer. He should have done more research, but he'd never expected to end up here.

She showed them into a suite that opened its arms to them in luxurious welcome. Fresh bathrobes and towels were folded on the expansive king-size bed. An office area furnished with a desk and printer took up one corner. She showed off the bathroom, complete with tub and a two-person shower, and a sunken living room with an entertainment center.

"This suite usually costs fifteen hundred a night," she told them. "But to be honest, I would never turn away a stranded hiker. You have ID, I assume?"

They both put down their backpacks and rummaged for their wallets. Kelsey scanned Jessica's first, taking a picture of it with a pad she drew from the pocket of her bathrobe.

When Ethan handed his over, she glanced up at him sharply. "You're a PI?"

Oops—he'd handed her his official California investigator license instead of his ID.

"Yeah. Sorry, you probably want my real ID." He tried to hand her that instead but she didn't release the first one.

"What kind of private investigator?"

"A retired kind. I'm just here on vacation with my sweetie." He slung an arm over Jessica's shoulder.

She narrowed her eyes at him from behind her horn-rimmed glasses. "That would explain the bickering."

"Everyone says we're like an old married couple."

Jessica snorted next to him. "Do you need anything else from us? We're literally about to collapse, and my *sweetie* here could really use a shower."

She still looked suspicious. "That must be tough, living so far away from each other."

"You have no idea. But it works because we're just so perfect for each other. When you find your soulmate, it doesn't matter how far away they live." Jessica beamed at Kelsey, radiating that bright angelic innocence that no human could resist. Ethan suppressed a laugh. "How about you? Are you married?"

But Kelsey seemed to have no interest in sharing any of her own personal details. She handed back their IDs and left them on their own, with the instructions that breakfast began at six and ended at nine.

And then...finally...bed.

CHAPTER TWENTY-TWO

"Why did I even bother to try to change things up?" Jessica often talked to herself in the shower. Technically, she usually talked to her favorite rubber ducky, but he wasn't available out here in the wilderness. "So far, nothing's different. Still not having sex, not even the unromantic kind. I should have just stuck to the old Jessica."

She tilted her head under the showerhead and let the delicious water flow through her hair. She'd turned both of the showers on, so water came at her from two directions. Blissful, especially when she lathered herself with the luxury jasmine-scented soap the lodge provided.

A hot shower might not be the same as sex, but right now it felt pretty darn orgasmic.

Ethan hadn't so much as moved a muscle since he'd landed on the bed. He hadn't even gotten under the covers. She'd removed his hiking boots and socks, wrinkling her nose at the stench. Then she'd rolled him from side to side to get his jacket off. The entire time, she kept glancing up at him, checking to see if he was waking up.

They had a date, after all. *Next time we're anywhere near a bed.* That was a bed in there, a very luxurious bed with an oyster goose-down comforter and a solid mahogany headboard.

And an unconscious man splayed across it.

Oh well. More time to think about the fact that her recipe for walnut-cinnamon rolls was paying their way. She hadn't realized her pastries were practically famous all the way across the bay. That gave her quite a confidence boost, and opened up a world of possibilities. Could she expand the business and yet stay true to the quirky Sweet Harbor style?

Or should she sell it and try something new?

Ugh, decisions.

Squinting her eyes closed, she let the water flow across her face. Her thoughts inevitably came back to Ethan. She should have known their flirting wouldn't actually lead to anything.

"I am who I am," she murmured out loud. Anyone looking for a fling or a hot night wasn't going to want her. "Deal with it."

"Deal with what?" On the other side of the shower curtain, Ethan knocked on the tiled shower stall. The curtain was made of a shimmery fabric through which she could see the lines of his body. He was completely naked. Just like her.

Her hands flew to cover her breasts and private parts. "You can't come in here."

"But we had a date."

"For a bed, not a shower."

"You really want me to skip the shower before we get into a bed together?"

"No, but..." She hesitated. Team Romance Jessica would probably wait for a better moment for him to see her naked. Low lighting, a touch of incense. So maybe she should do the opposite of that. She should invite him to share the shower with her, despite the fact that...

"You can come in, but I don't want you to be disappointed, so you might as well know that my thighs are not perfect."

"Neither are mine," he said gravely. "I have a scar."

"Also, there's a botched tattoo on my ribs. It was supposed to be a jellyfish but it ended up being more of a...cupcake."

"I like cupcakes. But I don't have any tattoos. Had enough of needles by the time I was twelve."

"I don't like my elbows."

"I've already seen your elbows." Amusement ran through his voice. "They're spectacular."

"Nobody's elbows are spectacular. That's ridiculous."

"Would I lie about elbows? They're much too important for that. If you let me come in I'll prove how much I like yours."

The funny thing was that he could simply part the shower curtain and step inside whenever he wanted. But this was kind of sexy, talking to each other through a flimsy layer of translucent fabric.

"When did you even notice my elbows?"

"When we were talking to S.G. at the peony farm. You were wearing a green t-shirt that showed off your elbows perfectly."

"Teal," she corrected.

"Teal. Right. It's getting a little chilled out here. Now that we've settled the elbow issue, any chance—"

"My butt is not exactly petite."

"Woman! You're going to be in big trouble if you don't stop bashing on yourself. Believe me, after all that time on the trail staring at your ass, I know its exact dimensions and I can't wait to get my hands around it. Did that sound weird? I'm very tired."

He was also very adorable, and the idea of him ogling her ass all the way up and down the trail got her kinda hot.

So she reached for the shower curtain and slid it open. She took his hand and tugged him inside. He closed the curtain behind himself and there they were, alone in the steamy world of the most luxurious shower she'd ever encountered.

As the water cascaded over his body, he groaned in bliss. When she tried to move to her own showerhead, he braceleted her wrist with one hand. "Don't leave me," he murmured. "I might drown on my own."

With a laugh, she stepped back to his side. At such close quarters, it was hard to fully take in his body. His naked physical presence overwhelmed her. He was lean and hard and extremely fit, not in a musclebound way, but in a "just right" way. As if his muscles were all there for a purpose and knew exactly what they would be needed for.

Her heart hammered in time with the water buffeting her body from the other shower head. She wanted him with such fierceness that it almost scared her. She sure hoped Team Sex Jessica knew what she was doing getting naked in the shower with Ethan James.

She glanced down his body and saw that he was half-aroused already, his penis rising from a soft nest of dark brown hair.

"That's what happens when you get me thinking about your ass," he murmured. "And your thighs. And your very odd-looking tattoo."

"Don't say I didn't warn you."

"You didn't warn me. Not even close." He reached for her and clamped his hand on her ass. "You didn't warn me about how fucking sexy you are." That last bit ended up as a growl somewhere over her head. Pleasure shot through her—at his words, the way his hand felt on her, his long body hard against hers.

"Same," she managed through the din of excitement flooding her. "Same, city boy."

"Take that back, Tasty Cakes. Don't I get a little respect for all that wilderness trekking I just did?"

"Pffft. We call that a gentle stroll here in Alaska."

She gasped as he squeezed one of her butt cheeks. Heat pooled between her legs. Her skin was flushed and extra sensitive from the shower steam. God, she wanted him to touch her everywhere. Especially between her legs, where her clit throbbed with anticipation. Every nerve in her body pulsed with the same cry —*touch me. Feel me. Tease me.*

Venturing a hand onto his body, she took the same position as him—her hand on his ass. The firm hard flesh slid against her palm. His muscles flexed as he shifted position, putting a tiny bit of space between them.

He bent her backwards so the water sluiced over her chest. Her already sensitized nipples hardened under the barrage of water droplets. Biting her lip, she wrestled with the intense sensation until she finally gave in to it—just in time for him to chase it away with his mouth. Warm and commanding, it engulfed her nipple. A sizzle of pleasure snaked through her body on a direct line to her sex.

He set a slow and luxurious pace as he suckled her nipples. As if they had all night, as if they hadn't been sleep-deprived for the past two days. He toyed with her breasts until the rest of her body was one long throb of desire.

God, was he ever going to touch her?

Needing it *now*, she took his hand and planted it between her legs. Ah God ... just what she craved, those strong fingers touching the heart of her arousal.

His muffled chuckle vibrated through the tip of her breast. "I see what's going on here. You're in a hurry because you want to get into that fancy bed out there."

That wasn't it, but it didn't matter as long as he kept going with what he was doing. He stroked her sex with a mix of delicacy and strength that drove her wild. Sometimes he brushed his thumb against her clit, other times he used the heel of his hand. Wherever he touched, she lit up.

With his other hand, he gripped her hip to hold her steady as her body began to hum and vibrate. Then he released her and slid his hand up her body, along each curve of her torso, all the way to her breasts. He seemed to have more hands than one human normally possessed—or at least she lost track of his hands. He was touching every part of her and there was no part that didn't want it.

She slipped her hand between his legs and found him fully aroused. Wrapping her hand around that thick shaft, she felt him pulse with the same drumbeat that sounded through her veins.

"Did someone say something about a bed?" she murmured. Water ran down her lips as she spoke.

"Mm-hmm." But he didn't seem interested in the bed. He turned her around so her back was to him and leaned her against his body. Water pelted her entire front. She gave a soft cry of need.

As if he completely understood, he nudged her legs apart. At first there was only showering water where she wanted a man's hand—but just as she was about to beg him to come back, there it was. The Hand. Right where she craved it. She looked down at the strong forearm reaching between her legs. Corded muscles moving as he played with her clit. Tanned skin against her paler stomach.

She closed her eyes against the excitement surging inside her. Spreading her legs farther apart, she urged him on. *More. Faster. A little harder. No, too much. Like that. Just like that.* She wasn't sure how she communicated all that to him. He seemed to pick up on every twitch of her over-sensitized body. And he didn't seem at all worried about himself yet. Even though his erection burned against her lower back, he seemed completely dedicated to making her come.

"No one can hear you," he whispered in her ear. "But I want to. I want to hear you scream my name when you come."

Oh God, she could feel it, like lightning on the horizon. Any moment now, it would strike her into a sizzling pile of whimpering joy. But she had to get a little joke in first. She just had to.

"Remind...me...your name?"

He laughed against her neck and moved a hand to her nipple, which he plucked as if he was playing guitar. As if he knew perfectly well that there was an invisible string connecting nipple and clit, and all he had to do was thrum it, and she'd shatter into a thousand pieces.

She resisted the sensation, not wanting this pleasure to end. But she had no defense against the fingers toying with her clit. They drew ever wilder sensations from her, pleasure that felt new and feverish—along with sounds she didn't recognize.

Since when did she make that *noise*, that weird sob in her throat? Since when did she grind her pelvis like that? It must be a Team Sex Jessica thing. Or maybe it was an Ethan thing. Maybe she was writhing and moaning like this because he knew how to work a woman into a frenzy of desire. Maybe it was a skill he happened to know.

Or maybe—the thought occurred just as the first bright explosion burst across her nerve endings—maybe it was a Jessica-*and*-Ethan thing.

CHAPTER TWENTY-THREE

Lust must give a guy superhuman powers. That was the only explanation for how Ethan was able to carry a boneless and satisfied Jessica all the way from the shower to the bed.

She wrapped her legs around his hips and giggled into his neck as he staggered across the floor. "Bakers aren't generally known as featherweights," she pointed out.

Everything about her felt perfect to him, though he was relieved when he made it to the bed.

"*You can do it, buddy,*" he murmured out loud. "*Hang in there.*"

He tossed her onto it with a hard grunt of effort.

She laughed up at him, all flushed and scrumptious. "Were you talking to your leg? Giving it a pep talk?"

Oops. Busted. "So?"

"It's cute, that's all. Like talking to birds or—" She broke off with a shriek as he flung himself on top of her. He crouched over her like a beast with its prey.

Then he paused. Damn it. Protection. He hadn't packed any. "Do you have—"

She drew her bottom lip between her teeth. "No. I didn't bring anything. I didn't think any of this would be happening."

"Okay." Hauling air into his lungs, he rolled away from her, onto his back, and wrestled his arousal into submission. He hadn't imagined this happening either. Well, he'd imagined it as in *fantasized* about it. But he hadn't anticipated that it would actually happen.

"Hang on a sec." Jessica swung her legs off the side of the bed. In the shower, she'd seemed kind of shy about being naked, but maybe a good orgasm had chased that away. She moved freely across the room, not bothering to hide her ass or her thighs or even her elbows. All of which made his mouth water.

She disappeared briefly into the bathroom, then emerged with an expression of triumph as she brandished a condom in the air. "I knew this was the kind of place that thinks of everything."

"Thank you, Kelsey," he breathed.

"It was probably Kelsey's minions." She ripped the foil wrapper and tossed it over her shoulder, then prowled toward him with the condom. "Stay right where you are. I got this."

He spread his arms wide to indicate he had no plans to move. She kneeled over him, one of her luscious thighs on each side of him, and lowered herself down. The sweet contact of her flesh on his thighs sent his senses reeling. His erection had subsided while she'd been gone and he thought they'd hit the end of the road. But as soon as she scooted down his thighs and bent her head to his cock it came roaring back.

With each swirl of her tongue on him, his cock hardened further until it pulsed against her pretty lips. She kept gathering more of him into her mouth, tugging him deeper and harder. The sight made him absolutely mad with desire. Those rosy lips working up and down his cock—her hands touching his balls, his thighs—her wet hair swinging against his skin—he couldn't get enough of any of it.

When the tension became unbearable, and he knew he was about to explode, he tugged her mouth away from him. The innocent way she ran her tongue across her lips nearly ended him right then.

"Condom?" he managed.

"Oh yeah. Right." She shook herself back to attention. He loved the fact that she'd been so lost in the act of sucking him off. That meant that she'd enjoyed it too—though probably not nearly as much as he had.

She straightened up and plucked the condom from the comforter. "Do you know that I used to practice this on a cucumber so I'd know what I was doing? Maya saw me once and laughed her ass off."

"Let me do that." He plucked it from her hand. "I ain't no cucumber."

He quickly rolled it onto his erection.

"Wow." She clapped her hands in mock applause. "That's at least point-six seconds faster than I could do it. We should have a competition some time. A condom-off. See who can—"

He shut her up by lifting her bodily into the air and shifting her toward his erection. It arrowed toward her, thick and eager and safely covered.

She followed his lead and poised her entrance over his cock. Her beautiful breasts, swaying so close, tempted him with the fragrance of damp flesh and jasmine soap. He flicked his tongue across her swollen nipple and savored her instant response. He could feast forever on those nipples and take breaks only to lick her pussy. Sounded like a nice life to him.

He placed both of his hands on her hips to guide her down. The soft give of flesh under his palms added another layer of arousal. Inch by inch, she lowered herself down until she was fully seated on the pole of his erection. *Ah God.* Tension gathered in his balls. He gritted his teeth to stop from ramming into her before she was completely ready. Her body was so tight around him, her channel still slick from their encounter in the shower. But he wanted to make sure she was completely able to take all of him into her before he unleashed the full force of his need.

He moved gently at first, sliding into her slick channel until she moaned and arched backwards. He feasted his eyes on the glorious line of her torso, the heavy sway of her breasts, the wine-dark color of her aroused nipples. *Too much, too much.*

He reached up and filled his hands with the flesh of her breasts, squeezing her nipples between his fingers. She cried out and he felt liquid well against his cock, lubricating his strokes.

He pumped his hips in a powerful motion that she met with her own push and pull. At first their movements were at odds with each other. When he wanted to be fully seated inside, she was pulling back. It was maddening. So close and yet tantalizingly out of reach.

He gritted his teeth and clamped his hands around her hips to still her. Then he moved her to the rhythm that was beating through his body. Up, down, just like that, oh yeah, fuck yes, there it was, the perfect coordination designed to pull his soul from his body.

Or so it felt, anyway, when that freight train gathered speed and carried him down the tracks. And boom—right off the cliff. His climax just about blew his head off. He pumped into her soft body, eyes closed, dimly sensing the brush of her hair against his chest, her moans.

He nearly blacked out for a moment—the "little death," wasn't that what the French called it? Chalk up another near-death experience, apparently. The kind he didn't mind.

He was half-laughing when he came out of it. "I think I just died and went to heaven, isn't that what they say?"

"Really? Again? How many times does that make?"

She raised herself up, freeing his penis from her body. He

didn't want to be free. He wanted to be there, *with* her, joined with her. He loved the fact that she got his little joke about dying. They were in sync now, in so many ways.

"Not enough. Can we do that again soon?" His eyes were already heavy with sleep. His little cat nap only went so far.

"Maybe. We'll have to ask my crystal."

Such a tease. "When did you get so mean? Wait—" A horrible thought struck him. "Did you come? I thought you came. I tried to wait. You were making that sound."

"Yes, I did. Relax." She patted his shoulder, then stretched her body alongside his with a huge yawn. "Mostly, I came in the shower. Then a little one just now. But it's sweet of you to be so worried about it."

"Just your regular average jaded cynical sweetheart, that's me." He had to get his ass off this bed and into the bathroom so he could clean himself up.

Her eyes fluttered shut and a moment later he heard the snuffling snore he'd gotten familiar with over the past couple of days.

He rolled himself off the bed and went into the bathroom to remove the condom and clean himself off. When he caught sight of himself in the mirror, he realized that he looked different. What was it? He couldn't quite put his finger on it.

When he got back to the sumptuous bed with the copper-haired princess sprawled willy-nilly across it, waiting for her turn in the bathroom, he finally realized what the difference was.

Happiness. He hadn't seen a happy expression on his own face in a very long time. Smirks, sure. Laughter. Satisfaction with a job well done, enjoyment of a good movie. That kind of thing. But happiness looked different. It looked like...peace. It was written all over his face.

He was here, with Jessica, and that made him happy.

SLEEP MADE him pretty damn happy too. He didn't wake up until light was pouring into the suite through the picture windows. Jessica was already gone. He sensed immediately that she wasn't in the suite with him.

Maybe she was off sharing her recipe with the manager.

He dragged his tired body into the bathroom and indulged in another hot shower.

Then he remembered that the lodge probably had cell service. He dug his phone out of his grungy borrowed backpack. Somehow it had made its way to the bottom of his pack, so he had to dislodge everything to find it.

The battery had drained, so he plugged it in while he got dressed. All of his clothes smelled like wood smoke and spruce needles. He knew that scent would always make him think of Jessica, even once he was back in West Covina staking out some lowlife outside an In-N-Out Burger.

His phone beeped. He saw that his landlord had texted. Last month he'd given notice that he was ending his lease on his office space. But now his landlord was offering him two hundred dollars off the rent to stick around.

Pretty good deal. He should take it.

But there was really no rush.

He ignored the text and went in search of breakfast.

The sunshine must have drawn all the guests outside, because he encountered no one on his way to the great room. It too was deserted, but he heard voices floating from down a hall-way, so he went that direction.

In the daylight, the lodge was even more spectacular. Luxurious touches were everywhere—genuine antique cabinets and blown glass vases overflowing with delphiniums and sunflowers. Every surface gleamed with polish and a pleasant scent of beeswax hung in the air.

He found Jessica in the kitchen, an immense space dominated by an eight-burner commercial oven and other stainless-steel appliances. She was perched on a stool at the long butcher block table that took up the center of the room. An Asian man in a chef's hat was rolling out dough on the floured surface. He and Jessica were chatting up a storm as he worked. Apparently they had a lot to talk about.

He pushed back a ridiculous niggle of jealousy. Of course he couldn't chat with Jessica about baking. The only thing he'd ever baked was chocolate chip cookies from a tube.

"Good morning." He included both of them in his greeting, lingering on Jessica's bright face.

"Good morning. I saved some breakfast for you." Jessica reached behind her to a counter and grabbed a covered plate of food. "Coffee's on the stove. This is Ren, he's the five-star chef I told you about. I had no idea he was so young."

"I'm not as young as I look." When the chef smiled, Ethan could see it was true; the grooves alongside his mouth indicated he was probably in his thirties.

"But still, you're not in your sixties, which was what I imagined a retired chef would look like. This is Ethan."

They exchanged nods of greeting, while Jessica handed Ethan the plate. Sausages, potatoes, biscuits, pancakes.

"I snagged a little bit of everything except the eggs," she explained. "I just can't condone eating cold eggs."

She and Ren both shivered with repulsion.

Talk about soul mates...apparently she'd found hers.

He dug a fork into a crisp potato and popped it into his mouth. He never got jealous. Where was this feeling coming from? He didn't like it one bit.

"So Ren was telling me that he's been working here for three years," Jessica told him. Her legs were crossed, showing off purple leggings under her hiking boots. Her hair, now that she'd washed all the forest debris from it, shone like bright autumn leaves.

"Most of the staff is pretty transient. People work here for a season or maybe two, then they move on."

So she'd been investigating while he'd been sleeping in. All those five o'clock mornings had paid off. "Most, but not all?"

"Right. According to Ren, the only long-term staff members are the head of landscaping—"

"Big Tom," Ren inserted. "He runs the greenhouses that grow all our produce."

Cross Big Tom off the list. Honestly, to him it was a long shot that S.G.'s mother would still be here. Aurora Lodge had been an exchange location, nothing more.

"And the other one is Kelsey, the manager." Jessica shifted on her stool, eyes aglow with excitement. "She's been working here since she was seventeen, according to Ren."

"She started as a waitress," he confirmed. With lightning-quick movements, he sliced the dough he'd rolled out into long strips of noodles.

"And then she became the head of housekeeping, and then eventually the manager. So she's been here a long time, isn't that wonderful? She's the perfect interview subject for my book."

She sketched a wink at him—as if he wouldn't pick up on her cover story on his own. Unnecessary, but cute nonetheless.

"Ren already texted her, and he says she'll meet us in her office whenever we're ready. She's doing accounts." Jessica rolled her eyes. "Which is always the worst part of my day, so she'll probably be grateful for a distraction. I was just waiting for you to wake up."

Ethan shoveled the rest of his food into his gullet. He was used to eating on the fly. "I'm ready."

He looked up to find both of them gazing at him with looks of pure dismay.

"Ethan, you should take your time with this food. It's a work of art."

He grimaced at the chef. "Sorry, Ren. I tend to get caught up in a—" He caught himself just in time before he said case. "Project. This book we're researching is really fascinating. I promise to savor every mouthful of the next meal."

Ren accepted his apology with a dignified nod. Ethan slid off his stool and took his plate to the sink.

"Leave it," Ren told him. "Guests don't do dishes here."

"Unless they can't pay," Ethan whispered to Jessica as they left the kitchen.

"Good thing you have me along to pay our way with recipes." She took his hand and squeezed it lightly.

"I can think of better reasons than that to have you along." All those sexy reasons turned his voice into a growl. "Last night—"

"Shh. Let's not talk about it." Flushing, she shook her head. "I don't want to get distracted. We have a job to do."

He cupped her ass. "Then let's get it done so I can get back into your—"

"Shh." Another guest was coming down the hallway toward them. He gave her one last caress, then dropped his hand.

As soon as the other guest was gone, he dropped a quick kiss onto the top of Jessica's head. "To be continued," he murmured. "Again."

CHAPTER TWENTY-FOUR

Kelsey's office was situated at the back of the lodge, facing the forest. He knocked on the doorjamb.

"Enter at your own risk," she called, with the same bluntness he vaguely remembered from last night. "I had a late night."

They stepped into the office. The casement windows were cranked open to let in the midday breeze, which danced in like a flower girl flinging rose petals. Ethan's nostrils widened at the dizzying scent of peonies and roses and other floral fragrances he couldn't identify.

"Sorry for the late night part," Ethan said.

Kelsey rose from behind the desk, where she'd been frowning at a desktop computer. "Good morning, you two. How'd you find your suite?"

He bumped Jessica's shoulder slightly as he answered, "Outstanding in every way."

"Good, good. Ren said you want to interview me for a book." She looked at Jessica, then back at Ethan. "Or is it both of you?"

"It's both of us." With a quick glance at him, Jessica took charge. It was her cover story, after all. "I'm working on a historical book about unsolved mysteries in Lost Souls Wilderness. Ethan is my research assistant."

"I thought you were a baker."

"Oh, I am. But I'm also a lifelong resident of Lost Harbor and I like researching its history."

Nice save. He had to give her credit.

But she still didn't soften. "And I thought Ethan was a private investigator."

"Yes. Exactly. With a special interest in, uh, cold cases. I hired him to help on this book."

Kelsey perched on the edge of her desk and folded her arms across her chest. She wore a denim overshirt with the sleeves rolled up. "You must have some serious funding. His day rate is..." she whistled. "Sky high."

Goosebumps rose on Ethan's skin. Something didn't feel right here. Why had she looked into his day rate? "I made a deal with her," he said lightly. "Recipes in exchange for my services."

That explanation went over like...well, like cold eggs. She adjusted her glasses. "Sounds unlikely. But it's your business, not mine. What unsolved mystery in particular are you interested in?"

Jessica glanced again at Ethan, but he gestured for her to take the lead. He watched Kelsey closely as Jessica posed her first question. "Were you here about fifteen years ago when a twin-engine plane crashed after taking off from the Aurora Lodge airstrip?"

"I was. I had just started working here, in fact. So awful. A couple died. The...Berengers, I believe?"

"Berensons."

"Right. The Berensons. Surprised I remember that much, it was so long ago."

"What else do you remember?" Ethan asked her.

"I remember there were helicopters out here searching for the wreckage, but it was never found. Is that the mystery you're writing about?"

"Do you remember *them* at all? The Berensons?"

Kelsey answered smoothly—maybe too smoothly? Ethan wasn't sure, but he made note of it. "We get a lot of couples like that here. Wealthy older man, beautiful younger woman. I don't recall any other details. I do remember that they left me a very generous tip. I was sad when I heard about the crash."

"Do you remember the other people working here back then?"

"Oh no. That's so long ago. But I can pull the employee records for you. They go back to the first year we were in business."

"That would be great," Jessica said eagerly. "Especially any female employees."

Kelsey looked at her sharply. "Why female in particular? What would their gender have to do with the crash?"

"Oh, well..." Jessica stammered, then glanced at Ethan for help.

He was in charge of information flow, after all.

"We understand that the Berensons were here to meet a young woman. We're hoping to talk to her and see what she remembers."

Even though he was watching her closely, he didn't notice any visible reaction.

"Are you sure she was a staff member? Perhaps she was a guest."

"We were told she worked here."

"By who?"

His mental alarm bells sounded. Why was *she* interrogating them?

Kelsey checked her watch. "Sorry, I have to end this. New guests arriving. I'll pull those employee records when I get back. I doubt they'll help you much, so don't get your hopes up."

Jessica shot him a disappointed glance. He decided to toss one more question out there before Kelsey left. "What about a drowning? Do you remember a case like that?"

Finally, a reaction. Her head shot up. "What do you mean?"

"We heard there was a couple that drowned somewhere in the area. Possibly in one of the lakes. Does that ring a bell?"

She slowly came off the desk and stood facing them. "Where did you hear about this drowning?"

Jessica piped up. "From a possible eyewitness."

Shit. He would *not* have shared that. First rule of investigating—never give out more information than absolutely necessary. Kelsey slid her gaze over to Jessica.

"What did this eyewitness say?"

Ethan surreptitiously touched Jessica on the arm, hoping she'd get the message to stay quiet. All of his red-alert systems were blaring now, and he didn't trust Kelsey at all.

"I'd have to check my notes," Jessica said vaguely.

He touched her arm again. *Good girl.*

Kelsey studied them for a long moment, as if trying to decide what to do next. "You aren't being straight with me. I don't like that."

Jessica shot Ethan a pleading glance. He knew she wanted to trust Kelsey, just like she'd trusted Alastair at the cabin. And sure, life would be much easier if you could go around trusting everyone you came across. But that wasn't reality. At least it wasn't *his* reality.

"What makes you think we have anything to hide?" He spread his hands open.

"You didn't mention anything about a book when you showed up last night. And then there's this." She reached behind her, into

a desk drawer, and pulled out his Ruger. Still holstered, fortunately. "Weapons aren't permitted inside the lodge."

"Did you search our room?" he demanded. "That's illegal.
We didn't consent to a search."

"You aren't paying guests. I comped you the suite."

"That's a technicality."

She shrugged that off. "So sue me. The chambermaid
knocked over your backpack and it fell out."

He didn't believe that. Or maybe he did—he'd left his backpack a mess, after all. "I have a concealed carry license. It's
completely legal."

"Our policy is that all firearms are supposed to stay in a safe
until they're needed for hunting. And usually, they're rifles. This
—this thing makes me nervous."

"We didn't know the rules. Feel free to lock my gun up until
we leave. It's standard equipment for a PI, that's all."

"Even one researching a book?"

When he didn't answer, she pointed the holster at them. He
tensed, ready to snatch it from her hand if things got too weird.
"Know something funny?"

"What's that?" he asked warily.

"We have so few people out here in Lost Souls Wilderness
that I've been deputized by the sheriff. I have the power to detain
anyone I deem to be suspicious and hold them until law enforcement can get here."

"That's interesting," said Jessica, brightly. She didn't seem to
be picking up the same ominous vibe he was getting. "How many
times have you had to do that?"

"This will be the third."

CHAPTER TWENTY-FIVE

Jessica watched in utter shock as Kelsey pulled a set of old-fashioned steel handcuffs from a desk drawer. "I've already alerted the Forest Service, so don't waste time resisting. They'll be here in a couple hours. Then you'll be their problem."

"What the hell are you arresting us for?" Ethan demanded. "We have the right to know that. And a right to an attorney, a right to—"

"I'm not arresting you. I'm detaining you until the forest rangers get here. But if you resist, that'll change. Fast."

She slid one cuff around his wrist. Jessica could tell he was fighting with himself, wanting to object but not make things worse.

"Why are you doing this? We're not a threat. All we've done is ask questions."

Jessica finally found her voice. "We're just trying to find—" Ethan kicked her in the ankle. "Ow."

"I'll let law enforcement sort it all out." She snapped the other cuff around Jessica's wrist. The cold, impersonal steel pressed against her skin. "It's like the wild west out here. I have to protect this lodge and my patrons. Sorry."

She strode toward a door that opened onto a smaller side room, possibly a storeroom. "Come on. In you go."

"What's in there?" Jessica hung back. It seemed so surreal that she'd gone from sharing recipes with Kelsey to getting arrested by her. Or *detained*, whatever that meant.

"It's our holding cell. And my printer and copier room, but don't mess with my electronics or you'll get me even more pissed off. Make yourselves comfy, jailbirds. The Forest Service was none too happy to get a call from me. They won't be in a good mood when they arrive."

She pulled Jessica by the arm, which forced Ethan along after her.

"Don't we get to make a call first?" he demanded.

"Call away. I assume you have your cell phones."

The door closed behind them and a lock clicked into place. Jessica looked at Ethan in disbelief. "This can't be happening."

The room held a large copier unit along with stacks of paper and a set of folding chairs propped against the wall. It was tiny and claustrophobic, with only one small window breaking the monotony.

Ethan stepped toward it, bringing her stumbling after him. From the window they could see flower gardens to the left and a woodshed to the right. The wood shed was more of a wood condominium. It held at least twenty cords of wood, organized by size. Cut logs, rounds, kindling.

She took a moment to admire it. Could someone so conscientious about their firewood really be a villain? Or did the organized quality of the woodshed indicate a compulsive disorder?

Past the woodshed, there was a stretch of close-cropped lawn and then an area filled with tall grass already gone to seed. Beyond that, the forest loomed.

"Second damn arrest in less than a week in Alaska," Ethan muttered.

"At least you're used to it. This is my first arrest ever! It's not like what I imagined. No mugshot, no fingerprints."

"That happens when you get booked. If this goes that far, it'll happen when we get to an actual police station. Like she said, we haven't been arrested. Sure feels like it, though."

"Wow." She opened one of the folding chairs and sank onto it, nearly knocking him off balance. "I guess it's lucky I'm with such an expert on the subject."

"Very cute." He snagged another chair and sat next to her.

"Why do you think she did this? Was it really because of your gun?"

"I don't know. Something sketchy is going on. Did you see her face when you mentioned the drowning?"

"Ooh, what if *she* did it? The drowning?"

He shook his head impatiently. "She would have been pretty young when that happened. Well, seventeen, same age as when the plane crashed. We don't even know if there *was* a drowning. It could just be a symbolic dream about S.G. missing her parents or something."

"No." Jessica rubbed her hands down the front of her purple tights. She'd brought them as an extra layer to wear under her hiking gear, then had worn them with a t-shirt and black micro skirt to breakfast. She'd never imagined that she'd get arrested in them. "I checked with the crystal. It was a memory, not a dream."

"Oh for fucks sake, lighten up on the crystal talk. We're *in jail*." Ethan snapped at her, making her jump.

"Why are you yelling at me? And my *crystal*?"

"I'm not yelling. I'm just—Grrr." He plunged his head into his hands, his hair brushing against her cuffed hand. "Can't believe I'm jail again."

"Oh come on, it's not so bad. Think of it as a..." she glanced around the little room. "Store room. The kind you sneak into when you want some afternoon delight at work." She added a purr to her voice. "And look, we even have sex toys." She jingled the cuffs.

He snorted. Then the snort became a laugh. Then his entire body shook as the laughter came rolling out of him. "Is there no situation that you can't look on the bright side of?"

"Probably." She gave him a crooked smile. She could think of one right off the top of her head—the fact that she'd finally found someone she loved being with, but he wasn't her soul mate and had no intention of sticking around. That situation just plain sucked and she saw no silver lining. "Don't test me."

After his laughter died down, he went quiet for a while. He seemed to be turning something over in his mind, so she held her tongue too.

Finally, he spoke in a much more serious voice. "There's another possibility here. What if Kelsey is working with whoever shot your plane? She could be trying to shield whoever did it and get us out of Lost Souls."

She shivered at the thought. "Another message."

"Exactly."

This whole situation was so surreal. "She seemed so nice at first."

"You just think that because she praised your walnut-cinnamon roll recipe."

"I do love flattery, especially when it comes to my baking." She sighed. "I wish I could bribe our way out of here with pastries."

He chuckled. "They are pretty much magic. I'll never forget the first whiff of your scones in my last holding cell."

"So you *do* believe in magic!" She rubbed her shoulder against his. "I knew it."

"It was a figure of speech."

"No, you meant it. *And* you believe in my crystal. Don't bother to deny it," she teased.

When he turned his head toward her, his expression snatched her breath away. "No. I believe in you," he said simply.

"In...me?" she stammered.

"Yeah, the woman holding the crystal. You."

A smile trembled on her lips. "Even though I made you come to Lost Souls and get thrown in jail again?"

He snorted. "You wanted to step out of your comfort zone, right?"

Her smile grew even wider until it filled her face. "Not what I had in mind, but yes, that's true."

He gently traced the rim of her lower lip. "There's just something about that smile of yours. It's irresistible."

"Really? The mean girls used to tease me because my mouth was so big. I could show you photos of me when I was a kid and half my face was one huge smile."

He lowered his head and skimmed his lips across hers. "I hope it didn't make you stop smiling."

Her lips tingled as if he'd dosed her with champagne. "It did at first. Then I saw them tease Maya because her hair was so curly and I realized they were just jerks. That's when we became best friends, actually. We made a pact to laugh and whisper to each other every time they said something mean to either of us. It drove them *crazy*."

The little finger of his cuffed hand wrapped itself around her little finger. "Pinkie promise that you'll never hold back on your smile again?"

She laughed out loud. "That is the first time a man has ever asked me for a pinkie promise."

"Blame it on my sister. She would have beat my ass if I ever broke a pinkie promise."

"She sounds fierce."

"Oh, she is. She's a badass. Smart, too. She told me Charley wasn't right for me."

She wondered what kind of woman would inspire someone like Ethan to forget his convictions and propose. "Do you miss her? Charley?"

He snorted. "I've barely thought about her. That proves it."

"Proves what?"

"I'm not meant for marriage."

Her heart deflated like a punctured balloon. Which was stupid, because he'd been very clear about his stance on marriage and how he saw their relationship. She even agreed. They weren't right for each other—at least beyond the bedroom. So why did she keep getting her hopes up?

Maybe she was just a hopeless romantic and should accept that about herself. Team Sex Jessica was no different from Team Romance Jessica. *Deal with it, woman.*

She shoved aside her disappointment. "Well, I guess it's good that you tried. Now you know for sure. Maybe that was the point of the vision. It led you to try something, even though it didn't work out."

He stretched out his legs and absently rubbed the right one. "I never thought of it that way. I took it literally. Me, a bride, a meadow. Seemed pretty straightforward. But it could have been anything. A scene from a movie or an ad in a magazine. I shouldn't have taken it seriously and made an important life decision based on it."

"How could it be a scene from a movie? Didn't you see Charley in the vision?"

"No. I couldn't see the bride's face. I just saw our hands." He lifted their cuffed hands and wriggled his fingers. "We were holding hands and I was a little bit ahead of her so I only caught a glimpse of her dress. Enough to see that it was a wedding dress."

She stared at their two hands. His was big-knuckled and

calloused, while hers was smaller, with the familiar burn scars. If he hadn't even seen the bride's face, how could he possibly know if the vision was false? Maybe he'd proposed to the wrong woman. Had he even considered that possibility?

"And where were you? What was the setting?"

"Outdoors. A meadow with tall grass that looked gold in the sunshine. Like a prairie."

She slowly rose to her feet and tugged him up behind her. With him on her heels, she stepped to the small window. "Like that?"

He frowned at the pretty scene outside. Tall grass waving in the breeze, seed heads catching light from the sun. The fireweed was just starting to bloom, adding spikes of vibrant light purple. "Sort of, I suppose."

Looking uneasy, he shifted his attention to the window frame. "I wonder if we can climb out of this window."

"A jailbreak? Where would we go from here? We have no gear, no supplies."

"Good point." He heaved a sigh and turned away from the window. She followed him back to the folding chairs. "I think this common sense thing is catching on."

"You know, I do run a business," she said wryly. "I'm not completely immune to logic. I just believe there's more to life. Mystery. Magic. Miracles."

"Think you could conjure one right now?"

"I wish. We could call someone. I wish Maya was back from Anchorage."

"Not sure what we'd say anyway."

They turned as one so they could sit down together. "There must be a reason we're here, handcuffed together," she mused. "Maybe we're missing something."

"We're here because Kelsey the Extremely Sketchy Manager put us here. That's it. End of ridiculous story. It's my fault. I should have hidden my Ruger better. I shouldn't have let her cuff us. I'm the professional. I'm supposed to be in charge of this thing. I set the parameters." The longer he spoke, the more wretched he looked. "I let you down. I'm sorry."

She couldn't bear for him to beat himself up like that. Carefully, she maneuvered herself so that she was sitting on his lap, facing him. He tilted his face to look at her, his expression one of bemusement. "What are you doing?"

"Reminding you of last night." She squeezed her thighs with his sandwiched between them.

"Trust me, you don't need to remind me. But I'll take it. Any particular reason why?"

"Because you *didn't* let me down. We're in this together. We made all the decisions together. I pushed you into this whole thing. Without me, you would have gone back to LA days ago. So really, it's my fault."

"That is true," he said thoughtfully. With his free hand, he stroked the length of her back, kneading the muscles alongside her spine. "It's your fault I got to stay in a fifteen hundred dollar a night suite. Your fault I had such an incredible time last night. Your fault I haven't eaten this well in years. Even the crackers you brought were top notch. It's all your fault, baby."

She arched her back like a cat as he worked the tension out of her muscles. If she had to be in jail with someone, Ethan was definitely her pick.

"Now what are you going to do to make it up to me?" he murmured.

"Hmmm." She practically purred under his touch. "What do you want me to do?"

"I have some ideas. Lean forward. Yeah, like that. Put those pretty breasts right there, right against my chest. Oh yeah."

Smiling to herself, she pressed her breasts against him. It was what she wanted anyway. She moved side to side, seeking the abrasion of his clothing through her t-shirt. Her nipples immediately perked into tight peaks.

With his free hand, he gently pushed her back so he could see for himself. Through her t-shirt, he pinched one nipple, rolling it between his fingers. She bit her lip as sharp pleasure coursed through her, as if it had been lurking inside waiting for a signal. One spark of a match and she was on fire again.

She closed her eyes and hummed as he toyed with her nipples. Her hips moved on their own, grinding against him. She wanted friction there, too, between her legs. He adjusted his position so one thigh bone pressed against her mound. When she tilted her pelvis, there it was, just the force she needed.

He groaned as the bulge in his jeans swelled against her. "I had plans for this morning, you know. You were gone when I woke up, but if you'd been there I would have had you spread out like a breakfast buffet. You'd have been hanging onto that headboard for dear life while I ate you out."

Heat jolted through her. "Oh yeah?" she managed.

"Oh. Yeah. I would have kissed your pretty lips. The other ones. I would have put my mouth on your clit and tasted your sweet honey running across my tongue. Captured every little flutter and pulse. I can feel it now, you know. You're so hot on my thigh. Your mound feels like it's burning up."

"It is." She rubbed against him, a frantic feeling racing through her. As if an orgasm was out there but she'd never be able to reach it like this, with so many clothes between them.

"I bet it is. That hot little clit's in charge right now. It knows what you want. It wants to fuck." As he spoke each naughty word he tweaked her nipples. Every time he did that a wild flood of sensation carried her deeper and further.

She gave a strangled moan deep in her throat. She had no idea who could hear them. Probably no one. Only two people here even knew they existed, Kelsey and Ren. Ren wouldn't question it if he never saw them again.

Nope, she and Ethan were alone in the world. And she was about to come against his thigh. If she could just get there...

Then came more hot words flowing into her ear. "If I had my mouth on you right now, you'd be coming so hard you'd forget we're in jail. I'd be licking every drop of cream off your lips. I'd be tickling that little clit, I'd be putting my fingers inside you, so hot and soft, I'd find all your secret spots that make you scream, I'd—"

She came with a hard shudder, tight against his thigh. She couldn't control her body; it kept convulsing again and again. The orgasm went on and on, sweet waves of pleasure gripping and releasing. Ethan kept whispering in her ear. "That's it, give it to me. Let it go. You're so hot, so beautiful."

She wasn't even sure if he knew what he was saying. He seemed almost as carried away as she was.

After the last spasm was wrung from her body, she slumped over him. "Oh my God..." she murmured. "What did you just do to me?"

"Hopefully something good." The rough humor in his voice brought her back. Trust Ethan to say something practical at a moment like this.

"Oh yes." She spread her hand against the bulge in his jeans. His penis was hard as a rock under there. "But what about you?"

"Rain check. No condoms. No desire to come in my pants."

With one last lingering touch, she drew her hand away. He shifted under her, clearly trying to reduce the pressure on his erection. She extricated herself from his lap and collapsed onto her chair.

Raincheck. She liked that idea. It meant they'd do this again sometime, though she couldn't imagine where or when. Their time together was running out. Either they were going to be sent to separate male and female prisons, or he was going to get the hell out of Alaska before he got thrown in jail again.

A sound from somewhere outside caught their attention. After sharing a quick glance, they got to their feet and stumbled together toward the window and peered out. A convoy of three four-wheelers was cruising down the road toward the lodge. They could only catch glimpses between the tall spruce trees lining the road.

"I see Kelsey," Jessica murmured into Ethan's throat. They had to crowd together so they could both see.

"And I don't see anyone with a badge or a uniform." His voice sounded grim. "I don't like this at all."

"She said she was picking up some guests. Do they look like guests?"

"I don't see a single piece of luggage."

Jessica's imagination was going wild now. "What if that's *them*? The bad guys? What if she notified them, threw us in jail and went to pick them up?"

The four-wheelers disappeared from sight.

She swallowed hard. "My intuition is screaming at me that we should get out of here."

"My common sense is saying the same thing."

CHAPTER TWENTY-SIX

Knowing they didn't have much time until the four-wheelers reached the lodge, Ethan came up with a plan and they set to work. Jessica used the edge of one of her bracelets to slice the old putty that held the window in its frame. When it was cut all the way through, Ethan was able to crack the frame and remove the entire window without breaking the glass and making a racket.

The hardest part was getting them both out the window while they were still handcuffed together. They set up one of the folding chairs under the window to make it easier to climb out.

Ethan went first so he could scope out any dangers that might be lurking outside. The logistics were ridiculously uncomfortable. He had to go head first, scooting on his back, with both hands planted on the upper frame to pull himself through. That meant Jessica's hand stayed above her head, adjusting to his every move so he didn't yank her shoulder out its socket. Tricky operation, and it took a lot of whispered coordination.

When his rear was entirely out the window, he used all his upper body strength to lift himself up off the window frame. He was hoping there would be enough room for him to extract his legs next and jump down to the ground. Not even close.

"Okay, plan B," he said quietly. "I'm going to fall backwards and you're going to come with me."

"That sounds like a very bad idea."

"It's not. Trust me, I know how to fall. It's nothing but grass down there, I already checked it out. Just come closer and put your arms around me."

"Are we both going to fit through the window?"

"It's just my legs now. We can do it if we stay close together. Come on, they're getting closer. We got this."

"I'm never eating chocolate croissants again," she grumbled as she crawled up his body.

"Take that back. Your chocolate croissants are ma—"

"Magic, I know. Just help me up."

He used his free arm to assist her, then wrapped it tightly around her.

Strange how they kept having to get closer and closer to each other, and how it never felt like too much.

When she was plastered against him like a second skin, he scooted his rear backwards until he reached a pivot point. "On the count of three, push off."

"Push off what?"

"Just let your weight fall forward. I need to keep my legs straight so they don't snag on the frame. We need gravity and momentum to take us down. After you push forward just pretend you're a rag doll. Don't fight it, just fall. Ready?"

"I guess?" Her answer was buried against his chest. "I can't even see anything. I'm totally trusting you here."

"Remember how you said I didn't let you down?"

"Yes, but we've never tried to tandem dive out a window before. I'm not sure—"

"Three, two, one. Go."

The weight of her body pushed him backwards into a freefall toward the ground. *Good girl.* He felt a rush of air, then his back thumped onto the ground. It knocked the wind out of him, and his lungs heaved for a moment, gasping for air. His mouth was full of Jessica's hair. He tried to tell her so, but couldn't get enough air to speak.

"Are you okay?" Jessica planted her hands on the ground and lifted off him.

"Yeah," he wheezed. "You?"

"No damage." She turned her head one direction, then the other. "And no witnesses. Let's get out of here." She crawled off him and helped him up with her cuffed hand. He shook out his leg to make sure it was still functioning. Considering he hadn't done his stretches in a couple days, it was holding up pretty well.

He gestured with his head toward the thick forest beyond the grounds. "Think we can make it?"

"Only one way to find out."

"Let's make it look like we're just going for a stroll. If we run that might attract attention."

She nodded admiringly. "That's a great idea. You're so good at this. You think of everything."

He snorted. None of this investigation had gone remotely according to plan. The whole in-and-out, one-last-job approach was out the window. Now it was think on your feet and try not to get shot at.

He clasped her hand, so it looked as if they were a happy couple out for a romantic walk. They ambled across the closely cropped lawn surrounding the lodge. Beyond that grew the taller grass, and after that the forest. If they could just get to the trees, they might have a chance. But if Kelsey and her cohorts spotted them before they disappeared, they'd have to get even more creative.

One step at a time. He smiled down at Jessica, playing the

part of the besotted lover. She gazed up with a similar expression of head-over-heels infatuation.

A warm thrill traveled through him.

What would it be like to have someone *really* feel that way about him? What would it be like if *Jessica* was that person? It would be like living in a world made of honey and sunshine.

It took a few excruciating minutes to reach the taller grass, with its feathery seed heads. It was easier to blend in with this grass—some of it was over their heads—and yet it was more unlikely that anyone ever walked out here.

They should make it look as if they were so wrapped up in each other they had no idea where they were.

He dropped a kiss onto the top of her head. In the short time they'd been out here, the sun had warmed her hair. Its fragrance sent a rush of visceral memories through him. The shower. His fingers between her legs. Her face when she came. Desire punched him hard in the gut and time seemed to slow.

Her hand tightened in his. The high grass rustled as a light breeze whispered through it. A butterfly flitted past his head. Sunlight glanced through waving grass and suddenly he was back there again.

In his vision.

Holding hands with a woman who was his bride.

Not Charley. *Jessica.* Haloed in golden sunshine.

The stunning moment was shattered when voices shouted at them from the direction of the lodge.

"*Run,*" he told her.

Their hands fell apart and they took off, thrashing through the grass as best they could. The voices came closer, and now he heard footsteps racing after them. At least there were no gunshots.

"Just get to the woods," he panted, trying to pick up the pace.

It wasn't easy with grass tussocks getting in their way and their hands cuffed together.

"I'm trying! Stop yanking my wrist around."

"Just hold hands, that'll make it easier." He snagged her hand again.

"Running while holding hands is *not easier*."

"Maybe you should stop talking and focus on running."

"Maybe you should stop talking and kiss my ass."

A new voice broke in. A somehow familiar voice. "Are you two *still* fighting?"

Jessica stopped in her tracks, nearly causing Ethan to fall on his face. He staggered to a halt. "*Maya?* What are you doing here?"

He spun around. Sure enough, there was the Lost Harbor police chief herself, in jeans and a casual black-and-purple striped sweater, hands on her hips, panting from her dash across the meadow.

"I was hitching a ride back from Anchorage on a Forest Service chopper when I heard that you two were detained. They let me come out here and take you off their hands."

"Where's Kelsey?" Ethan asked.

"The manager? She's right behind me."

"We don't trust her," Jessica said urgently. "We think she might be working with some bad people out here."

Maya's forehead wrinkled in a frown.

"I don't know about that. She followed protocol by holding you until someone could get here. She's on her own out here, so she has to act if anything makes her suspicious." She fixed a stern glance on Ethan. "What's going on here? Last I knew you were heading back to LA."

Uh oh. This was a hell of a way for Maya to find out about Jessica's plan. He glanced at Jessica, letting her decide how much to reveal.

"I hired him," Jessica said after a brief moment.

Good call. With someone like Maya, it was best to tell the truth because she was likely to find out anyway.

"For what?"

"Same thing you hired him for. To solve S.G.'s case." Her voice trailed away as Maya glared at her. "And I'm working with him. Surprise!"

A variety of reactions flitted across Maya's face. Confusion. Astonishment. Disbelief. None of it positive.

She swung toward him. "And you went along with this? Jess doesn't know anything about investigating. She's a civilian."

"Actually, she's been great, especially as a guide out here. We've made a lot of progress."

"Is that right?" *Siri, show me skepticism.*

He reached for his most professional tone. "I think you'll be happy with our report. I can catch you up on everything we've learned as soon as you let us out of these damn cuffs."

"First of all, I don't have the key. Second, you're both on my shit list right now. I'm supposed to be getting Dad's house ready for him, not dealing with two crazy cowboys."

Jessica's face lit up. "Oh, is he coming home? That's great news!"

"Yes, I was really excited about it until all this broke out." She waved at them. Then her face softened. "I'm still happy about it. He's doing well. He'll be home in a few days."

Jessica clasped her hands together, which of course dragged his hand into the gesture as well. "That's fantastic."

Ethan winced as the cuff chafed his wrist. He glanced past Maya and caught sight of Kelsey hurrying toward them. He hoped she had the handcuff key with her and could put an end to this crap.

As he watched Kelsey cross the lawn, he noticed that she was moving strangely. There was a hitch in her gait, sort of like his except it had more of a twist to it. Had she walked like that last night? He'd been so weary that he hadn't paid much attention to her beyond the night robe and the glasses. But now that he thought back—yes, she did have an unusual gait.

He didn't know what it meant, but maybe it was an important data point. He filed it away.

"Ethan! Ethan, are you okay?"

Jessica tugged at his arm. He wrenched his gaze away from Kelsey.

"Yeah. What's up?"

"What's *up*?"

His thoughts were still focused on Kelsey. She'd called in law enforcement rather than the bad guys, whoever they were. But that didn't completely rule out the other possibility, that she was working with or protecting someone nefarious. If that was the case, he didn't want to let her know anything about S.G. He had to make sure she was legit first.

He lowered his voice and spoke rapidly as she closed the gap between them. "Don't say anything about S.G., Maya. Please."

Her eyebrows climbed up her forehead, but she nodded.

Kelsey finally reached them. In her rush across the lawn, her round black glasses had slid down her nose. "You guys broke my window!" she said furiously. "You couldn't just stay put until I got back?" She turned to Maya. "Are you vouching for these two?"

"I know, they're a pain in the ass. I promise they won't cause you any more trouble." Maya gave the two of them a pointed glare. "I'll take them back to Lost Harbor and deal with them there."

"Are you sure? Why would they try to run if they weren't up to something?"

Maya swung her gaze toward Ethan and Jessica. "Anyone want to take a crack at that?"

Ethan cleared his throat and reached for the first explanation that came to mind. "We had to pee."

Maya's eyebrows shot up, but he forged ahead. This whole situation had already gone beyond parody anyway.

"Sorry, but we had no idea when you were coming back. Desperate times..."

Jessica added to his story by hopping in place. "We still haven't been able to pee, by the way."

Kelsey looked flabbergasted, while Maya burst out laughing. "I'm here trying to figure out which one of you is the instigator. I thought it'd be Jess, but Ethan, you're right up there. Come on, let's get you back to civilization. Pit stop on the way."

"We also need to get our things," Ethan said. "They're still in our room."

"I'll take you up there." Kelsey narrowed her eyes at him. "But I'll be watching every second, so no bullshit."

"Fair enough." He stepped forward, then jerked back, having completely forgotten about the handcuffs. "Can we get out of these damn things?"

Kelsey bristled, but Jessica aimed one of her bright smiles at her. "Please, Kelsey. We promise to behave. And I really need to talk to Maya alone."

Kelsey glanced at Maya, who gave a nod of approval.

He held up their cuffed hands so she could insert the key. "Most people use zip ties nowadays," he told her as the metal ring fell away. "Just for future reference."

"I guess we're just old-school out here. Deal with it."

As he followed Kelsey across the grass, it occurred to him that it felt strange to be separated from Jessica after so much time plastered to her side. He wasn't sure how long they'd been in the storeroom, but it was probably a couple of hours.

"I suppose I should thank you for alerting me to my faulty

window," Kelsey grumbled. "We've never had a jailbreak here before. Very creative."

"We can pay you back for that."

She waved him off. "The owners of this lodge are billionaires. They can afford it."

He glanced at her cautiously. She seemed more relaxed now, maybe because an actual police officer was taking charge.

Maybe it was scary being in charge of such a remote location.

Or maybe she had another reason to be nervous.

Or maybe she was a straight-up villain.

But sometimes even a hard-boiled investigator had to go with his intuition. His gut told him that Kelsey wasn't a real threat.

"What do you say we put our cards on the table?" he asked her as she unlocked a side door to the lodge and they stepped inside.

"What cards?"

"I'll tell you what we're doing out here and you tell me why you felt you had to toss us in that storeroom."

CHAPTER TWENTY-SEVEN

Jessica rubbed the red mark the cuff had left on her wrist. It was sore and painful, but that was nothing compared to the way Maya was looking at her—as if she didn't know who she was.

"Surprise?" Maya folded her arms across her chest. "You want to explain what you were thinking?" Her rich brown skin picked up hints of bronze in the morning sunlight. Unfortunately the sun also emphasized the pinch between her eyebrows and the puffiness of her eyes. She'd been through a rough few days.

"It was for you." Jessica flexed her hands and rotated her wrists. Now that she was on the spot, trying to explain, nerves were setting in. "I knew you didn't really want to drop S.G.'s case. It was such a great opportunity, with Ethan here. So I asked Ethan to move forward with it."

"Do you know how much he charges? I was going to work out an arrangement with him to cover his costs."

"Don't worry about that." She flung up her hand. "I got it. I told him from the start that I'd pay for it."

Maya shoved her hands in the back pockets of her jeans. "So

what, you decided to play savior? That's why you're out here in Lost Souls Wilderness getting detained?"

A mosquito whined near Maya's face. Jessica wanted to swat it away, but would that be like playing mosquito savior?

Maya shooed it away herself. Problem solved. "How'd you get here, anyway? The float plane? Where is it?"

"Someone sank it. It's in a lake." Jessica kind of wished she was at the bottom of that lake herself.

"Your float plane sank? Damn." Maya shook her head a few times, speechless for a moment. "Then you came here and frightened the manager of Misty Bay's fanciest resort so much that she locked you up."

"I wanted to tell her the truth, but Ethan is so untrusting."

"Goes with the territory. He's a PI. You're..."

"A baker. I know. And a bad decision-maker." Ugh, that rhymed, unintentionally, and just sounded goofy. "But I figured something out, Maya. Maybe I just make decisions in my own way, in my own time. There's nothing so wrong with that, is there?"

"No. There isn't."

"That doesn't mean I always have my head in the clouds. It doesn't mean I live in a bubble."

Maya stared at her. "That's why you did all this? Because I said you live in a bubble?"

Jessica straightened her spine. "Partly. But mostly I did it because you're my best friend and I love you, and in the hospital I could see how exhausted you were by everything. I know you hate letting people down. You always have to be strong and handle everything by yourself. I wanted to share some of that burden for you."

"Jess..." Maya stepped away from her, as if she was trying to get herself under control.

"What? Say it. You don't have to tiptoe around my feelings."

Maya turned back, head tilted curiously. "You think I do that?"

"I know you do. I figured that out in the hospital. But you don't have to."

"Okay," Maya finally said. "Here's the thing. I know how you like to focus on the positive, and I love that about you, Jess. You always look on the bright side and bring that everything's-for-the-best attitude. But sometimes it feels like you're whitewashing things because you never want to think about the bad stuff. You only want to think about the good stuff."

Jessica bit down on her lip to stop the automatic response that wanted to jump out. *That's not true. I can think about bad stuff too.* But did Maya have a point? "Go on," she said instead.

Maya gave her a dubious glance, probably testing to make sure she was sincere.

"Really. I want to hear more. I can handle it."

"Okay," Maya said slowly. "You want to know why I tiptoe around you. That's why. It's not always easy being the first black police chief in a town that's mostly white. But I don't think you want to hear about that. You'd rather think everything's groovy and rainbows and flowers and magic."

A soft wind whispered through the swaying grass around them. The sunlight made everything crystal clear—gilding the delicate seed heads of the stalks. She had the sudden sense that she was seeing her friend clearly for the first time.

And maybe herself too.

"You're right, Maya. I have this...thing." She played with a piece of grass to help her focus. "I look on the bright side because I'm so afraid of how bad things could be if I don't. You know how it was for me growing up. I guess I got in the habit of putting on those rose-colored glasses just to escape. I like to believe in magic because reality was always so crappy. But it's not anymore. I like my life now. And I can handle a lot more than I thought I could. "

Maya's serious expression softened. "It's a Jess thing. I get it."

"No." Jessica threw up her hand to stop her. "I don't want excuses. I didn't realize all that was interfering with our friendship. Nothing's more important to me than my friends."

"I know. You're a fantastic friend."

"Not if you can't tell me things, I'm not."

"Okay. I'm getting the message." Maya smiled slightly. "You know, we could have just had a conversation about all this. Coming out here, reliving the Nancy Drew days, it's a little extra, don't you think?"

Jessica burst out laughing. "You think? I lost my float plane and I don't even mind."

Maya snorted. "I never trusted that thing. For real, though, I'm pretty impressed. For a head-in-the-clouds type, you really put it on the line out here."

Ethan's comment floated through her mind. *I believe in you.*

Just look at everything she'd gone through on this crazy-ass adventure. Sure, proving something to Maya was good, but she'd proved something to herself too. She could push out of her comfort zone. She could even thrive out there in the big wide world—or at least the wilderness part of it.

Maybe it was time she started believing in herself.

She jumped as Maya touched her on the shoulder. "I can't officially approve of you and Ethan going rogue, but unofficially, I'm touched you wanted to take care of business for me."

Jessica flung her arms around Maya and they hugged each other tightly.

"But there might be a problem." Maya's "police chief" voice brought Jessica back to reality as their hug came to an end.

"Uh oh, what now?"

"You might have a record after this. It's going to look bad for a police chief to be friends with a criminal."

"I'd say I'm more criminal-adjacent. It's a gray area."

Maya smirked at her. "Look at you, hanging out with criminals instead of soul mates. I guess you really did change things up."

If Maya was teasing her, everything was definitely back to normal.

"Want to go finish solving your case now?" she asked her friend. "I'm pretty sure Ethan's about to crack the whole thing wide open. He's a really good investigator, you know."

"Something tells me that's not all he's good at. Got anything else you want to confess while we're out of earshot?"

Jessica gave a dreamy sigh. "All I can say is, Team Sex is a lot more fun than I ever imagined."

Maya burst out laughing.

As they neared the lodge, a strange sensation crawled across the back of her neck. Not an insect, which was her first theory. She glanced behind her uneasily.

"Do you get the feeling that someone's watching us?" she asked Maya in a low voice.

"Someone is," Maya answered. "There's a man in the woods about fifty yards in. I don't spot a weapon, but he's using a set of binoculars. Don't react, and don't look back again. I'm trying to draw him out, so make it seem like you don't see him."

Jessica followed her instructions and tried her best to act normal. "I *don't* see him. How did you even spot him?"

Maya shrugged. "You know me, I never relax out here. No one should. If it ain't mosquitos, it's bears. Or bad guys with binoculars. Come on, let's get inside."

CHAPTER TWENTY-EIGHT

Kelsey turned her back on Ethan and marched into the lodge. "I don't care what you're doing out here. You're about to leave."

"I think you would care if you knew the real reason. I think you're afraid."

He saw her shoulders tense, and knew he was right.

"What's scaring you? I know it's not us. You know we're not dangerous. Why did you arrest us?"

"Because I found a weapon and I have to protect my guests. As I've said."

"And because we were asking questions."

They reached the suite where they'd stayed last night. She unlocked the door, then ushered him in. "Go ahead and grab your things."

He stepped through the door, brushing past her in the process. He grabbed the opportunity to deploy his brand-new secret weapon—his nose. Surreptitiously, he drew in a solid lungful of her scent. He didn't know what he was after—just something different from a normal healthy woman in her thirties.

Something acrid filled his nostrils. A spice of some kind. It took a moment to recognize it. *Turmeric.* Mixed with a menthol-ish scent. He'd tried turmeric once to bring down inflammation in his leg. Unless she was cooking curry, maybe she leaned on turmeric for the same reason.

Did Kelsey have a medical condition?

He thought about the sharp edge in her personality. Some people were like that naturally, of course. But for others, it was a reaction to chronic pain. He'd seen many examples during his time in hospitals.

Alastair's words came back to him. *She had a good reason to give up her baby beyond being young. But they never said what. It was something beyond the usual family issues.*

Ethan had assumed it was a family reason or a religious one. Or even financial. But what if it was medical? He knew very well how a medical condition could force your life in new directions.

What if...could it be?

Still speculating, he moved deeper into the room. Her scent faded, replaced by jasmine and the memory of last night. Had it just been last night? It felt like a lifetime ago. Maybe time moved differently out here in Lost Souls Wilderness. One of those "strange things" people talked about happening here.

He squatted down to put yesterday's clothes in his backpack. "Why did you search our suite to begin with? Because we were asking questions?"

"I don't have to explain. It's part of our policy, which you accepted when you stepped onto the property."

"Okay. I get it. You're very strict and I have no argument with that. But we were two stranded hikers who wandered in out of the wilderness with hardly anything with us. Why would you think we'd be any kind of a threat? Why search our room?"

She didn't respond, but the answer clicked into place anyway. "*Because* we'd come in from wilderness. There's something going on out there, and you know about it. That's why you're afraid."

She ran her tongue nervously along the seam of her lips. Behind her glasses, she blinked.

"Whatever it is, we're not part of it. And maybe we can help. I'm an investigator with a lot of experience—"

She interrupted him with a brisk shake of her head. "You should go home and stay out of it. Whatever your experience is, it won't help."

Bingo. So he'd called it right. There was something bigger going on. Whoever had sunk Jessica's float plane hadn't done it for kicks. It was part of something larger and more menacing.

"We also have a police chief right outside."

"She should go back too. You should all forget you came here." Her gaze drifted to the window that looked out on the back meadow. Maya and Jessica were now making their way toward the lodge, still deep in conversation.

In the forest beyond, he caught a flash of something. He strode to the window and flattened himself to the wall next to it so he could peer out without being spotted.

"Someone's surveilling us."

Kelsey hung back by the doorway. "Get your things and let's go. This isn't your problem."

"How do you know? You don't even know why we're here, do you?"

"You're investigating them, aren't you?"

"I don't even know who 'them' is. That's not it. We're here to find a woman. The one we mentioned earlier, before you put us in jail."

Her eyes went flinty behind her glasses. "Why?"

From across the room, he held her gaze for a long moment. He didn't see a downside anymore to telling her. She was warning him away, after all. Trying to protect them. He didn't have to mention S.G. at all.

"Okay, I'll put my cards on the table, like I offered. This woman—or girl, at the time—had an appointment here at the Aurora Lodge with the Berensons. She was pregnant and was giving up her baby for adoption."

As he spoke, the color slowly faded from her face, even though she didn't move a muscle. He kept going.

"But she broke the agreement and the Berensons left without the baby."

He watched her closely. She opened her mouth and shut it again. Swallowed hard. He waited patiently, more and more sure that he was onto something here.

"Why...who...who sent you?"

"I can't tell you that unless you tell *me* something. I don't know if I can trust you."

She stepped inside the room and closed the door behind her. In an urgent voice, she said, "Will you go away and stop asking questions if I do?"

Adrenaline rushed through him. He was closing in. He knew it.

And hell, Maya was taking over after this anyway. It'd be her job to ask questions from now on. "I swear."

She swallowed convulsively. "The agreement wasn't broken."

It was a start. Baby steps. He kept his voice neutral so as not to scare her away. "What happened?"

"They said they were the Berensons. They checked in under that name and they looked like the photo they'd sent."

"So someone else posed as the Berensons and took the baby?"

"Yes." Every word came out in a halting way, as if her speaking muscles were rusty. She sounded like a different person than the acerbic woman who'd tossed them in jail. "They left right away. Then the next day the real Berensons came. Everyone was horrified when we realized what had happened. The other couple—" She shivered as if the room had suddenly gone ice cold. "They sent the Berensons a ransom demand."

How could she possibly know all these details unless she was close to the situation? Her age was roughly right. Her behavior had been so strange since they'd started asking questions. It all pointed in one direction.

Adrenaline surged through him, but he controlled himself and kept asking patient questions. "What was the demand?"

"Money. They said they'd kill Stephanie if they didn't give them the money."

"That was the baby's name? Stephanie?"

She continued as if he hadn't even spoken. "They hadn't even *seen* the baby yet. It wasn't clear they'd pay the ransom."

"The mother couldn't pay?"

"Of course not! She...she was just a waitress here."

Maybe it wasn't Kelsey. Maybe she was protecting someone else. How could he pin her down?

"That must have been terrifying for the girl. If she didn't even have the money to keep the baby, she wouldn't have enough for a ransom—"

"It wasn't about money!" she cried. "She couldn't—I wasn't —" She snapped her mouth shut.

My God. It *was* her. This was S.G.'s mother. This woman— who'd been right across the bay the entire time.

The satisfaction of solving the mystery flooded through him. God, he loved this job.

Why had he thought for more than a second about quitting?

He and Kelsey stared at each other for a long moment.

"So you decided to give Stephanie up for adoption," he said gently.

Kelsey wiped her hands on her denim overshirt. The fight seemed to have gone out of her. "Yes, but Stephanie was the name the Berensons chose. I didn't dare to name her. But when I sang to her I called her Maggie."

Finally S.G. would learn her real name. *Maggie.* Pretty name. It even suited S.G.

"Maggie was short for Magpie," she went on. "Magpies had always brought me good luck. Now I hate the sight of them and chase them away whenever they come near the lodge."

A shiver traveled down Ethan's spine. S.G. had named herself after a bird. Was it possible that some part of her remembered that her mother had done the same?

Impossible. And yet out here in this wild land, impossible was a moving target.

"So the Berensons went somewhere to pay the ransom?"

"Yes, that's what they told me. They promised to let me know as soon as they had Maggie back. But I never heard anything, and they never got to where they were going. They were dead."

She leaned against the doorframe, looking spent. "Sorry. It's been so long since I talked about any of this."

"Don't apologize. Do you want to sit down?"

"No." She looked beyond him, out the window, and he remembered that they were under some kind of surveillance.

"Who's out there? Are they connected to what happened?"

"I can't talk about that. It's not what you're here for anyway. You said you're looking for the woman who turned out to be me. So here I am. Why are you looking for me? Do you know something about Maggie?"

Anxiety swam in her eyes.

BEFORE HE COULD ANSWER, he was interrupted by the sound of footsteps and pounding on the door. Kelsey stepped aside as Maya and Jessica burst through the door.

"There's someone out there watching us with binoculars," Maya warned them.

"We know." Ethan edged around the perimeter of the room to the door. "Let's get out of here so we can talk freely."

He shot Jessica a complicated look meant to communicate everything that had just happened. That was impossible, of course, so all he got in response was a frown and a shrug.

"It's her," he mouthed silently, gesturing toward Kelsey.

Jessica mouthed something back, but he couldn't interpret it. He tried again, only to catch Maya frowning at them. Apparently their attempt at charades was more annoying than anything else.

Kelsey led them all into the empty kitchen. A gigantic bowl of rising dough sat on the long worktable. The comforting aroma of flour and yeast filled the room.

Jessica was still mouthing things at him but he didn't want to make Kelsey uncomfortable by repeating her story for her. Kelsey seemed lost in her own thoughts and gave him no guidance about where to take things from here. Maya checked all the windows of the kitchen to make sure no one was watching them.

When she was satisfied, she turned to Kelsey and folded her arms across her chest. "Who's out there, Kelsey? Why are they watching this place?"

Kelsey's head jerked up. "I really can't talk about it. I *won't* talk about it." She turned on Ethan. "It's time for you to talk now. I told you about the Berensons. I told you about my baby."

Jessica's eyes went wide. "*You're* the one?"

Kelsey swung toward her. "Who are you people? How do you know about Maggie?"

"*Maggie?*"

"Hold on, hold on." Maya's voice of authority cut through the chaos. "Some of us need to catch up here. You had a baby, Kelsey?"

"A long time ago. I was seventeen and I—couldn't keep her. I gave her up for adoption to the Berensons, but we were tricked and another couple stole Maggie. Then I found them drowned."

Jessica gasped. "Just like—"

Ethan clapped a hand over her mouth. What if she was about to blurt out S.G.'s name? Blurting wasn't the best way to deliver the news to Kelsey that her child was still alive. She pulled his hand away from her mouth. "I was going to say, just like we heard. The couple drowned in the lake."

"Yes, but how did you know about that? I only found them because I was looking for Maggie. I never reported it. I was too scared. No one ever knew about it—except for whoever drowned them, of course."

"So that's why you detained us."

She nodded. "I didn't know what your involvement was."

Ethan and Jessica shared a glance. He could see that she now understood the situation. Learning that her baby was still alive might be overwhelming. Kelsey should probably be sitting down. With a strong drink in her hand.

"Would you maybe like to sit down?" Jessica suggested.

"No." Fierce fire burned in Kelsey's gaze. "You know something about Maggie, don't you? She's my daughter and you need to tell me, right now."

Maya came to the rescue. She stepped forward and placed a hand on Kelsey's shoulder. In a calm, matter-of-fact voice, she delivered the news. "There's a very good possibility that your daughter is alive. She's the one who asked us to find you. She asked me first, but these two stepped in for me."

That was a kind way to put it. Ethan appreciated that.

"If your baby is the same girl as the one we know, she lives in Lost Harbor now," Maya continued. "She's known as S.G."

"Lost Harbor..." Kelsey clutched at her throat. "How long has she been there? Who does she live with? How is she?"

A touch on his hand made him look down. Jessica was

sneaking her hand into his as they both watched, spellbound. He squeezed her hand. This was it. What they'd been working towards. Sharing the moment with Jessica made it all the sweeter. Sharing *everything* with Jessica made it sweeter.

Maya filled Kelsey in on the details of S.G.'s short but very unusual life. Kelsey kept gasping and dropping her head into her hands. "So she ran away? All on her own?"

"She did. Gutsy kid. She's very resourceful." Maya paused, then asked a question of her own. "Call me crazy, but you didn't seem surprised when I told you she was alive."

Ethan had thought the same thing, though he hadn't known what to make of it.

"No, I—" Kelsey gripped the edge of the table so tightly her knuckles went white. "I was afraid she wasn't anymore. I knew she had been alive. But—" She transferred her death grip to her own throat, choking off her words. "No more. Don't ask me anything more."

Ethan fielded a questioning glance from Maya. *What's going on?* He couldn't be sure. But he could certainly speculate.

He turned to Kelsey. "You knew she was alive. Did they use her as leverage to get you to turn a blind eye to whatever they're doing out there?"

Bulls-eye. Kelsey went as white as the flour scattered on the table. She swayed slightly.

Jessica stepped to her side and put her arms around her for support. Always the sweetheart, his Jessica.

He banished the thought—*his* Jessica? Where had that come from?—and focused on Maya, who was pacing back and forth across the kitchen floor.

She continued the thought process that Ethan had initiated. "You knew she was alive, but you didn't know *where* she was."

Kelsey nodded.

"And you didn't contact the police because you were afraid they'd hurt her. They threatened to hurt her."

Kelsey nodded some more. Jessica rubbed her back in soothing circles. "That must have been so terrible. Being afraid all the time that something might happen to her. You poor thing."

More nods. More convulsive swallowing. "They sent me photos now and then. I saw her grow up that way. I knew she was okay. But then the photos stopped coming last year. They tried to fool me with some old photos, but I could tell she hadn't grown since the last one. I was so afraid she was gone."

"That's why you stayed here all these years?"

"No." She shook her head fiercely. "I stayed because I thought I'd find her eventually. I thought I might be able to rescue her."

"Looks like she rescued herself." On impulse, Ethan pulled his phone from his pocket and scrolled through to the picture of S.G. that he'd taken at Petal to the Metal. She'd been tossing feed to the chickens, and was addressing a glossy rooster like a teacher scolding a naughty child.

"That's her," Kelsey choked out. "She looks like my mother. Talking to birds. My little magpie."

"Oh yes, she says she can talk to all kinds of animals," Jessica said eagerly. "I confess I do the same thing, but I never expect a response. She can actually *communicate* with them. She told Nate—he's the one who found her in the firehouse—that the birds told her to leave the trapper's cabin."

Kelsey struggled to hold back tears. "And that trapper, he's been arrested?"

"Yes, but he's in Texas on preexisting warrants. He's not saying a damn thing about anything that happened here in Alaska."

"No, he won't. He must have been working with—" She stopped abruptly. Ethan ground his teeth together. If only she'd trust them, maybe they could actually get somewhere. There had to be something he could say or do.

Maya shot him a warning glance. Her message was clear: his role in this was over. He'd done his part; he'd found S.G.'s mother. *Maggie's* mother. The rest of this situation was in the hands of law enforcement. AKA Police Chief Maya Badger.

He held his tongue. He didn't want to get thrown in jail again, after all.

Jessica gave Kelsey one last comforting pat on the back. "Do you mind if I ask how you want to handle things from here? Do you want to come with us to Lost Harbor?"

A look of intense longing spread across Kelsey's face. "More than anything," she breathed. "But I don't think I can."

"We can make sure no one follows you," said Maya.

"That's...nice of you, but sorry. I can't be responsible for bringing danger to Maggie's doorstep. I won't allow that. It's better for her if no one makes the connection between us. Except for you all."

"Can we tell her we found you?" Jessica asked. "That's what she wants most. She wasn't sure her family was even alive."

"You can tell her, yes. But make sure she doesn't come here. It's not safe for her. Tell her I'll come to her when I can do so safely."

"You know we're here to help, right?" Maya sounded almost offended that her police expertise wasn't being called upon. "You got a police chief, a highly rated if overpriced PI, and a crystal-wielding intuitive genius on your side."

"Overpriced?" he muttered. Ironic, since he didn't plan to charge anything.

"Genius?" Jessica lit up. "Maya, you *have* forgiven me."

"I'm getting there." Maya kept her focus on Kelsey.

The woman was wavering, he could tell, but then she shook

her head. "I'm sorry. I've been handling this on my own for fifteen years. It's a little hard to give that up."

If there was one thing Ethan had learned in his time here, it was that Alaskan women were tough. Imagine a teenage girl giving up her baby, then being the target of threats for the next fifteen years. And she was still protecting her child. Truly remarkable. As was her daughter, of course.

"I understand." Maya signaled to Ethan and Jessica that it was time to clear out. "Come on, you guys, grab your stuff and let's hit it. Chopper can't wait much longer."

He remembered that everything was still in their suite, and gestured to Jessica to follow him back upstairs. "Be down in a flash."

"Good. I'll let the Forest Service guys know we're on our way."

As soon as they left the kitchen, Ethan twirled Jessica into his arms and planted a deep kiss on her lips.

That flustered look on her face was adorable. "What was that for?"

"Making up for lost time, Tasty Cakes. I didn't like being apart from you for so long."

Her eyes glowed with golden light. "Aww. That sounds almost...romantic, city boy."

Romantic? Hell no, that was taking things too far. He had to bring them back to reality. Lighten the moment.

With a grin, he tweaked a lock of her hair—the same way he used to tease his sister Olivia. "Guess I'm hooked on Japonica."

Her smile vanished and she stalked away from him, down the corridor to the stairs that led to the upper floor.

He wrestled with the urge to go after her and tell her he *was* hooked on Japonica—but not as a joke. As the real thing.

But what was the point? They both knew where things stood. The sensible thing was to walk away and move on.

He slowly followed her up to the suite where their baggage waited. They'd completed their mission. They'd found S.G.'s mother. They were about to get on a helicopter and leave Lost Souls Wilderness, where "strange things happened." They'd only known each other for a few days, after all. This was the perfect moment to end things between them. That was just common sense.

So what if a big part of him wanted to say: *Screw common sense. Screw logical decision-making.* That was what he knew. That was what worked for him. Always had, always would.

CHAPTER TWENTY-NINE

Oh hell no. Jessica knew exactly what Ethan was doing. She wasn't about to fall for his attempt to be flirtatious while he walked away from her. How dare he try it with his "hooked on Japonica" line and his "Tasty Cakes" and his "making up for lost time"—when he wasn't pulling her hair like a teasing older brother?

No. He could take his charming act somewhere else. She intended to keep her feet on the ground and her eyes firmly fixed on reality. No more deluding herself with rainbows and flowers and wishful thinking and all the other head-in-the-clouds Team Romance stuff. *Boots on the ground.* And those boots were going to kick Ethan to the curb before he stomped all over her heart.

Besides, things started moving fast as soon as they'd grabbed their backpacks and met Maya outside.

Ethan tried to make small talk with her, but she ignored him. He could find someone else to fool with his beautiful hazel eyes and his sexy forearms. Besides, every time he spoke, some kind of engine noise interrupted him.

First there were the four-wheelers that brought them to the

lodge's private airstrip. Very loud. Then there was the Forest Service helicopter. Even louder.

Once they'd landed at Lost Souls Airport, Maya drove them to Trumpeter Lake where Jessica had kept her late lamented float plane. They spent the drive discussing—loudly—how to handle the delivery of the big news to S.G./Maggie.

They all agreed that Maya would be best suited to tell S.G. about Kelsey. Now that she was back, she would take the reins of the case. That included talking to S.G. and contacting state and federal authorities about the goings-on in Lost Souls.

By the time Maya dropped them off at Jessica's car, Ethan had given up on his small talk attempts. They drove in silence back to Sweet Harbor Bakery.

The awkward silence continued after they'd both exited the car and claimed their backpacks.

The bakery had already closed for the day, so the lot was largely empty. Judging by the smell of molasses, the staff had made Anadama bread today. The wheels of the bakery had kept on turning in Jessica's absence. As if she hadn't gone on the wildest adventure of her life.

Ethan broke the silence. "You did well out there," he said. "Good job. We found what we were looking for."

She glanced at him briefly, enough to realize she was still irritated with him. Or maybe she was irritated with herself for getting too attached. "We lost a few things too."

Her naïveté. Her inhibitions. Her float plane.

"Yeah, I'm really sorry about your plane. You can take the cost off my bill. That probably puts you in a negative range, so consider us square. I wasn't going to charge you anyway."

"That's very generous of you," she said stiffly. "But I'm more than happy to pay your regular rate."

"No need. It was an experience I'll never forget."

Was there a hidden meaning in that statement? She didn't

want to delve too deep, since she knew it would just be more teasing. Nothing had changed. He was still leaving.

"Thank you. You can have the first shower."

An uneasy expression crossed his face. "That's, uh, kind of you."

She allowed herself a smile, remembering the fun of pranking him. "Don't worry, Old Crow's probably out fishing. He won't be back here for another month."

"Good to know. Is there anyone else I should be worried about hopping into my shower?" He lifted his eyebrows in invitation.

Okay, now he was definitely flirting with her. She bit her lip, tempted just for a moment. She still wanted him even though he was about to disappear back to his regular life. That was the problem. *She still wanted him.* She'd fallen for him, just like the Team Romance sap she was. Sleeping with him again—or showering with him—wouldn't make it any easier to say goodbye.

"Just lock the bathroom door and you'll have no need to worry. Enjoy."

She turned away from him and hauled her backpack toward the laundry room at the rear of the building. She might as well throw all her grungy hiking clothes into the wash instead of schlepping them to her room.

On her way to the laundry room, she noticed a FedEx letter that had been slid under the side door. It must have arrived after the staff had brought the mail inside. She pried it out.

Through the plastic window of the envelope, she saw that it was another certified letter from *Gary.* Which meant it was serious and she wouldn't be able to ignore it—or pretend to ignore it.

All the buzz of adrenaline and excitement from the trip to Lost Souls drained away. Nothing had changed in her absence; if anything, things had gotten worse. *Gary* had probably found a way to corner her and make her sell the bakery. He'd sue her and force her to hire a lawyer and...

One thing at a time. Laundry came first. Then came certified letters from horrible stepfathers.

The laundry room had been carved out of the space allocated for utilities—water heater, boiler, etc. It had no windows, one washer and one dryer. It was often the warmest spot in the building other than the work area near the stonework oven.

As soon as she closed the door behind her, she dropped her backpack and stripped off her outer layers of clothing. Hoodie, in the wash. Thermal layer, in the wash. She unloaded everything else from her backpack and dumped it in too. Might as well add the t-shirt she was wearing. And her purple leggings and micro skirt. As soon as she heard the pipes clang, indicating that the shower had turned on, she'd run upstairs in her underwear and grab some clean clothes.

When she was down to nothing but bra and panties, she hit the start button on the washing machine. And that was the last of her energy.

A wave of dizziness struck her, as if she'd just plunged off the edge of a cliff and was free falling toward the unknown.

What now?

She slumped over the machine, gripping its familiar pistachio surface as it filled with water.

What now?

She'd had her adventure. She'd played on Team Sex. She'd stepped way outside her comfort zone. Now she was back to her real life. No more running. She had to make a decision about selling the bakery. Her borrowed time had run out.

What would she do without Sweet Harbor Bakery? Who *was* she without it? She'd never gone to college, never traveled outside Alaska, never tried anything other than running this place. She loved it. But was that because it was the only thing she knew?

Now that she'd stepped out of her comfort zone once, should she do it again?

"This is my safe haven," she said out loud. "I'm stuck to it like a barnacle on a rock."

Realizing that she was addressing the laundry detergent, she snapped her mouth shut.

What about the other side of the coin? If she agreed to the sale, where would she go? What would she do?

Her breath sped up, heart galloping in her chest until she was practically wheezing. Without Sweet Harbor, she'd be all alone. With no purpose. A barnacle without its shell was nothing—just a translucent little wisp of a creature that drifted with the currents. That would be her. She'd have no home, no anchor, no refuge, no work. Nothing to wake up to in the morning, nothing to plan for at night. And she had to make this decision—no one else.

Her throat went tight and her vision blurred around the edges. No matter how hard she gulped, she couldn't get enough air. Her entire life was crumbling around her, as if she was standing on a bluff that was eroding beneath her feet.

Through the fog of panic, strong arms came around her. "Jessica? Are you okay?"

Ethan.

Trembling, she tried to answer, but couldn't manage it. He turned her around and cradled her head against his chest. She clung to him and let the steady hypnotic beat of his heart whisper to her. *It'll be okay. It'll be okay.*

Finally she was able to get enough air into her lungs to take a normal breath. She eased away from him and glanced up, wondering how much she'd embarrassed herself. Could he tell she'd teared up from sheer panic? His face showed nothing but concern.

"I'm okay now," she muttered. "Sorry, I just had a moment there."

"Is it me?"

"*No.*" A little arrogant for him to think that, no? "Of course not. It's...everything else. I have to decide what to do about selling this place. I have to deal with my mother and *Gary*. It's just...a lot. I got overwhelmed for a minute there."

"Understandable. Have you consulted your crystal?"

She scanned his face closely, but try as she might, she detected no signs of mockery. "No."

"Why not?"

She dropped her gaze to his throat, to the little hairs that curled just above his Henley. His throat might be even sexier than his forearms; his voice came out of it, after all. That husky gravelly baritone always sent shivers down her spine.

"I'm afraid of what it will tell me," she admitted. "Whether it says sell or don't sell, I'm not ready."

"Then give yourself more time."

She blinked at him to clear away the remaining moisture in her eyes. "But I have to make a decision. I'm terrible at decisions. I have been ever since...since I was eight."

"But this is a big one. You don't have to rush it just because they want you to. Tell them you need more time."

That advice was so logical. Such common sense. It brought her a rush of sheer relief. She drew in a long breath, steadying herself.

"You're right. It *is* a big decision. I can make it in my own sweet time. I don't have to do anything until I'm ready."

"Exactly."

"I always blame my decision paralysis, but it's not that, is it? This is a really important decision. It's a hard one. Not like whether or not to kiss."

Her face flamed. Why had she picked *that* decision to use as an example?

One corner of his mouth crooked up and he dropped his gaze to her lips. "Best decision ever."

"Don't do that."

"Do what?"

"Look at my mouth like that. We're not going to kiss."

"Okay, I won't look at your mouth." Instead, his gaze lowered even farther, to her breasts."

She remembered that she was wearing nothing but bra and panties. Just like that, her nipples swelled against the cups of her bra. If he looked farther down her body, he'd probably see that her inner thighs were trembling.

Oh sweet heavens.

She could take one more little trip to Team Sex, couldn't she? Drown her troubles in orgasmic bliss? One more time. The last one. Then she'd say goodbye and not look back.

"Lock that door," she told him tightly.

His eyes flared and he reached back for the door to slide the deadbolt into place. In the meantime, she rested her elbows on the washer and arched her back. The provocative pose made her feel outrageously sexy.

It did the job; his jaw worked as he brought his body against hers. "God, Jessica. Just one look at you and I want to touch you."

"Then do it." She spread her legs farther apart, then shoved her pelvis against his. She trailed her hand across the skin above her bra. "How about here? Or here?" She tucked her other hand under the upper edge of her panties, headed for her own clit.

Her teasing had exactly the effect she'd been hoping for— except more so.

He slid his hands onto her ass and cupped the fleshy globes. Liquid heat seared between her legs. Lust gripped her with a fierceness that shocked her. With an easy motion, he hoisted her onto the washing machine. Its vibrations traveled through her already aroused body. "Oh!" she said, surprised. "Oh."

She leaned back, her hands propped behind her on the lid of the washer. It was warm under her thighs.

He was entirely focused on her panties. "I'm taking these off," he warned her. "I want to see you, and do all those things I only talked about before."

She flashed back on their time in the holding cell, when he'd painted a picture that had sent her into a pulsing dry-humping orgasm. Now they were alone in another tiny room, but here they could do absolutely anything they wanted.

"Okay." She squeezed the word through her tight throat, and arched her back for his clever fingers to do their thing. He put his hands on her inner thighs, thumbs reaching inside her panties. The roughness of his palms made her gasp.

"Ethan," she moaned.

"Shh. I'm busy." His stare drilled down on her sex, amping up her arousal level even more. His thumbs made their way to her sex and slid between her slick folds. She gave a cry and arched back even farther. Waves of tingling pleasure swamped her senses.

She closed her eyes to give herself fully to the sensations he was teasing from her. Stars spangled her vision and thrills ran up and down her system. The vibrating washing machine gave her no mercy with its steady oblivious rhythm. Oh God, the way he touched her, the friction, the heat, the juice, the intensity. And then something changed. Cool air briefly came across her sex, then wet warmth latched onto it.

She glanced down to see his head deep in the vee between her legs. Tousled brown hair brushed against her pelvis. He'd pulled down the front of her panties to expose her sex, and was now stroking his tongue against her clit. The surge of sensation made her body tighten like a bow. She wanted to draw her legs together, to clamp him between her thighs. But his hands were still braced on her inner thighs so she couldn't move.

Giving in to the pleasure, she relaxed and let him take command with his hard hands and firm mouth. He devoured her as if she was more delicious than her cinnamon buns. He licked her and teased her as if there was no rush at all, as if he could do this all day long. As if right there between her legs was exactly where he wanted to be.

He set the pace, not her, no matter how her hips twitched and her body writhed. As he worked her with his thumbs and his tongue, she lost all sense of where she was. She could have been on a cloud somewhere, or deep within a cave. This little room with this vibrating machine became the entire world. Nothing else existed. No one else could hear. No one else mattered.

The orgasm hit her like a steamroller, blasting pleasure all the way through her, from her curling toes to her tingling fingertips. She gripped the edges of the washing machine and rode out wave after wave of ecstasy. Ethan kept pace with her, keeping his tongue right where it was. He didn't release the pressure until every last speck of bliss had been wrung from her body.

She sat up, panting with deep ragged breaths, as he straightened. The sight of him running his tongue across his mouth, lapping up her taste, would have made her blush once upon a time. But she was way past that now.

She slipped off the washing machine with an assist from Ethan. She ran her hand across the gigantic bulge in his pants as she stepped to her backpack. "I have a surprise for you."

"Oh yeah?" He adjusted his jeans.

She bent over her backpack, making a provocative show of it. When she stood up, she held a condom in her hand. It took him a moment to drag his gaze away from her body to notice it. Very satisfying.

"I grabbed this from the Aurora Lodge. Those billionaires will never miss it."

He grinned widely and snatched it from her fingers. "Have I mentioned that I love you?"

As he bent his head to unzip his pants, she froze in place. How dare he drop another of his flippant flirty comments at a time like this? How dare he toy with her heart like that?

When she took a step away from him, he glanced up.

"What's wrong?"

She didn't answer. If he didn't understand, she wasn't going to explain it to him.

Awareness flashed in his eyes. "I..." He closed his mouth. She turned away, ready to put an end to this. The next thing out of his mouth shocked her even more.

"My God. I said it as a joke but it's not."

She spun around to face him. "What?"

He wore a stunned expression. "I love you. I do. I know it doesn't make sense. We don't make sense. You're all wrong for me. But there it is. I love you anyway."

In her bra and damp panties, as confused as her laundry in the spin cycle, she stood frozen to the ground. *She was all wrong for him? But he loved her anyway?* What kind of backhanded non-romantic thing was that to say?

Maybe that would work for Team Sex, but when it came down to it, she was Team Romance all the way.

Her wash cycle came to an end. She elbowed him aside and flung up the lid. With her arms full of laundry, she pushed past him, then dumped it all in the dryer. Jabbed the start button and headed for the door.

"Good luck working all that out."

"Jessica." He called after her. "Please, don't walk away."

"It's the sensible thing to do. We're all wrong for each other, after all."

"You're really going to go out there in your underwear?" She heard him coming after her, but didn't look around.

"This is Lost Harbor. The first time it hits zero degrees the crew at the Olde Salt streaks naked down the boardwalk. I think they can handle a woman in her underwear."

She was so furious she didn't even care if anyone saw her. If she stayed in that little laundry room with Ethan one second longer she might explode.

"You said the same thing, that we were all wrong for each other," he pointed out from behind her.

That was true. She had said that. But she hadn't loved him at the time.

Oh dear God. Did she love him now? Was that why she was so outraged right now?

She shook that notion off and stalked around the corner toward the side door that offered a shortcut to the bakery and the upstairs staircase. "Which is why I'm doing the logical thing and walking away. You should too. It only makes sense."

"Maybe sense is overrated."

Maybe? *Maybe?* She was sick of his maybes and his common senses. She flung the door open and charged inside.

There, on the floor of the bakery, she found herself face to face with perhaps the last people she wanted to see her in her underwear.

Her mother and *Gary*.

CHAPTER THIRTY

In the short time he'd known Jessica, Ethan had never seen this side of her. It was simultaneously arousing and confusing. But one thing he knew for sure: the part about him loving her was real and he had to make her understand that. He'd never said that to anyone other than family.

As she stormed into the bakery, he followed after her. He nearly collided with her when she skidded to a stop.

A fifty-ish woman in an embroidered kaftan top and a burly guy in a camo hat faced off with Jessica.

"What are you guys doing here?" Jessica demanded. "We're closed."

"Good grief, I started this bakery!" the woman exclaimed. Putting two and two together, Ethan figured she must be Jessica's mother. "It doesn't matter if it's open or closed. It's my bakery."

"No, Mother, it's mine now. You dumped it on me, remember? Why do I have to remind you of that all the time? It's *mine*. Which is why it's not getting sold unless I say so."

"Well, make up your mind! That's all we're asking. Oh!" She threw up her hands. "You always were a disaster when it came to decisions. I know you, Japonica. You're dithering because it's so hard for you to choose. You've always been like this. Remember when you couldn't decide which college to apply to so you let all the deadlines pass and never went?"

"I remember that. Yes. But I didn't go because you left and I had to run the bakery." Her voice sounded thin and tense.

"I offered to hire a manager. You took forever to decide and by the time you did, she'd moved on. Remember? And the time you couldn't decide between cross-country and debate so you missed them both? And the time—"

"I remember. I remember it all." Visibly shaking, Jessica clenched her fists by her sides. "Do *you* remember when you made me choose which parent to live with?"

Jessica's mother clucked at her. "Of course kids should have a say. I was giving you a choice."

"I was *eight*. It broke my heart having to choose." That confession seemed wrenched from Jessica's soul. "It drove Dad away. Didn't you care about that?"

Behind her, Ethan put a steadying hand on her back, just to let her know he was there. She stepped back until his chest was pressed against her. Maybe she was using him as a wall. Whatever she needed, he was there.

"That was his choice. Why are you blaming me?"

Jessica's chest heaved with emotion. "We just met a woman who hasn't seen her daughter for fifteen years and still she's doing everything she can to protect her. I can't even imagine what that would be like. You made me choose between you and Dad. That was a terrible thing to do."

"Well." Her mother shared a look with her husband. He made a little motion with his head. "I always encouraged you to express your feelings. At least I did that right."

Jessica's shoulders stiffened. "Justify it however you want.

You shouldn't have done it. If I struggle with decisions, maybe that's why."

Her mother blinked a few times, as if she couldn't quite believe this new version of her daughter. "I'm sorry, then. I'm sorry if that hurt you. But now there's another decision to make, honey, and we can't just let it hang forever. Gary says there's a window and we won't get as much if we wait."

Jessica didn't respond right away. Was the family pressure getting to her? Ethan bent down and murmured in her ear, "Remember what we talked about, Jessica."

"Who are you?" Jessica's mother asked.

"Must be the lawyer Hutch mentioned," Gary said.

"Oh yes, of course."

"No." Jessica finally spoke in a firm tone; she seemed to be standing up to the pressure just fine. "He's not my lawyer, he's much more than that. But this isn't about him. This is about me." She drew in a long inhale and declared, "I'm ready to make my decision."

Ethan squeezed her shoulder before she could do something she couldn't take back. "Jessica, can I speak to you for a moment?"

She nodded, and he tugged her back outside the building and closed the door. He stood so she was shielded from any onlookers who might wander by.

"What are you doing?" he asked her.

"Announcing my decision." Color still glowed along the tops of her cheeks. Her chest moved up and down with her fast breaths. He hadn't seen her so riled up since she'd walked away from him at the lodge.

He spoke in his most calm and soothing tone. "What about giving yourself some time? You can't make this decision on pure emotion."

"What's wrong with emotion? Didn't you just tell me you love me?"

"Yes, but..." He trailed off, realizing that for the first time in his life, he'd acted from his heart alone when he told her that. And it felt very, very right. "What about consulting your crystal?"

"I don't need my crystal. I can do this. Want to know why?"

"Okay." She was on some kind of tear he didn't understand.

"Because I finally figured out that I can *trust myself.*" Her eyes blazed with fire. She was magnificent. His heart turned over in his chest and he knew that he would do anything for her. Even abandon all his common sense and take a leap into new, unmapped territory.

"I can step out of my safety zone," she continued. "I can do things I haven't tried before. I can be real. Feet on the ground. Sex on a washing machine."

He had to correct her there, because he hadn't even gotten the condom on before she'd stormed out. "Technically, that hasn't actually happened yet."

"*The point is...*" She straightened her spine and shoulders. "I can handle my business. I don't always have to put my shit on the back burner for everyone else. That's another thing Maya told me, and she was right."

"Maya's a smart woman."

"She is. Usually I run to her when I need to make a big decision. But the truth is, our whole trip, I was thinking in the back of my mind about what I want to do about the cruise line offer. I can do this. I got this."

"I know you do. I don't doubt it for a second. You're spectacular. I believe in you all the way."

"You do?"

"Absolutely." He noticed goose bumps rising on her arms. The bra-and-panties look, much as he loved it, made it hard to concentrate on the important part—her inner fire.

He took off his Henley and handed it to her. Underneath he wore a t-shirt saturated with wood smoke. The scent brought their adventures in Lost Souls rushing back. "How about a little extra support while you take on the world?"

She glanced down her body, as if she'd completely forgotten her half-naked state. "Thank you." She pulled it over her head. It hung halfway down her legs and didn't diminish her sexy appeal one bit. "That's very kind of you."

With a much softer expression, she tugged her glorious hair from under the Henley. His heart twisted and he realized that he couldn't wait another minute to throw himself at her mercy.

"Jessica, I screwed up before. I'm no good at saying things romantically. I don't have any practice with it because I've never done it. I was talking from the wrong side of my brain. Will you give me another chance?"

She twisted her mouth to the side, as if unsure. He'd really hurt her with his flippancy, and he hadn't even realized it. He couldn't let that stand. He had to make her understand.

He set his hands on her shoulders and met her gaze, letting his entire heart show in his eyes. "I'm not used to falling in love, Jessica. I've never let it happen before. Not even with Charley. It came at me sideways. I'm sorry I ruined it. Will you please give me another shot?"

"Another shot?"

"Another shot at telling you that I love you." Now that he'd said it again, it felt even more real. "I promise I can do it better."

She leaned toward him and lifted herself on tiptoe. He bent his head so their lips could meet. Fresh and sweet, the touch of her mouth sent hope rushing into his heart.

"You're cute when you grovel," she whispered against his mouth. "How could I say no?"

The relief made him sag. He hadn't ruined everything. He

was getting a retake. He planned to blow her away with romance the next time.

And then she was gone, back into the bakery, and he had to follow her and find out what her future held.

Because he absolutely intended to be part of that future.

CHAPTER THIRTY-ONE

Just as she'd told Ethan, in the back of her mind Jessica had been weighing the pros and cons during the entire trip through Lost Souls Wilderness.

Now that it was time, her decision came out easily. "I'll agree to sell the bakery, but only on one condition."

"Name it," Gary said.

"I want an executive role in the development of whatever they build. A meaningful role, not just for show."

Gary was already shaking his head. "That's not in my power—"

"Then tell whoever does have the power. It's not negotiable. I won't let some non-Lost Harbor-ites come in here and build something that doesn't suit the town. I know this place and I know the tourists who come here. I know what people are looking for. They're not after a prefab experience they can get anywhere else. They want something authentic. You go back to these people and tell them that I can be a real asset to their project. I'll meet with them whenever they like if they want to discuss it further. If they're not interested, I'm happy to walk away from their offer."

Her mother scrunched up her face. "I don't know, honey. You don't have a head for business."

"Haven't I been running this business for the last decade? Stop telling me what I'm bad at. Stop telling me who I am. This is my decision, and I'm not changing it. That's my offer, Gary." She turned to him, Ethan's Henley swinging around her legs. It gave her an extra layer of confidence, she had to admit. "You can try some kind of lawsuit or whatever to change the terms of the contract, but this is much easier. One of my best friends is a total shark of a lawyer when she's not harvesting peonies, and Ethan is a fantastic private investigator. I'm not afraid of your shenanigans."

He grunted as he absorbed her seriousness.

"Shenanigans?" Her mother bristled. "We wouldn't—"

"Process servers, intimidation, big dudes with hairy eyebrows, anything along those lines. It's just a waste of time and money. The best way to get this deal done quickly is to accept my terms." She crossed her arms over her chest, more than ready to be done with this conversation. "After all, I'm perfectly content staying here in my bubble. Such a lovely little spot by the beach. Have you seen the wild roses?"

Her mother surveyed her with a look of speculation. "Are you really? Content here? I'm starting to wonder."

"You bet I am. Especially now that I have this guy." She reached behind her and grabbed the neck of Ethan's t-shirt. She pulled him toward her. At first his body language registered surprise, but then he caught her drift. When she turned her head to the side, he was there. Their lips met in a passionate kiss. "I love you too," she whispered into his mouth.

With a start, he deepened the kiss. A sense of perfect rightness came over her. She hadn't meant to say that to him. She hadn't even known for sure that it was true. But now that she'd said it, it felt like the truest thing ever.

She was a Team Romance girl to the core, after all.

Her mother cleared her throat. Jessica ignored the sound. Gary said something along the lines of, *I'll let you know what they say.* She ignored that too. Then her mother added a question about what shenanigans she was talking about.

Jessica tuned it all out.

After all, Mother and Gary were the ones who had crashed her sex-turned-argument-turned-romantic moment. Next time, maybe they'd call first.

As she and Ethan continued to kiss, she turned to face him and fully abandoned herself to his embrace. Her mother and Gary muttered their goodbyes and departed through the front entrance.

And still she and Ethan kissed.

Of course she had no idea what any of this meant in terms of a future. He didn't live in Lost Harbor, and if Prince Cruise Lines accepted her terms, she'd be staying here. But luckily, she didn't have to decide all that right now. They'd figure it out together. Or they'd argue about it and then use the argument as foreplay and hash it out in bed. If none of that worked, they could always call on her crystal—together. It hadn't led them wrong so far.

———

"I FIGURED something out at the Aurora Lodge." They were in her bed. Naked. Freshly showered. Blissful. Half-asleep. Ethan was murmuring in her ear, the sound like river water over pebbles.

"Hmmm?"

"My near-death vision was right."

She lifted her heavy eyelids. He was braced on one elbow over her as he traced a finger along her jawline. He'd finally been able to use the condom he'd been carting around during that entire showdown with her parents. And a couple more. "It was?"

"But it wasn't Charley, it was you."

"You saw me in your vision?"

"Not exactly. But I saw that meadow behind the lodge, and I saw us running through it holding hands."

"Because we were handcuffed together."

"I didn't see the handcuffs," he admitted. "But, you know, close enough. The rest of it fits."

"What about the wedding gown?"

"I figure that part was metaphorical. The vision was telling me that I was going to hold hands with my future bride in a meadow."

She blinked at him, taking in his words. "Future bride?"

He cringed and fell back onto the bed. "Crap, I ruined it again."

"That was a proposal?" Wide awake now, she sat up, clutching the sheet to her chest. "Ethan, you can't propose to me. That makes no sense. We just barely met."

"I know. I agree. It makes no sense. But it's all I can think about." The usual cool of his hazel eyes was gone, replaced with heart-stopping passion. "I want to be with you. I want you to be my future. If you want to give it time I'm okay with that. I know this must sound crazy."

She wrapped her arms around her knees. Usually she was the one who jumped right into imagining a future, so it didn't seem crazy to her. But it *should*. Shouldn't it?

"If you're counting on me to be the sensible one here, we're in big trouble."

A smile tugged at the corner of his mouth. "I'll take that chance. The question is, will you?"

She knew what he was getting at. His history with cancer, his propensity for close calls. His reluctance to bring someone else into the red zone that he considered to be his life. Those were very serious roadblocks. She didn't take any of that lightly. She'd gotten involved with him knowing exactly where he stood.

"Have you changed your feelings about the future?"

"I have," he said gravely. "I'm making a conscious decision this time. I never expected to fall in love, but I have. I'm in love with you. I'm choosing you and a life with you, if you'll have me."

A warm feeling, like the best hot cocoa on a winter day, swept through her. "How can you be so sure, after such a short time?"

He picked up one her hands and laced his fingers through hers. "I've dealt with a lot in my time. I think having cancer made me grow up fast. I had to think seriously about life from an early age. I had to make decisions like an adult. So when I tell you that I love you and that I'm here for whatever you want, you can believe it. If you want to spend the next decade dating, I can do that. If you want me to go back to LA so you don't have to worry about my next brush with death, I will do that. I won't like it, but I'll understand. If you want to get married tomorrow, well..." He grinned and kissed her hand. "My family would be pissed that they missed it, especially my sister, but I can handle them. They're used to me doing things my way."

A rush of incredible feelings overwhelmed her. Gratitude, amazement, wonder...but most of all, love for the man holding her hand and looking at her with such perfect understanding.

But she had to be logical about this—at least a little.

"If Prince Cruise Lines accepts my terms, I'll be stuck here in Lost Harbor," she warned him. "We'll have to be long-distance."

"Not necessarily. I already have a client waiting for me across the bay."

She tugged her lower lip between her teeth. "You think you can work here in Lost Harbor as a private investigator?"

"I don't see why not. The cases will probably be a little different, but I could use a change. I like my work. I don't want to change careers. But if it makes you anxious the way it—"

"No, no. I don't want you to change what you do. I think you love it. You should do what you enjoy and what you're good at. I..." She tilted her head at him with a tender smile. "I believe in you. I've seen you in action. You're careful and you think things through. And maybe sometimes you'll even want a partner on the—"

"No," he said firmly. "I don't think my nerves can take that again."

She laughed at him. "Gotcha. Don't worry, my Nancy Drew days are done. Watching my float plane get murdered was pretty much the last straw for me. Or was it nearly getting caught under the hemlock? Or getting thrown in jail for no good reason?"

He let out a long relieved breath. "As long as we agree on that, I think we can handle anything. I've already wrapped things up in LA, so it's easy for me to relocate here. I guess the James Agency lives another day."

She thought about the job for Alastair, and how it might involve whatever criminal things were happening in Lost Souls Wilderness.

"Will you mind if I occasionally check with my crystal about what jobs you should take?"

"I'm counting on it." His sweet smile sent an arrow of love right through her heart. "I feel safer already. I learned my lesson when it comes to magic."

"Yeah, well, don't feel bad. I had it all wrong about soul mates."

"You don't believe in them any more?"

She echoed his words, the ones that had meant so much to her. "I believe in *you*."

With his arm around her, she settled back under the covers,

nestling her body alongside his. His delicious heat radiated through her skin into the deepest part of her soul. Was this what it felt like to find her "soul mate?" Or were they just two people who'd found each other and fallen in love while spending an intense few days together facing danger in the wilderness? There was really only one way to know for sure.

"Yes," she murmured.

"Yes to what?"

"Yes to everything. We can figure out the details later."

Some decisions were just so easy.

CHAPTER THIRTY-TWO

Three weeks later

"SO, S.G. Since it turns out you have a name—a couple of them, actually—what do you want us to call you?" Ethan smiled at the teenager. He had a special affection for her because her case was the first success of The James Agency 2.0 Everyone on the Misty Bay peninsula had heard about it by now; his reputation was made before he'd even signed a lease for office space.

He and Jessica had answered a call from Maya to meet in her office at the police station. Jessica had brought a box of pastries, of course, which S.G. was already happily consuming.

"I like Maggie," she declared. "Magpies do like to gossip, but they're more optimistic than Spruce Grouse. The Spruce Grouse complain too much."

"Alrighty then." Jessica put her hand up and they exchanged a high-five. "How was your first conversation with your mother?"

"It was good. I told her I was afraid she'd drowned. But she said that was someone who was trying to kidnap me."

Maya was flipping through photos in a file folder. "We think that most likely Murchison was the one who drowned those two, but we don't yet know who they were. That's probably when he found you and decided to keep you."

"Was Murchison the one who sent Kelsey updates on S.G.? I mean Maggie?" Ethen took a peek at the photos Maya was going through. They were all snapshots of S.G.—Maggie—throughout her childhood.

"I don't know. It could have been someone he was working with. It's unclear what role he played. But Kelsey was right. He's not talking because there's something big out there." She turned to Jessica. "Which is where you come in, Jess."

"Oh no. I'm retired from my short but brilliant investigative career." She blew a kiss at Ethan.

"You sure? The two of you solved that case like—" She snapped her fingers.

"She's sure," Ethan said firmly. He tugged Jessica's hand into his. What a gift, to be able to sit and hold hands with the woman he loved. Such a simple thing, but it meant so much to him. "Besides, she's going to be busy with the Sweet Harbor expansion as soon as the sale goes through. I already barely see her."

At least it felt that way, even though they still spent all their extra time together.

"What do you need, Maya?" Jessica asked her friend.

"Well, the Lost Harbor Police Department is officially taking an interest in the shenanigans out in Lost Souls."

"I thought it wasn't in your jurisdiction."

"When one of my residents gets her float plane shot up, that changes things. Assuming that resident wants to file a complaint."

"Say no more. That resident most certainly does," Jessica declared. "Where do I do that?"

Maya slid a clipboard across the desk to her. "Here. I can take your statement right now."

"Got a pen?"

Maya handed her a black Bic and Jessica set to work.

"As for you, Ethan, I hear you're in business again."

"Yup. Spread the word."

"I need someone to fly down to Texas and try to get something out of Murchison. I'd do it, but I can't leave my father right now. And none of my crew here has the interview chops to handle it."

Jessica looked up from the clipboard, her face glowing with pride. Adorable really, how great she was at moral support.

"I'm already committed to a job for the man we ran into at Maggie's old cabin. Hey, did you hear that, Maggie? Your new name slid right off my tongue."

The girl beamed widely at him. "You're the first one. My boyfriend still keeps calling me S.G."

"You mean Dylan?" Jessica slid another walnut-cinnamon roll her way. "Are you two making it official?"

"He asked me to be his girlfriend. I said yes, as long as I don't have to do boring things I don't want to do."

"Good policy. I support that. And may I be the first to welcome you to Team Romance." Jessica gave her a little squeeze around the shoulders.

Maya snorted as she put the photos back in a file folder and picked up a scone. "I'm feeling outnumbered here."

"See, that's the thing. You never really chose a team, Maya. I think you were keeping your options open depending on who you happened to meet. I think it was on a case-by-case basis for you."

"Can we get back to the point of this meeting?" Maya fixed her with that stern glare she pulled out for police matters. "Fill out your paperwork."

"Yes ma'am." Jessica turned back to the clipboard and got to work, while Maya turned to Ethan.

"How long do you think this other job is going to take?"

"I don't know. But it's connected to your case. The client is Carole Berenson's brother. He's looking into her plane crash."

Maya rolled her eyes over a bite of scone. "Just what I need. Another civilian getting involved in this thing."

A knock sounded at the door of the office. "Ethan, could you answer that? I have my hands full here." Maya waved half a scone at him.

He got to his feet and swung open the door. And blinked. Some kind of large Viking warrior stood on the other side of the door. Eyes calm but watchful, shoulders almost too big to fit through the door.

"I'm looking for the police chief," he said.

Ethan ushered the man in. He moved with the kind of controlled power that Ethan always associated with athletes. Maybe a Swedish skier or something?

"Maya, Thor's here to see the police chief."

Both Jessica and Maya looked up; he wished he had a photo of their faces as they took in the full impact of this dude. Even Maggie looked impressed.

Unfortunately Maya had a mouthful of scone; a few crumbs spurted onto the desk. She covered it up quickly, swallowed, and got to her feet. "Hi, I'm Police Chief Maya."

Jessica cleared her throat discreetly.

"Police Chief Badger," Maya corrected quickly. "How can I help you?"

"I'm Rune Larsen."

Her mouth fell open again. "You're my father's new home health care nurse?"

Jessica put down her pen and propped her chin on her hands, as if she were watching a show. "I didn't know Harris was getting a nurse."

Flustered, Maya explained. "Yes, I need help. My dad isn't the easiest patient, so I called in—"

"Can we speak in private?" Rune Larsen interrupted. "Alone."

"Sure. Yes." Ethan had never see the badass police chief quite so rattled. She looked around the office, which was filled with their little group, then the outer bullpen area, which held two sergeants working at their desks. She squared her shoulders. "It'll have to be the holding cell if you want privacy."

Ethan laughed out loud. "Don't worry, my man, it's a pretty good jail. Four and a half stars on Yelp. Changed my life."

With a scolding look, Maya shepherded the big man out of the office and firmly closed the door behind her.

"Whew." Jessica whistled as she got back to work on her statement. "I think Maya just joined Team Sex, judging by the look on her face."

Ethan came back to her side and peered over her shoulder. She'd already written an extensive description of the incident with the float plane. "Wait, you're really going to put in the part about the crystal?"

"Well, the crystal did warn us. I think it's only right to give it some credit."

He opened his mouth to object, to point out that his professional credibility could take a serious hit if it got out that he'd given any credence to her crystal.

But then again—love Jessica, love her crystal. He dropped a kiss on her hair, breathing in that fragrance of all-good-things, and sat down by her side.

Which was the only place it made any sense to be.

THANK you so much for reading! Maya Badger's story is coming out next. You can find all the Lost Harbor books here. Want to be the first to hear about new books, sales, and exclusive giveaways?

Join Jennifer's mailing list and receive a free story as a welcome gift.

ABOUT THE AUTHOR

Jennifer Bernard is a *USA Today* bestselling author of contemporary romance. Her books have been called "an irresistible reading experience" full of "quick wit and sizzling love scenes." A graduate of Harvard and former news promo producer, she left big city life in Los Angeles for true love in Alaska, where she now lives with her husband and stepdaughters. She still hasn't adjusted to the cold, so most often she can be found cuddling with her laptop and a cup of tea. No stranger to book success, she also writes erotic novellas under a naughty secret name that she's happy to share with the curious. You can learn more about Jennifer and her books at JenniferBernard.net. Make sure to sign up for her newsletter for new releases, fresh exclusive content, sales alerts and giveaways.

Connect with Jennifer online:
JenniferBernard.net
Jen@JenniferBernard.net

Lost Harbor, Alaska

Mine Until Moonrise

Yours Since Yesterday ∼ Book 2

Seduced by Snowfall ~ Book 3

Wicked in Winter ~ Book 4

Naughty All Night ~ Book 5

The Rockwell Legacy

The Rebel ~ Book 1

The Rogue ~ Book 2

The Renegade ~ Book 3

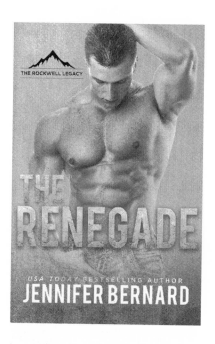

The Runaway ~ Book 4

The Rock ~ Book 5

Jupiter Point ~ The Hotshots

Set the Night on Fire ~ Book 1

Burn So Bright ~ Book 2

Into the Flames ~ Book 3

Setting Off Sparks ~ Book 4

Jupiter Point ~ The Knight Brothers

Hot Pursuit ~ Book 5

Coming In Hot ~ Book 6

Hot and Bothered ~ Book 7

Too Hot to Handle ~ Book 8

One Hot Night ~ Book 9

Seeing Stars ~ Series Prequel

The Bachelor Firemen of San Gabriel Series

Love Between the Bases Series

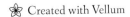